WHERE THERE'S SMOKE

ALSO BY E. B. VICKERS

Fadeaway

WHERE THERE'S SMOKE

E. B. VICKERS

ALFRED A. KNOPF
NEW YORK

THIS IS A BORZOI BOOK PUBLISHED BY ALFRED A. KNOPF

Text copyright © 2023 by E. B. Vickers
Jacket art copyright © 2023 by Iana Kunitsa/Getty Images

Visit us on the Web! GetUnderlined.com

Educators and librarians, for a variety of teaching tools, visit us at RHTeachersLibrarians.com

Library of Congress Cataloging-in-Publication Data is available upon request.
ISBN 978-0-593-48069-4 (trade) — ISBN 978-0-593-48071-7 (ebook)

The text of this book is set in 10-point Berling LT Std.
Interior design by Stephanie Moss

Printed in the United States of America
10 9 8 7 6 5 4 3 2 1

First Edition

for Lucy and Halle and Ally and Hope

and all the brave women in my life

and all the brave women in your life too

Monsters are real, and ghosts are real, too. They live inside us, and sometimes they win.

—Stephen King

in the beginning

He wasn't always a monster.
It's important to know that.
He was once so small,
he curled into the space
beneath his sleeping mother's chin.
So helpless, that was the only place
he felt safe enough to close his eyes.
He once fed with a mouth that held no teeth at all,
only a red ridge where they would soon appear.

He wasn't always a monster.
And that is always the case.

1

The day we bury my dad, I am almost a ghost myself.

My mom waits at the cemetery already—she's been waiting there for five years. But her old friends are with me today in her stead: Maggie wakes and dresses me, Sofia brushes my hair and pulls it up. Trish makes toast and eggs just in case I'll eat a few bites, and she won't stop hovering until I do.

After that, it is Ben at my elbow all day, best-friend-turned-babysitter even though, technically, we're both adults now. He leads me into the church, where the whole town of Harmony has gathered for the funeral and every speaker makes Dad sound like a saint. He guides me out of the church and walks beside me through the cemetery, where Dad will be laid to rest next to Mom. The grass over her grave has transformed from a patchwork of sod strips into an unbroken extension of the greater field of green. When did this happen, and why didn't I notice? How long will it take until the seams of his grave disappear too?

A memory comes, then, of sneaking into their bed on cold, dark mornings, not because I was afraid, but because I knew there was no safer place in the world. "A Calli sandwich," they would say as I wedged myself between their warm bodies. I want so much to climb back into my own past life, into that warm, safe bed, that I drop to my knees in the grass, stretching one arm forward—

—until Ben pulls me back and whispers my name, and it strikes me how wrong this is. Not just because we're in a cemetery and there's a hole and a headstone instead of a down comforter, but because my parents are on the wrong sides.

He should be on the right.

She should be on the left.

That is where they belong, and I belong between them. But they are mixed up with no safe space between them, and they will be like this forever. Couldn't we have gotten at least that small thing right?

Ben loads me back into the passenger seat of his old white truck and pulls the seat belt across my body. *What does it matter?* I almost ask, but it's easier to click the buckle into place and look away.

Before we turn out of the cemetery, I see Dylan Rigby climb into a backhoe next to the storage shed, and I realize he is coming to move the dirt.

It is Dylan Rigby, my first boyfriend, who will bury my dad.

Back at home, Maggie, Sofia, and Trish are here again, helping the women from church serve lunch. Long, rectangular tables covered with taped-on, dollar-store tablecloths wait under the two tall cottonwoods in front of the house. Even in early June, it's hot enough in our corner of high southwest desert that we're all seeking the pockets of shade wherever we can find them.

Up by the porch, they've set up a serving area for the food. Lines of people pass by on both sides of the serving tables, taking thin slices of ham and scoops of cheesy potatoes—funeral potatoes, we call them around here—and wilted salad from a bag. I'm not sure I can eat any of it.

I'll have the prime rib.

Dad's voice cuts through the crowd, so clear and sudden that it startles me. I know he's gone; it's not like I look around to see if he's standing beside me somehow. But still, there's a comfort in knowing it's exactly what he would have said, just to lighten the moment—and in feeling like the words didn't come entirely from me. I've been flooded by memories ever since he died, but the voice—this is new.

I find myself hoping to hear him again as I accept the plate that's been assembled for me, hoping this hallucination can bring me back into myself somehow.

Because from the moment I got the news of the fire, I've felt myself fading from my own life. Maybe part of me has wanted to show Dad that this is how it's done; you don't just leave all at once. I know he didn't have a choice, but I'm still angry at him for disappearing so suddenly, so completely. No smell of shaving cream in the morning, no slightly off-key singing while we fold laundry, no guilty smile when he peeks into my room at night to check that I'm home in bed and not off with Ben. (Or Dylan Rigby, once upon a time.) When he left, it wasn't a slow fade, a gentle ride into the sunset, but the click of a light switch. Binary. There, then not.

He was there at my graduation ceremony, just over a week ago. When they talked about all the ways we'd change the world, I looked out and found him. We locked eyes, and he said to me, without a sound, that I didn't have to change the world to be his whole world.

And even though it helped, I wanted to say back to him, *What if that's not enough? What if who I am is average? What if I never become brave or strong or sure?*

Because I wasn't anything special in high school. Average height, average grades, average social status. Brown hair that can't decide if it's curly or straight, blue eyes that are more winter fog than clear summer sky. Nothing noteworthy or even very noticeable.

I tried to be something more. I joined cross-country and Future Health Professionals and half a dozen other extracurriculars. I tried out for *Into the Woods* and got cast—but only as Ensemble/Villager #4. I got good enough grades to get into a good enough college that's close enough that I could still live at home and help out. But was any of it really enough?

I wanted to ask him, but afterward, the stadium was crowded, and there were pictures to take, and Dad had to leave for Cedar Falls soon anyway, and then Ben was waiting, ready to force me to come to the grad party and be social for once. So I only told my dad I loved him and would see him tomorrow.

After the party, Ben and I lay in sleeping bags on his trampoline, drifting off under the canopy of stars just before the morning light began to wash them out. We were still there, baking on the slick black surface, hair matted to our foreheads, when Bishop Carver came to tell me Dad was gone.

The first words out of my mouth were: "But what about my questions?" Which, of course, Bishop Carver misunderstood and therefore answered in the absolute wrong way with details about the fire itself. I sank to the ground, not because my dad had died but because I had traded my last chance to talk to him for a night of loud music and meaningless conversations, and who would understand me or have answers for me now? In spite of my questions, I knew in that moment that every part of who I was and who I wanted to be was built squarely on the foundation of my father: all he was, and all he believed. So who was I without him? And how dare he leave me with the inevitability that I would crack and crumble in his absence?

Selfish, I know.

I know.

Now, in the heat of this impossible afternoon, Ben scoots a chair next to mine and sits down. I hadn't even noticed he wasn't right beside me. I should have noticed, though. I should hold on as much as possible to everyone who's left.

"People are starting to go," he says.

"But not you?"

"Not me. Not until you kick me out." He hands me a cold bottle of Dr Pepper under the table. "You look like you could use a stiff drink."

Our bottles hiss as we open them, sighing at the relief of a little less pressure. Together, we sip and watch as the women begin to untape the tablecloths and the men begin to fold up the chairs.

Bishop Carver turns and catches my eye, and a strange thought strikes me that maybe he's the closest thing I have to a father now. Not just because a bishop is the "father of the ward," but because he's also my dad's cousin and has known me all my life. He even looks a little like Dad: same sandy hair, same barrel chest, same crinkly smile. He ambles over and sits a safe distance from us, always the model of love—but also propriety.

"Calli, I'm so sorry. He was a great man, and a great example to me."

They're not empty words. Bishop Carver always said he learned everything he knew from Dad, from throwing a fastball to casting a fly line to raising a kid. They were both natural leaders too, charming and charismatic. Everybody said so.

Which is probably why they were both chosen, one after the other, to be the bishop. Dad went first, as always, and I was so proud to see him sitting at the front of the congregation. To feel important because of his importance.

When Mom died, he insisted that he wanted to keep serving, even though it was already a lot with raising a kid and running a veterinary practice. But somebody higher up decided it was time to release him from that role anyway, three years into what's usually a five-year calling.

The blow should have been softened a little by the fact that it was Travis Carver, the younger cousin who'd always tried to follow in his footsteps, who replaced him. But things were never quite as natural between the two of them after that, maybe because Dad even insisted that he and I both call his cousin Bishop from then on—even though we'd only ever called him Travis, and it took a lot of getting used to. "He is the presiding high priest over us now," he said, "and it's too easy to forget that if we call him by his first name, even outside of church settings." Dad didn't mention the fact that his cousin had never used the title for him.

Now Bishop Carver rests his hands on the table, clasped together like he's ready to start praying any second. "We've got folks lined up to mow your lawn and bring in meals, and any bills you get, you send them straight to me. I'm happy to handle the financial end."

"Okay," I say.

"Anything else you need, you know where to find me."

"Okay," I say.

"Or you tell him," he says, nodding at Ben. "He knows where to find me too."

"Okay," I say. And "Thanks," because maybe then we can be done.

Soon everyone is gone but Ben, because he promised to stay until I kick him out. He would stay forever to keep that promise, but as much as I want him to, his brown eyes are sunken and his broad shoulders stooped.

"You can go," I say. "I think I want to be alone for a while."

He probably knows I'm lying, but he also knows I don't want him to call me on it. That's the kind of best friend Ben is. So he leans his forehead against mine, his hairline prickly against my skin. "You know where to find me," he says in his best Bishop Carver voice. Then he wraps me in a hug that smells like laundry and home before climbing into his truck and leaving me behind.

Inside, I change my clothes, then wander around the empty

house, which is cleaner than it's been in years. The funeral flowers are at the graveside now, since the one thing I managed to decide in all this was that I'd rather let the deer eat them than watch them die, day by day.

So instead of flowers, there's a little bouquet of gifts in the center of the table: a pair of thick-soled shoes from Maggie, a molecular model kit from Trish, a set of soft scrubs from Sofia. No cards, but I know who each gift is from all the same. I can even hear what they'd say if they were here: *For your future. You still have one, you know.* They would make some joke about how the minute I pass my NCLEX, they'll take somebody out so there's an opening on the med/surg staff. "Your mom did that for each of us," Maggie told me once. "Made us feel like there was a place for us, and we could belong here. Like we belonged to each other."

That's been the plan ever since we lost her: As soon as I finish nursing school, they'll find a place for me where Mom once was. I never had the guts to tell them that I think I mostly agreed to it all because it seemed to mean so much to the people who love me best.

I hardly felt a thing as I watched everyone gather today, and even less as I watched them leave, but somehow their leaving has still left me empty. Outside, the sun's finally setting, spilling a last splash of warmth across the sky. I can't bear the beauty of another sunset he'll never see, so I turn my back on it and walk east instead. When I reach the fence at the back of our property, the wind takes my shoulders, and I turn left. Or maybe I turn left for no reason at all.

North.

North to Alaska . . .

It's a ridiculous song from a terrible John Wayne movie that Dad and I laughed and cringed our way through when it randomly popped up as "Recommended for You" a couple of weeks ago.

A couple of weeks ago? Is that possible?

Go north, the rush is on. . . .

I smile. I mean, I'm crying, but I smile too, because he'd sing that song at the most random times after that, and I can still hear the sound of his voice, singing that stupid song.

Maybe if I keep moving, he'll keep singing.

Go north, the rush is on. . . .

I'm almost running toward the tallest cottonwood in the northeast corner of the field. The tree towers above me, whispering with its leaves, beckoning with its branches. Maybe I'll climb it. Or maybe I'll hop the creek that forms the northern border of our property and keep going, all the way to Alaska. Whatever it takes to keep this voice, this memory. To not forget.

Then something shifts beneath the tree: a scrape and scramble of a shape, retreating beneath a heap of burlap. One ragged breath and a rancid smell. An animal. Not dead yet, unless that was a trick of the wind rippling the edge of the fabric.

The moment feels like it's already been scripted, so there's no conscious choice in what to do next.

I inch forward.

Pull back the burlap in one quick motion.

At first, only the long flannel shirt tells me this isn't an animal but a girl, since the shape in front of me seems so dirty and wild as to blur the line between the two. She's sunburned—blistered and peeling—everywhere her shirt doesn't cover. A long gash across her leg still seeps. Her fire-orange hair is matted against her scalp, but still, patches of scabbed scalp show through.

Who is she? How did she get here? She's smaller than I am, but it's hard to tell how much younger. Maybe eleven? Twelve? She opens her mouth, lips cracked and bleeding. Reaches out a blistered hand.

And I recoil. Bile fills my throat.

I want to look away.

Turn away.

Run away.

I can't do this. Not today. I'll get Bishop Carver or my trio of nurses or literally anyone else in Harmony. She needs help, and I am still hollow.

"I'm going to call somebody," I say, reaching for my phone before remembering it's back at the house.

The girl shakes her head.

"I'll be right back," I tell her. "We should get you to the hospital."

She shakes her head harder. Groans in a way that's painful even to me.

Then Dad's voice, clear and firm, reverberating through the caverns of my heart.

Take care of her, Calli.

Love thy neighbor.

That's when I know it's really him, because those are the words he would always say when someone needed our help. Everyone was our neighbor, our family.

She's your sister, when the Chapman girl showed up, clothes too small and eyes wild, asking if I could play.

He's our brother, when we'd see somebody with an out-of-state plate stopped on the side of the road, staring helplessly at his flat tire.

I look down at her, and as I do, the sound of the creek brings me back into my own body, the vessel filling again.

"It's okay. I'm here."

I'm not sure if the words are mine or his. The girl winces as I slide one hand under her knees and the other behind her shoulders, but she wraps her arms around my neck. "I'm going to pick you up now," I say, hoping I'm strong enough.

I am—but she shouldn't be this easy to lift. As I carry her to the house, she buries her head against my neck and cries quietly, and I speak the words he said to me every time I had a skinned knee or a broken heart.

"This will heal," I promise her. "God will help."

The day we bury my dad is the day he comes back to life.

And because of the girl, so do I.

harmony

is a pleasing arrangement of parts
is agreement and accord
is balance and unity
is an interweaving of different accounts
into a single narrative

and Harmony
is a high-desert town
named after all these ideas,
where folks borrow sugar
and return favors
and sing together every Sunday
in perfect, four-part . . .
well, harmony.

But underneath the surface,
Harmony
is violence
and heartbreak
and skeletons in closets
just like any other town,

and some of those skeletons
are just like yours.

2

The girl whimpers softly when I lay her on the couch. I scan her face—from her green eyes and patchy orange hair to the slight upturn of her nose, from the freckle near her eye to the small chip in her front tooth—to see whether I might know her underneath all this. But I've never seen her in my life.

"I'm going to get you some water," I say. She may have followed the creek all the way through the canyon, but that doesn't mean she's not thirsty. The creek might keep you alive, but it could also make you sick enough to kill you all the same.

I fill a glass and try to give it to her, but her hand shakes so badly, she spills half of it before I take it back. "Let me help," I say, and she leans forward, lips parted. We start off easy, a sip at a time, but soon she grabs the glass from me, steadier now, and starts drinking in great gulps.

"Maybe you should slow—"

It's too late. She pitches forward, heaving it all back up across the coffee table. The acidic smell fills my nostrils, making me realize how far I'm in over my head.

She's crying now, so I open my arms, and she climbs into my lap. She wipes her face against my shoulder, leaving a streak of dirt and vomit and tears across my T-shirt. Even though part of me wants to lean away, I hold her closer. "Hey, it's okay. I mean it will be. I'm going to call Maggie. She'll know what to do." The girl looks up at me with big, scared eyes. "She won't hurt you," I say. "Or take you away. Whatever you're afraid of, it shouldn't be Maggie. Okay?"

The girl searches my face for a few seconds that feel like forever. Finally she nods.

I slide her gently off my lap and cross to the kitchen, where my phone waits, facedown on the counter. I've been avoiding it for days, because every time I pick it up, it's filled with so many well-meaning messages that it's exhausting to read them, let alone think about replying.

Once again, missed calls and texts fill the screen when I flip it over.

So sorry, they say.

I can't imagine, they say.

Thoughts and prayers, they say.

I ignore them all and call Maggie, who answers after the very first ring.

"Calli? You okay, honey?"

"I need you." Because it's Maggie, that's all I have to say.

"I'm packing up your dinner right now," she says. "Sit tight. Stay strong. Breathe."

Then she's gone.

"She's coming," I tell the girl. "Sit tight. Stay strong. Breathe."

Maggie's probably getting into her car any second now, but she's a good ten-minute drive away. What do I do in the meantime, besides clean up the mess? Try another drink? Make her lie down? Get her into the shower?

"I can't do this alone," I whisper, partly to God and partly in hopes of hearing Dad again. "I'm trying to help her, but please, help *me*."

I look for answers in the too-clean kitchen, which offers only one left-behind vase of flowers and a stack of funeral programs as an answer. I'm not even sure who chose the photograph on the front, but it's one of the last pictures we ever took with all three of us. Dad's telling a story and Mom and I are listening, laughing, soaking it up.

The printed picture feels more real in that moment than all the digital ones. So I tear it from the program on top of the stack and tuck it inside my phone case so I can have both of my parents with me, always. Then I grab an old dish towel to mop up the sick on the coffee table.

The girl tries to take the towel from me and clean up her own mess, but I gently guide her hand back to her lap. "No, that's okay," I say, wishing I had any idea what to say next.

Talk to her. Just talk. About anything.

He's right. And knowing this, knowing *him*, a hope sparks inside me. Maybe somehow I will be able to not only keep him with me but see him more clearly now that he's gone. Like getting a better view by taking a step back. Maybe I can know him in new ways, even now.

So I try to follow his advice. I start rambling about the first thing that comes to mind.

"I'm glad you found this place. The house and the land have been in my family for three generations," I say, like this is some casual conversation and she's some ordinary houseguest. But then I falter; Dad's childhood wasn't an easy one, and I don't know much more of that story.

I search for something else to say, and soon my mind lands on a memory: Mom and me, sitting on this same couch. There's a big white bowl next to us, and she's pulled my hair into a ponytail in case I throw up again. She's combing through it with her fingers as she tells me a story.

"Once there was a girl," I begin, recalling the story the best I can, "who went on a great journey to find her true home. . . ."

When Mom told me her own story, she always began with those words. She came all the way across the country for college because of a postcard the recruiting office sent her. "The people looked nice enough, but it was all the green trees against the red rocks that really got me." It's the same college where I'm already signed up with a full schedule of pre-nursing classes once summer's over. But for me, the campus feels more like a foregone conclusion than a life-changing adventure.

Mom fell in love with this land first, but her love for Dad wasn't far behind. And I came along only a year later. *After that, there was no going back*, she always said. Not like she was stuck, but like she'd finally found where she belonged.

I keep telling it as true to Mom's memory as I can—until a sharp knock interrupts. Then I give the girl's hand a little squeeze before getting up to let Maggie in.

But it's not Maggie. When I swing the door open, it's Dylan Rigby, covered in dirt from his curly brown hair to his untied work boots. He reaches for the handle of the screen door with one long, toned arm—then lets it drop to his side, remembering that, unlike Ben, his invitation inside isn't automatic anymore.

"Hey," he says, eloquent as always. Still, seeing him on my doorstep takes me back to a time when things were, if not easy, at least easier than this. Of course, back then I probably would have made a little effort to look nice instead of answering the door in a vomit-splashed T-shirt.

"Hey," I say, keeping the door open wide enough to talk to him, but not so wide he thinks he can come in.

Behind me, I hear the girl moving, and then she lets out a yelp. I glance back and see her standing in the kitchen, shaking her head, staring toward the open door with wide, scared eyes.

"What was that?" he asks.

I turn back, try to smile. "TV, I guess. It's just me here." I wait for him to remember that he's the reason we're having a conversation at all.

After a few seconds, he does. "I wanted to say I'm sorry. About your dad. Fires can get out of control so fast." He brushes his fingers absently along the faint scars on his left arm. "And I'm sorry I couldn't be at the funeral. I . . . had to work."

"I know," I say. It's unreasonable for me to expect him to have been by my side all day like Ben was. Ben and I are still best friends, and Dylan and I are . . . nothing. Still, I'm tempted to ask if he watched the graveside service or just showed up to run the back-hoe, but I decide to let it go.

"And I wasn't sure I belonged there," he says. "He was always nice to me after we broke up, but I don't think he liked me that much when we were together."

"What do you mean? He always loved you."

Dylan bites his lip, like there's something more he wants to say. Finally, he finds the words. "Look, I get it. He was just . . ."

Then a crash from behind me and the sound of breaking glass. I sneak a glance into the kitchen, where the girl is backing away from the mess on the floor: water and fallen flowers and sparkling shards of blue.

"Cal, there's somebody in there. Or some*thing*. Do you want me to come in and check it out? LuEllen said there was a raccoon in her pantry last week. And, no offense, but . . . do you smell that?"

He breathes in, leans in like he's trying to look around the door, and I have to put my hand on his chest to push him away. Between working for the parks department all summer and varsity football and swim the rest of the year, he's built enough that he could get past me if he wanted to.

But he doesn't, of course. For all his faults, Dylan was never like that. He takes the hint and steps back, hands shoved into his pock-ets. "I still care about you, Cal." Dylan's the only one who calls me Cal, and the shorthand reminds me that he does know me better than almost anybody, even now. "That's what I came here to say, I guess. So if you need me, I'm here. I can do little repairs, inside and out. Fertilize the lawn this summer, winterize the sprinklers when it gets cold. Stuff like that, whenever you need it." He squints past me. "You sure nobody came back inside with you?"

Now I shut the door behind me and face him on the front porch. "How do you know I even left the house? Have you been watching me?"

Dylan sighs, like he knows he's busted. "It looked like you left all the flowers out there with him, and I wanted you to have some here with you, I guess. So I bought some at Food Town. In a blue vase, because one time you said it was your favorite color."

So they weren't just left behind when the rest of the flowers were taken to the cemetery. The idea that I don't even know who's been coming and going from my own house makes me shiver.

Dylan pulls a tiny, crumpled envelope from his pocket. "When you didn't answer the door, I put the flowers on the counter. But then I got home and saw the card had fallen out, and I was really afraid you'd think I hadn't done anything at all."

It costs a lot for him to say this. Rigby boys aren't supposed to have a softer side, let alone show it. They're not supposed to be afraid of anything but government conspiracies.

But I've still got to keep my boundaries with him.

"So you just invited yourself in, even though I wasn't here. Did you look for me out back?" I ask, wary.

"No," he says, and I want to believe him.

"Thank you for the flowers," I say, taking the envelope from his outstretched hand. "I think you should go now."

Dylan nods. "I'm sorry," he says again. He scratches at the back of his head, oblivious to the faint puffs of dirt he's stirring up.

"Thanks," I say, slipping back inside. "Let's talk again when it's time to winterize the sprinklers."

Dylan gives one more long look at my door before he climbs into his truck and turns the key, but I'm backed far enough into the darkness of the front hall that he can't see me watching him. Once he disappears around the corner in a cloud of dust, I turn away. "He's gone," I say to the girl.

But she's nowhere in sight. There's a noise, low and rhythmic, from the kitchen. So I follow it, rounding the other side of the island to find her cowering, knees clutched to her chest again. She claws at her scalp so the wounds reopen, chanting something that sounds like "Tsm, tsm, tsm, tsm."

"Hey," I say, kneeling beside her. "He's gone. It's okay."

The chant gets louder. So loud I barely hear the knock before Maggie comes through the door without waiting for me to answer.

"What the hell?" she asks, taking in the vomit-soaked towel and the broken glass and scattered bouquet and then, with a sharp breath, the girl on the floor.

"Calli, who is this? What's going on?"

The girl looks up at Maggie with more fear in her eyes than I've seen yet, and that's when her chant turns from the rhythmic beat of *tsm* to *tsim* to something more. Something that sends every inch of me to chills.

"It's him," she says, again and again and again.

It's him.

ingredients, part 1

Every first grader in Harmony learns
what it takes for a plant to grow:
seeds and soil and sunlight,
water and fresh air.

Put all those things together,
and soon
tender leaves and a small stem
break free and stretch forth.

Look, the teacher says,
drawing their attention
to the wide world beyond.
It is happening around you
all the time.

ingredients, part 2

To make a monster like ours
takes more than simple ingredients,
and no one talks about where they really come from.

So these monsters are harder to recognize
and almost impossible to bring down—
nurtured by narcissism,
protected by patriarchy
and their own power and charisma
and our need to believe
the world is right and good.
They are able to hide in plain sight
thanks to the blinders
we put on ourselves.

Look.

It is happening around you
all the time.

3

Maggie drops her bags on the table and brushes past me, heading for the kitchen like a missile in scrubs. But when the girl flinches away from her, she abandons her trajectory. Instead, she kneels right where she's at, so they're eye level but still ten feet apart. "Now, honey, I'm not here to hurt you. I'm only here to help. We're going to get you to the hospital, okay?"

The girl starts shaking and moaning, banging her head against the cabinet. This time, what she's saying is unmistakable. "No. No. No."

"Okay, okay," Maggie says, her voice strong but calm. "No hospital. At least, not right this minute. But we'll need to call social services or the police or—"

More moaning. Deeper thuds against the cabinet. "No hospital. No police. No. No. No."

I move to step in, but Maggie holds me back.

"Nobody else," she says. "I get it. You decide what happens next. Okay?"

The girl and Maggie watch each other for a minute. Finally, she gives a wary nod.

"Can we get you settled somewhere, up off the floor?" Maggie asks.

Another nod—this time more sure.

"Can you walk, or would you like us to help?"

The girl tries to get up, closing her eyes against the pain.

"I'll help you this time," I say, stepping forward and scooping her up. "I think you've walked enough."

I carry the girl, limp and whimpering, toward the couch—but Maggie stops me before I put her down. "What if we get her settled in bed?"

There are only two beds in this house: mine and my parents'. The choice is an easy one.

"Let's put you in my bed," I tell her, hoping to ease the worry on her face. "It's closer to the bathroom. And it's cooler on that side of the house."

I don't tell her the real reason: I've been sleeping in my parents' bed all week anyway, and if I lay her down there, I'm afraid her scent is so strong, I won't be able to smell my dad on his pillowcase anymore.

Maggie darts around me and into my room, covering the bed with towels she's grabbed from under the bathroom sink.

"What are those for?" I ask.

She answers me with a question for the girl. "Could I clean you up a little?"

The girl shakes her head as I lay her down.

"Maggie knows what she's doing," I say. "And I'll stay here the whole time."

This time, the girl groans, and she holds my gaze with pleading eyes.

"I can see that you trust Calli," Maggie says. "What if she cleans you up?"

The girl pauses, nods, then stares so blankly at the ceiling, it's hard to know if she's still in there.

"Okay," Maggie says. I could tell her I'm not sure about this, but it wouldn't do any good. "Grab two big bowls of warm water and a bar of soap," she adds. "And more towels, if you have them."

I find two mixing bowls and bring them to the bathroom. As I sit on the edge of the tub, filling the first bowl, Maggie rummages through the bathroom cabinets.

"I don't know what I'm doing," I say.

Maggie pulls out a bottle of aloe vera. "You'll be fine. Get a clean sheet to lay over her, and only uncover the part you're washing. Start with her face and her hair. Be gentle."

I slide the first bowl back and begin filling the second, testing the temperature again to make sure the water's not too hot. "What if I mess this up?"

Maggie starts piling supplies on top of the towels: shampoo, antibiotic ointment, bandages. "We're not getting her ready for the prom, Calli. If you miss a spot, we'll get it tomorrow, maybe when she's able to get to the bathtub. Or, better yet, when we take her to the hospital."

I think of the look in the girl's eyes when Maggie mentioned the hospital earlier. "I don't think she wants that. And you told her she could choose what happens, remember?"

Maggie sighs. "I'm hoping she comes around."

I'm still not sure the girl actually wants me to clean her up, but when I bring the warm cloth to her cheek, her eyes drift closed. I stroke her face in smooth circles, then return the cloth to the bowl to rinse and wring it out as she releases a long breath.

"Maggie's not in here to tell me if I do anything wrong," I say, making the same small circles on her other cheek, "so I'm counting on you to let me know." She gives a little nod, eyes still closed.

Maggie hasn't abandoned us, though. She stands outside the door the whole time, her back to us, and answers every question I call out.

"What if a blister has popped?"

"That's what the nail scissors are for. Cut the extra skin away and get it cleaned and covered."

"What about the sunburns? I don't know if I should touch them."

"Cleaned and covered, honey. That's our new motto. That and 'be gentle,' especially around the wounds."

I try to be gentle, but still, tears slide down the girl's cheeks after I accidentally catch the edge of a scab with my washcloth, and again when I rub aloe vera on the burns. There are gashes across her belly and back to match the one on her leg, angry and red like they're more recent than some of the others, and I dab antiseptic on them as gently as I can.

I want to be finished, but I know I'm not. "Maggie," I ask, struggling to keep my voice casual. "Am I supposed to wash . . . everywhere?"

"It's best," she says, and I can tell she's caught my meaning. "If she'll let you."

"Is that okay?" I ask the girl. She nods once, and I take that as my cue to go ahead but make it quick.

I'm extra careful as I wash between her legs, grateful there's not anything noticeably wrong. Not that I know what I'm looking for. Not that I want to know. Not that I'm looking any more than I absolutely have to. The girl's eyes are open now, and she watches a spot just over my head. But by the time I'm finished, I think she appreciates the bath. Maybe.

"Let's get you dressed in something clean and soft. Okay?"

Okay. She only mouths the word, but it still feels like a victory.

Of course, everything I own would be huge on her, but I do my best, sliding on the silk pajamas Dad got me three Christmases ago that I never wore but felt too guilty to give away. I spray some detangler on her hair and start working through the knots with a wide-toothed comb. But she cries out when I accidentally hit a tangle too hard, and I abandon the idea. Maggie's right: We're not going for prom-ready here.

"Should we be done for now?" I ask, and she gives a little nod. "Okay, then. I'm going to take these towels to the laundry room. I'll be back soon, though."

The laundry room is more of a laundry closet off the kitchen, which means Maggie can talk to me as I load the towels into the washer.

"You did good in there, honey," she says. "And no, I don't mean you did *well*, although you did that too. It was kind and selfless of you to take care of her like that, especially after the day you had. I don't know that most people could have managed it."

I look up from the machine. "You could have."

"Well, of course *I* could have." She smiles, but I can tell the compliment means something to her. Maggie is as tough as anyone I know, and you don't get that way by living an easy life. You get tough when you take your four kids and leave your abusive husband to start over in a small town called Harmony a thousand miles away. At least, that's one way it can happen.

I breathe in the smell of the detergent—because that's his smell too—before closing the lid on the gentle shushing sound of things getting clean. Maggie's already taken care of the flowers and broken glass, unpacked her grocery bags, and loaded a plate for me. Not funeral potatoes, thank goodness, but grilled vegetables and chicken and fresh strawberries.

I take the plate to my room, since the girl seems to like having me nearby. She's lying still, eyes closed, so I leave it on the nightstand and go to grab a chair from the dining room.

By the time I get back, she's sitting up and scarfing down my food.

"Um," I say, standing in the doorway. She doesn't even look up. "Maggie?"

Maggie joins me in the doorway and sighs. "Well, at least she has an appetite."

"Isn't she going to throw it all back up?" I ask, reaching for the trash can just in case.

"Probably. You'll have to 'accidentally' leave some broth for her next time."

The girl flashes us such a dirty look that I nearly laugh out loud. "I'm guessing you don't like us talking about you like you're not even here."

As if to prove her point, the girl finishes every bite—and doesn't throw it up. She just gives one satisfied belch before settling back in the bed and promptly falling asleep.

"Well, then," Maggie says. "You're officially on call instead of active care. Let's get you some food."

We go back to the kitchen, where Maggie fixes another plate for me and one for herself. "Maybe she's doing better already," I say.

"Maybe," she says. "But I've watched enough recoveries to know that healing isn't linear. It's always two steps forward, one step back, and it always takes longer than you think." She gives me a piercing look. "That goes for you too, you know. You have your own healing to do, and it's going to take time."

She's right. Of course she is. But I'm amazed how much more alive I feel than I did a few hours ago: how my thoughts have broken through the fog of my grief, how even my limbs feel light and capable again, now that I have purpose. For a moment, there's a brush of guilt that it's the girl's suffering that's easing mine.

But no. We'd both be worse off without each other. The only person she seems to trust is me.

"Did you hear what she was saying when you first came in?" I ask.

Maggie thinks a second. "I don't know that it sounded like words to me."

"It was," I say. "The same words, over and over. 'It's him.'"

She frowns. "Him who?"

"I think she meant Dylan Rigby."

Now Maggie sits up straight. "What does Dylan Rigby have to do with any of this?"

"He came by right before you did. To check on me, I think. Except he seemed to know there was somebody in here with me. And then she kept saying, 'It's him, it's him.'" I chew my lip. "What do you think she meant?"

"Well, maybe—"

"Because she's probably just delirious, right? She's got to be. Or she's got him mixed up with somebody else."

"I think—"

"Because I know him. I *know* Dylan Rigby. And—"

"Calli." Maggie's voice is sharp enough to get my attention. "It's my turn now for a minute, okay?"

She waits.

I nod. "Okay."

"Dylan Rigby has always seemed like a good enough kid to me. I never worried when you two were dating. But . . ." Maggie looks down at her lap for a long moment. A very long moment.

Maggie.

At a loss for words.

What am I supposed to do with this?

Keep listening. It's Dad's voice again, and he's right.

So I wait until she draws in a deep breath and straightens her shoulders.

"You're as strong as anyone I know. Stronger than we have any right to expect you to be. But you're barely eighteen and all alone in this house, if you're still set against moving in with me."

I'm about to interrupt again—I can't help it—when she reads my mind.

"And don't tell me you've got that girl, because I'm determined to take her to the hospital tomorrow."

"Not tomorrow," I say, trying to keep the desperation out of my voice. I know it's selfish, but if she takes the girl, I'll be alone, and the grief I felt at the cemetery will swallow me whole. "Give me some time to earn her trust and get her on board with it. You can check on us whenever you want. Doesn't that sound like a better plan than adding to her trauma and breaking our promises?"

"Negotiating *and* changing the subject at the same time," she says with the slightest roll of her eyes. "You are your mother's daughter, my dear. Okay, I'll give you forty-eight hours, but you call me if you get even the slightest 'yes' to health care or social services."

She's set her terms so firmly, she may not notice that I never agree to them, so I just let her go on.

"I did have a point to make before you derailed us, so listen up. You say you know Dylan, and I know it feels like you do. But people can surprise you in wonderful ways, and in terrible ways too. So here's the thing you need to know as you make your way through this world: You never truly know anyone else."

"But—"

"Yes, *but*." She takes my hands in hers and gives them a squeeze. "But you can know yourself, and that's enough. Be careful, is all I'm saying. And trust *yourself*."

Her phone buzzes, and the moment is broken. She looks down at it and shakes her head. "My kids will burn down the house if I'm gone much longer."

The words sear through me as Maggie's eyes snap up to mine. "I didn't mean . . ."

"I know," I say. "It's okay." One offhand joke about a fire isn't going to ruin me, but it does reopen the wound enough that I'm not ready for Maggie to go just yet. "He would know what to do, wouldn't he?"

Maggie gives a little nod. "Probably. But she would have known even better. Your mom was always so steady, no matter the situation." She looks down the hall to where the girl's still sleeping peacefully in my bed. "I'll let you have your forty-eight hours, but we'll need to take her in day after tomorrow," she says. "I'm sticking my neck out by not calling this in right now. Nurses are required to report when there's reason to suspect child abuse or neglect."

My stomach catches at hearing the possibility of the girl having been abused spoken so plainly—and at the possibility of turning her over to somebody else.

"But didn't you just tell me I can only trust myself? What if they send her back to whoever's hurting her? Wouldn't reporting be exactly the wrong call?"

Maggie looks at me long and hard, but I don't look away. Finally, she gives a little nod, like I've passed some test I didn't know I was taking. "I'll admit, it's complicated. Sometimes we try to simplify the world too much for kids. We try to make them believe that the adults in charge—parents and teachers and police and nurses and all the rest—know what we're doing and have their best interests at heart. But unfortunately, it's not always that simple."

"So tell me the unsimplified version."

Maggie leans back in her chair and folds her arms. "I'm not saying the system's broken, although there are some who would say exactly that. I'm just saying it doesn't always work perfectly for everyone. Especially kids. And that's the only reason I'm willing to take advantage of the fact that we trust each other enough in this town to bend the rules now and then. Did your mom ever tell you about—"

Then Maggie's phone buzzes again, and she hurries to type a message back, presumably to her kids (who hopefully haven't burned the house down yet). Before she goes, she pulls me in for a hug, which smells like fabric softener and feels like a favorite sweater. Even though the hug lasts a good thirty seconds, somehow it still isn't long enough.

"Lock the door, keep a light on, and call the police if you even think you see anybody hanging around," she says. "Just to be safe. I've got fresh milk and the rest of the strawberries in there for your breakfast, and a loaf of bread for toast. But if you need anything else, just say the word." She drops her voice for the next part. "I've been worried about you alone in this house, and I can't say this new development helps that. Is your dad's shotgun still in the hall closet? You remember how to use it?"

I nod, even though I'm not entirely sure of the answer to either question. It's not until she's gone that I realize she never finished *her* question.

Did my mom ever tell me about *what*?

the promise

Once upon a time
and many years ago,
a child left a dangerous home
and found her way to a safe place
in a nearby town
where four young nurses cared for her
and brought her back to life.

But the law said
when the girl was healthy again,
they had to send her home,
even though she begged them not to.

And the rules in the girl's community said
she must be punished
for running away.

Weeks later,
when the most fearless of the nurses
came to check on the girl,
the Brethren shook their heads sadly
as they told the nurse
that the girl had died
and how suddenly it had happened
and how sorry they were.

Then they escorted her
straight to her car
as dozens of blank faces
stared back at them
from under brimmed hats
and through sheer curtains.

The nurse gathered the pieces of her broken heart
and returned to her friends,
carrying the weight of what she knew
and the role they'd played in it
just by following the rules.

The four of them promised
it would never happen again.
Not on their watch.
No
matter
what.

The good nurse died
not long after that,
but
like dimples or freckles or curly hair,
she passed along the promise
to her daughter
without saying a word.

And the other three were there
to make sure they all kept it.

Not on their watch.
No
matter
what.

4

After Maggie leaves, I putter around the house for a minute, listening to the gentle shush and hum of the washer and sorting the giant stack of mail near the door.

One pile for junk.

Another for condolences.

And a third for things that look official and/or financial that I don't have the energy to deal with. Luckily, Bishop Carver already offered to take care of all that, and I have no doubt he meant it. He never blows smoke, even if it would save him from a hard or awkward situation.

He proved that to all of us at a fireside at his house last summer. There's never an actual fire at those things; they're just sort of casual mini-sermons, like if a bunch of people were sitting around a fire. All the youth gathered on folding chairs in his backyard and listened as he taught us about God's love and our Savior's atoning sacrifice.

After he was done speaking, he told us he'd left time so we could ask questions. "The hard questions," he said. "The ones you're not even sure you should be thinking about. I promise you, somebody else is wondering too. This whole church started because a young boy wasn't afraid to ask questions."

He really meant it, and we all knew it. But that doesn't mean it's suddenly easy to give voice to the things you've barely let surface in your mind, so we sat there in awkward silence for a long, long time. Finally, I felt so bad that I blurted out a question that surprised even me.

"What if you're not sure any of this is true? What if you don't know if you believe?"

I knew what the answer would be: Pray harder. Study the scriptures. Have more faith.

But he didn't say any of those things.

"You may not know this, but at my day job, I'm a wildland firefighter."

Everybody laughed, because of course we knew. He had just used an extended forestry metaphor in his message. Half the town called him Chief Carver, even though his title at the forest service was technically district fire management officer. But in spite of the joke, he was looking right at me in a way that meant he took my question seriously.

"For some of you, it might seem like your faith and your life are built on generations of history. Sometimes that feels really safe and protective, like an old-growth forest of interconnected roots. But sometimes in that same forest, you might feel like you're not even sure where you begin and somebody else ends. Or you're stuck somewhere you never intended to be and never really had any choice in the matter." He gave a half smile. "Not that I have any idea what that would feel like." Everybody laughed again.

He bowed his head for a moment, and when he looked up, straight at me, there were tears in his eyes. "If you're not sure yet what you believe, then you're being honest. And truth and honesty are absolutely what God wants. In this church, and in your life, you don't have to believe anything that isn't true.

"And how do you know something is true? Not just because I say it is, or your parents say it is, or even because the prophet or scriptures say so. You'll know it's true because you feel it inside you. Sometimes it feels like peace, and sometimes it feels like, well, fire." He shrugged an apology, but nobody was laughing then. "If you hang on to all that truth, *your* truth, it becomes a kind of compass. And if you let it guide you in all you do, even when it would be easier to go another direction, well, that's integrity. And that's the life you want to live." He looked back at me. "Did I even answer your question?"

All I could do was nod, because I'd felt that peace in small doses, like the water of the sacrament. And I'd felt that fire, even if it was only in tiny, fleeting sparks. I thought maybe I felt it then.

When I got home that night, Dad asked me how the fireside was, and I gave a vague "Good." Still, I couldn't stop thinking about Bishop Carver's trees and how thoroughly my roots were tangled in my dad's. How many of the lines of my own moral compass had been drawn by his hand. Dad had always had strict rules, tight curfews, and high standards, but I'd never doubted it was because he wanted what was best for me. But what if I could be trusted to know what was right too?

Now, alone in the empty kitchen, I'm not even sure that spark is still inside me. Because I just want him to be back here, telling me what to do next. I pull the matches from the cupboard and light my Summer Rain candle, both to cover up the lingering scent of the girl's vomit and to show myself I'm not afraid of a little fire. The flicker of the candle illuminates the stack of funeral programs on the counter, and I'm torn between wanting to hang them in every room and hide them all away.

Now that it's quiet, I swear I can hear him again.

You don't need my photocopied face all over this house. Nobody needs that. I'm here in all the ways that matter, whatever you do with that stack of paper.

He's right. Even so, I can't bring myself to throw them away, so I blow out the candle and take them to his nightstand, tucking them inside an open issue of *Veterinary Medicine*. When I flip it closed, there's a calf staring back at me from the cover, tawny body and white face and big, dark eyes. It reminds me of the one calving he let me watch—how badly it went, and how I was never allowed to go with him on an after-hours call again. The way he looked at me as I cried the whole ride home. "I'm sorry, Calli," he said. "It can all go wrong so quickly."

I spin away from the magazine, my mind flashing from the cold, glistening body of the dead calf to another image, blurred by its own burning, of my dad trapped inside a barn. Then all I can imagine is him under the ground, and Mom's down there too, and suddenly it feels like I'm the one who's buried. Because if she was a nurse and couldn't survive a disease, if he was a wildland firefighter every summer in college and couldn't survive a fire, then how in the hell does anybody survive anything?

There's a cry in the night, and for a second, I think it's me. But no. It's coming from my room. I cup my hands around my mouth and nose and breathe, breathe, breathe, until I can go to the girl without freaking her out.

When I can feel my feet on the floor again, I walk into my room, cloaking myself in false calm, and sit on the chair I've left beside the bed. "Hey," I whisper. Beads of sweat form along her hairline, and her face is hot to the touch.

I take the still-damp washcloth from the rim of one of the bowls. When I lean closer to rest it on her brow, her eyes are wide and terrified, and the words are back.

"It's him, it's him, it's him . . ."

I look to the window, which we left open to let the breeze in. "Who? Dylan?" I still can't believe he's dangerous, but he might not have been able to resist driving by or dropping off a raccoon trap.

The yard is dark. Only the trees and wheatgrass are moving at all. I shiver as I remember Maggie's words. *You never truly know anyone else.*

"There's nobody out there." I slide the cool cloth across her forehead. "He's gone. And I won't let him near this house again as long as you're here. Okay?"

She nods.

"Let me get ready for bed," I say. "And then I'll stay by you for the rest of the night."

I hurry to switch the laundry to the dryer, then take my own pajamas to the bathroom, where I change quietly. But as I finish brushing my teeth, something colorful catches my eye in the trash can.

The card from Dylan. I left it on the kitchen counter. Did Maggie throw it away? Did the girl? I pull it out, wary because it's already been opened even though it's clearly my name on the envelope.

Cal—I'll always be here. Dylan

What the hell am I supposed to do with that? Is it sweet, or is it kind of weird? Because this sounds like he's talking about being around for more than just winterizing sprinklers.

I shove the card back into its envelope and bury it in the trash, then hurry to my room, where the girl has saved a spot under the quilt Mom made for me when she was sick. "Night Stars," she told me. "That's the name of the pattern. And that's where you'll find me, when I'm gone." Even then, I didn't take it literally, but I do sometimes feel her near under the night sky.

I slide under only the quilt so the sheet's still between us, giving the girl a little protection in case I brush against her bruises or the tender skin of her sunburns in the night.

But when she rests her head against my shoulder, I can tell she wants to be protected *by* me, not *from* me.

"I'm here," I say. "I've got you. I won't let anything bad happen to you."

As soon as the words are out, I know I shouldn't have said them. Because I know better than anyone it's not actually a promise you can keep. No matter how much you want to.

waiting/watching

They waited
in the clearing,
watching.
Two figures moved inside,
only silhouettes and shadows
and small, familiar sounds.
They would have to come out eventually.
Until then,
waiting,
watching.

5

The next morning, I'm barely opening my eyes to the patch of sunlight on my bedroom wall when the sound of somebody pounding on the front door startles me fully awake. I jump up, banging my shin on the dining chair that's still right next to my bed.

Which is all it takes to open the floodgates of everything that happened yesterday.

The funeral.

And the girl.

The pain, and the purpose.

Somehow, the girl sleeps through the noise, her breathing gentle sighs, her eyes softly closed. I hurry out to the living room to answer the door before whoever is knocking wakes her and brings back her pain too.

"What the hell?" I ask when I see the faces staring back at me from the front porch.

"We're just coming off the night shift," Trish says, striding past me and into the kitchen, her soccer-star haircut flopping with every step. She played midfielder in college and could probably still run circles around our high school team.

Sofia is both her true love and her perfect complement, all warmth and soft curves. "I'm sorry if we woke you," she says.

"I'm not," Trish says, but her volume drops a notch after a look from Sofia. She opens the fridge and pulls out the milk Maggie left last night. "You're better off keeping your sleep schedule as normal as possible."

"Maggie already brought stuff for breakfast," I say, wondering how much longer the parade of food-bearing friends and neighbors will last.

"Sure," Trish says. "If you like organic multigrain bread with the density of packed dirt. We, on the other hand, brought doughnuts. And hot cocoa."

"And gifts, yesterday," I say, remembering what waited on the table when I got home. "Thank you."

Sofia waves the thanks away. "Tell me about the girl," she says, nudging the doughnut box toward me. I choose a maple bar even though it's not my favorite, because it was his.

"We're here on Maggie's orders," Trish says, returning to her typical Trish volume. "We're supposed to see if we need to take her to the hospital, but we're also not supposed to further traumatize either of you. Is she awake?"

There's a soft clattering from down the hall.

"She is now," I say, hoping I'll still get to eat my doughnut before I have to do anything else.

But the girl is already walking toward us like a fawn on first-day legs.

"Hey," I say, pulling out a chair. "You hungry?"

The girl ignores the chair, sitting herself down in my usual seat and diving in on my doughnut.

So I guess this is a thing now.

"What's your name?" Trish asks.

The girl keeps chewing, her eyes intent on the maple bar. "She can't really talk much," I say.

"Can't talk, or isn't talking right now?" Sofia says, with so much kindness in her voice that the girl looks up and holds her gaze. Then she dips her chin just enough to tell us all that Sofia's figured it out.

"That's okay," Sofia says. "But we'd love to have something to call you."

The girl scans the room, and Trish, unable to help herself, starts naming everything she looks at.

"Apple? Air? Plant . . . no, Rose? Rosemary? Wait, I've got it. Ikea!" She holds up her colorful plastic plate in triumph.

"Shut up," Sofia mutters, and I'm about to agree when I catch the first real smile I've seen on the girl's face. She likes them already, and that makes me love them even more.

Then the girl's gaze lands on the center of the table, and she reaches out and picks up my Summer Rain candle.

"Candle?" Trish asks. "Blue?"

The girl takes the wick and pinches it, then holds her fingers out to me, blackened at the tips.

"Ash," I say. "You want us to call you Ash?"

Definitely a nod this time. "Okay," I say. "Ash." I'm not sure whether she's given herself a new name or whether she's been Ash all her life, but something tells me not to ask. Not now, anyway.

Trish teaches Ash to use the microwave to warm up her cocoa, and Ash acts like it's the most magical thing in the world. A few minutes later, Ash's plate and mug are both empty, and she pushes the dishes away. When Sofia reaches out and touches one of the bandages gently, Ash lets her. "I'm a nurse," she says. "Would it be okay if I check your wounds and clean you up a little?"

"Okay," Ash whispers, which is infinitely better than the other things she's said out loud. She leads Sofia back to my bedroom, but before she sits on the bed, she stares at me, long and hard, reminding me that there's something like a contract between us.

"You're safe now," I say. "And I'll be here the whole time. Just call out if you want me to come in."

But hopefully she won't. I'm more than willing to let an actual adult take care of this for a minute.

Trish finishes up the last of her doughnut (and the last of

44

Sofia's), then starts in on the dishes. I try to help, but she shoos me back around the counter. "Talk to me," she says. "Or, who am I kidding? Just listen to me." She loads our plates into the dishwasher (facing the wrong way, but I let her) as she tells me about the difficult trauma patient she knows she's got waiting for her tonight and the prospects of her rec league soccer team.

"Ben says he could come over later today," she says. "If you want." Ben is Trish's nephew, and honestly, she might be the reason we became best friends. After Mom died, when Trish and Sofia and Maggie were here so much while Dad was sorting everything out, Ben got dragged along to keep me company. We played about a hundred rounds of slapjack that first week with a deck of cards we found in a drawer. There must have been something therapeutic about concentrating so intensely on something so meaningless. That and getting to slap somebody.

"He would have come with us this morning," she adds, "but he was trying to give you space."

"At least somebody is," I say with a smirk, but she knows I don't mean it.

Do I want Ben to come over, though? I think of the way I felt when he was beside me yesterday: anchored, and safe. "He can come by, if it's okay with Ash."

Which would have seemed like a pretty big "if" last night. But when I look down the hall and into my bedroom, Ash is letting Sofia comb the tangles from her hair with something like adoration on her face.

And then I wonder: What if she's not afraid of Dylan so much as afraid of men? Ben would be a pretty safe way to test the theory. And as much as I love my nurses, Ben's still the person I want to be with most right now.

I turn back to Trish. "Actually, tell him there's nobody I'd love to see more."

Ash and I spend the morning together. She's wearing some old shorts and a T-shirt of mine, plus a pair of worn-out canvas slip-ons I outgrew years ago, and I'm amazed what a difference it makes to see her in normal clothes.

I find a little green notebook and a mechanical pencil in my desk and give it to Ash, just in case she's more willing to write than she is to speak. Even though she doesn't use them right away, she carries them around like they're superglued to her hands, clicking the lead clear out with her thumb, then pressing it back in against the cover of the notebook.

When she finally scribbles a word, painfully and slowly, the word itself surprises me.

OUTSIDE, in messy capital letters.

"Okay," I say, thinking this has to be a good sign, in terms of both her strength returning and her fear subsiding. It's overcast and early enough that I'm not worried about the sunburns; I'm sure we won't stay out long.

Ash can't walk far or fast, but I give her a tour of the property. She still isn't saying (or writing) much, so it's up to me to fill the silence.

"Here's the garden," I say, which feels obvious. But you never know. Ash nods in appreciation at the tomatoes and zucchini and green beans, sprouting from the soil in the same neat rows Mom used to plant. She cups a tender shoot in her hand.

"I planted the whole thing by myself, since my dad had more out-of-town visits than usual this spring. The beans will be ready first, but the rest won't be far behind. I'll make you some ham-and-green-bean soup. It's my mom's recipe." I swallow. "She was a nurse like . . . well, pretty much everybody you've met here. That's how I know Sofia and Trish and Maggie."

Ash looks like she's ready to trample right into the garden, so I divert her. "And that's where I found you," I say, pointing to the cottonwood in the northeast corner as another memory surfaces.

The first time I climbed the big cottonwood by myself, my parents were there to cheer me on. I can still feel the bite of the bark against my fingers and the breeze cooling the damp of my hairline as I looked down at them through the branches. Towering over my dad in a way I never had before, I had the strangest moment of fully realizing, maybe for the first time, that he had been my age once.

"Did you climb this tree?" I asked. "When you were a kid?"

"Yes," he said, tears springing to his eyes in a way that startled me.

"Did you get hurt?" I asked, unable to think of any other explanation for his reaction.

"Not when I hid here," he said. "Nothing can hurt you in this tree." Then he turned and walked back to the house without another word. That night, he and Mom sat on the back porch, looking out toward the tree and speaking in low, secret voices that let me know the rest of the story wasn't meant for me.

I shake myself out of the memory. Ash and I are past the garden now and almost to the barn.

"This is the barn," I say, stating the obvious once again. "We can go in there later. If the back room looks like a veterinarian's office, that's because it kind of was. My dad started seeing some of his easier patients here a few years ago. None of the surgeries or anything, but just the basics. It let him be home a lot more, which is good for a single parent, I guess, but it also meant he never really got to leave work."

I turn to the older, emptier side of the barn. "Even before my mom died, though, he'd have animals in here he wanted to keep an eye on. We had a llama one time. And an ostrich. Man, I was terrified of that thing. Sometimes we'd bring the animals into the house, kittens and stuff like that, but mostly they'd stay out here. Especially the bigger ones. Definitely the ostrich. And one time I ran away to live here, but it only lasted a couple of hours before my mom found me and convinced me to come back."

I'm rambling now, and I look over in apology, but Ash seems to be soaking it up. She presses the notebook against the wall of the barn and writes out a question.

ALL GONE NOW?

"Yeah," I say. "No animals in there now. Well, mice, maybe, and I guess there could be a cat or two hanging around because of the mice."

And then it hits me: Maybe she isn't talking about the animals. I take a deep breath and answer the other question she may have been asking.

"My parents are gone now too. It's just me."

She pats her chest, and whether she means that I've got her now or that her parents are gone too, the gesture makes me feel a little less alone.

"What else should I show you?" I ask, mostly to myself. "There are petroglyphs only a mile or so up the canyon, by the creek," I tell her. "Pictures carved into the cliffs. We can go see them tomorrow if you want. The Fremont people carved them, maybe a thousand years ago."

Ash shows me the question again: *ALL GONE NOW?*

"Yes. They're gone now too," I say as another memory surfaces: fourth-grade Calli, out of breath and racing home, bursting through the door one day after a history lesson in school, desperate to ask my dad a question that had been burning inside me all day.

"Did Grandma and Grandpa steal this land from the people who lived here first?" I only had vague memories of my grand-parents, who died when I was little, but I didn't want to believe that of them.

"No, no," he assured me. "That all happened long before their time. They bought it from a rancher who was retiring. They didn't steal anything."

I felt better then, but not for long. The Fremont people who made the petroglyphs might be gone, but we had also learned about Paiutes and Navajos, who were very much still part of our community. Three generations on this land didn't seem like quite so many when I thought about it like that. *Grandma and Grandpa didn't steal it*, I thought as I lay in my bed that night, *but they didn't give it back either.*

Even now, the thought of the petroglyph panel is enough to remind me that this land isn't really mine at all. That even if it's true what they teach us at church and we're not responsible for the sins of our fathers, we're not entirely free from them either.

cottonwood

Once upon a time
and many, many years ago,
a boy and his mother
kept watch
for signs of their monster.

He wasn't always like this,
she said, blood smeared
across her cheek.
But for the boy,
always only extended back
as far as his memories,
and his very first memory
was not so different from this moment:
blood,
whispers,
waiting to make sure
the monster was really gone.
Wondering what they had done wrong
this time.

Later,
the boy learned to hide in the branches
of the big cottonwood
at the first sign of the monster's anger
crackling the air.

Sometimes, the monster would whip the boy
with a fallen branch
thick as the monster's own finger.

If he couldn't find one on the ground,
he'd stumble away, swearing,
and the boy could make his escape too.

That's why the boy whispered
what he did
in the branches of the cottonwood,
to the branches of the cottonwood
as much as to himself:

Hold on.
Hold still.
Stay here.
Stay alive.

coming home, part 1

Once upon a time
and many years ago,
a little girl from Harmony
made a big mistake that
made her daddy so upset,
she ran away
to live in the barn.

But it only lasted an hour or so
before her mother found her
and sat beside her
on the soft blanket she'd spread over the straw.

Do I have to come home?
the girl asked.

The mother shook her head.
Said,
Not until you're ready.

She took one of her daughter's hands in hers
and wrapped the small fingers into a fist.
You have power, she said.
Never forget that.

She took her daughter's other hand
and placed it over her six-year-old heart.
And, she said,
you have truth.
Never forget that either.
And never let anyone
take those two things from you.

The girl curled her fingers tighter,
pressed her hand closer to her heart,
and promised her mother—
promised herself—
she would never forget.

But she did.
For a while, anyway.

6

Ash is starting to look tired, so we turn back toward the house just as an old white truck rattles up the street and parks in the gravel at the edge of our lot. The first time Ben parked there, Dad was watching out the window. "He'd rather ask forgiveness than permission, wouldn't he?" Which is true enough, but my best friend seems to be able to charm his way into plenty of both.

"That's Ben," I tell Ash, trying to gauge her reaction to a pretty solidly male name. I can't quite interpret the look she gives me. "I think you'll like him, but if you're uncomfortable, tell me, okay?"

Ash considers this, then flips to the next page in her notebook to write another message:

HE LOVES YOU?

I'm not entirely sure if I'm allowed to laugh yet, but I can't deny how good it feels when I do.

"Well, yeah, he loves me, I guess—but just as a friend. If you're talking *love* love, he falls hard and fast, and he goes for girls with more curves than me, although there's more to him than that. . . ." I catch an uncomfortable look on Ash's face and trail off. She's at that in-between age when I have no idea whether the idea of a boyfriend is intriguing or absolutely disgusting to her.

Or something much worse than that. I shudder, wishing I knew where her wounds came from, but also grateful that I can hide from knowing.

Ben waves and starts walking out toward us in his smoothie-smudged uniform shirt. Instead of the nervous energy I felt last night when Dylan showed up, the sight of Ben puts me at ease. I want Ash to feel the same way, so I tell her more about him. How he works at the Dairy Freeze with me, how he can play any song you can name if you sit him down at a piano, how he pitched the first perfect game in school history last year.

Ash takes the notebook and scribbles another single-word message.

HAIR

I look up from the page to see some serious concern on her face. And I laugh again. I can't help it. I've gotten so used to Ben's hair situation that I don't even see it anymore. But when I look at him through her eyes, I realize how bad it is: patchy, uneven, sticking out in odd places at odd angles.

"Sometimes he thinks he can do anything," I explain. "And last month, he thought he could cut his own hair."

He's almost to us now, and I whisper to Ash, "Don't say anything about the hair. It's in an awkward stage right now, but it'll get better; I promise."

"Hey," Ben says in a low voice when he reaches us. "What are we whispering about?"

Before I can stop her, Ash shows him the notebook, and Ben lets out a laugh. "You like it, huh?" he says, combing his fingers through a particularly patchy spot. "I can cut yours like this, if you want." Ash shakes her head and backs away, and he laughs again, pulling me into a side hug this time. I'm breathing in the scent of him when he lets me go and turns to Ash.

"I'm kidding," he says as I wonder whether it's normal to breathe in your best friend. "Most people can't pull off this look, and I like your hair the way it is."

Ash puts a nervous hand up to her hair and gives him a smile.

She points to the barn, and I say, "Yeah, go ahead. We'll follow you in a minute."

I try to take a quick mental inventory to make sure there's nothing in the barn that could hurt Ash. The clinical stuff is all locked in the back room, so unless Dylan's right and she startles a raccoon awake or something, she should be fine. I can't even remember the last time we actually had an animal in there for more than a quick visit. Has there ever been a stretch this long when no animals stayed in the barn?

Ben searches my face, and I shake the question off.

"You good?" he asks.

"Oh, yeah," I say. "Never better."

He drops his chin to his chest. "Terrible question. I am the worst."

"You're not the worst," I say. "And I'm doing a lot better than yesterday. Which is weird, because . . ." I gesture to the barn, suddenly out of words.

"Yeah, Trish told me about the girl."

"Ash," I say, catching a slight movement out of the corner of my eye that tells me she might be watching us from the shadows.

Ben follows my gaze and lowers his voice. "Yeah, Ash. Are you sure you're up for this?"

"You don't think I can take care of her?"

"It's not that," he says, turning his phone over and over in his hand. "Not at all. But, Calli, you just lost your dad."

I look toward the meadow, blinking back the tears that have suddenly sprung up. "I promise I know that."

"So maybe you let other people help."

I roll my eyes, partly to clear the tears away. "Since he died, there's been a nonstop stream of people from every direction, trying to help. So tell me what you really mean, Ben."

He rubs his forehead. "I mean maybe she should see a doctor. Maybe somebody should talk to the police."

Then the voice. Dad's voice. Not from the barn, but from somewhere simultaneously beyond it and inside of me.

No police. No doctors. All she needs is you, just like all we needed was each other. Ben means well, but believe in yourself.

"Okay," I say, first to my dad's voice or memory or whatever, and then to Ben. "Okay, but maybe she ran away from something and police and doctors would retraumatize her. Maybe what she needs is a chance to heal and feel safe on her own terms. You've spent all of two seconds with her. How can you possibly know what she needs better than I do? Better than she does?"

Ben sighs. "You're right. You know her better than I do. But . . ." He gives up trying to explain and hands me his phone.

When I read the headline on the screen, my stomach drops.

Search Continues for Missing Girl from Ash Creek

Below the headline, there's a picture of Ash Creek, the religious fundamentalist community less than an hour's drive into the desert. Dad was one of the few outsiders they trusted, so he'd go there to help care for their animals sometimes.

I steal a glance into the barn, but Ash is on the far side, examining the shelves of tools and gardening supplies.

Ash.

Ash Creek.

Was she giving me a clue? But why, if she's trying to hide?

"A girl named Charity Trager went missing last week," Ben says, his voice low. "Thirteen years old. Red hair. They think she ran away, and they've been afraid she died in the desert."

"Why do they think she ran away?" I ask, remembering how young the girls in Ash Creek are sometimes forced to marry. "Did they tell the authorities that part?"

Ben shakes his head. "I don't know, but her parents even gave an interview, and you know how they feel about cameras down there. They're wrecked, Calli. If this is their daughter, they should know."

I shove the phone back at Ben. "Why? So they can send her straight down the aisle? If she ran away, she had a reason." I don't know if Ash is Charity—but if she is, the whole thing suddenly makes sense, and I'm more grateful than ever that she gets to have some control here. "She gets to decide what happens next—for forty-eight hours, at the very least. Maggie promised. So I'm not calling the police. And if she says no hospital and she keeps recovering here, I'm not going to force her."

Ben sighs. "Okay. But what are you going to say if they start asking questions? What am I supposed to say if they're making the rounds through town and they come into the Dairy Freeze and ask me? I can't lie to the police."

"Let's hope they don't ask you, I guess. But come on. We both know nothing ever happens at the Dairy Freeze."

Ben looks at me like there's more he wants to say, but whatever it is, I don't want to hear it. He can't know best if he doesn't even know Ash. "Come talk to her," I say. "She's already less afraid of you than she is of Dylan."

He pulls back. "Dylan came over? You talked to him before you talked to me?"

"Well, yeah, but only because he showed up unannounced. Trust me, I got rid of him as fast as I could."

Ben relaxes a little at this, a smile playing at the corner of his mouth. "If only that had always been your motto."

Inside the barn, Ben swings his leg over one of the saddles and smiles at Ash. "Calli might try to tell you that Dylan's the horse expert since he, you know, has horses. But I can show you a thing or two." Then he starts describing to Ash how to ride a horse—and getting all the details wrong, of course. She swings her leg over a saddle too, and soon they're laughing together. Ben's charmed her already, which shoots some serious holes in the theory that she's afraid of all men.

"Come here, Calli," he says. "I've got something to tell you."

I lean in close, thinking he's going to whisper, but then he leans back, closes his eyes, and starts crooning some corny cowboy love song as he sways back and forth:

"I love you more than a Tennessee rain,
But if you don't love me, then I'll drown in the pain."

I roll my eyes at him, but Ash bursts out laughing. I watch her, considering Ben's theory about who she is and where she came from. If she crossed the desert from Ash Creek, it would explain the dehydration, the name, and the utter astonishment at the microwave. It would explain almost everything, really. But why would she have been coming out of the canyon instead of from the south? And why was she wearing that flannel shirt instead of the long, plain dresses that are the uniform of the girls and women from Ash Creek?

After Ben leaves, Ash and I wander back to the house. She plants herself in front of the window while I start thinking about what to eat for lunch. I can't handle any of the foil pans in the fridge right now, so I find the notebook and flip it open, planning to take it to her and ask what kind of sandwich she wants.

But when I look down at the page, she's written something more while she watched us from the barn. One small scribble-out that changes everything.

HE LOVES YOU̶

She knew he wasn't serious with that song, right? I stare at the page for a few seconds before I remember that I'm supposed to be giving the notebook to her.

"Is a turkey sandwich okay?" I ask, handing her the notebook and forcing my thoughts back on track.

Ash thinks. Scribbles.

PB?

"Yeah, of course," I tell her. "It'll be ready in a minute." I tape the bandage on her leg back in place. "We might need to take a look at those after we eat, okay?"

She nods, then turns away and resumes staring out the window, so I start making sandwiches. I'm almost finished when I hear her cry out. This time, I recognize the word right away.

"No," she yells, again and again and again, as she digs her fingernails into her thighs so hard we're going to need a whole new set of bandages. "No, no, NO." She's shaking, searching for cover, running for my room. By the time I catch up with her, she's cowering in the closet, banging her head against the back of the wall. "No," she says again, this time in a whisper. Then she calms and stills, so suddenly it makes me shiver.

"Shhh . . . ," she says, closing her eyes and trying to clench her chattering teeth.

There's a knock at the door.

"Stay put," I say. "Whoever it is, I'll send them away, okay? You're safe here."

On my way, I glance toward the hall closet where Dad has always kept his gun. But then I hear his voice again. *Going into a confrontation with a gun just guarantees somebody's getting shot.*

So I keep walking, far enough down the hall that I can see out the front window. A truck waits at the curb, the word *SHERIFF* gleaming across its side in all-capital letters.

He wasn't asking permission, out by the barn. He was asking forgiveness.

"Ben," I whisper. "What have you done?"

correlation/causation

An aside:
Having a gun doesn't make you a monster.
But if you are a monster already,
having a gun sure doesn't help.

7

I don't know what I'm expecting when I open the door, but it's not Kasen Keller in uniform, gun at his hip.

"Oh," I say, trying to reconcile the picture before me. Crush-worthy Kasen, so strong and handsome and so very shy—but also Keller the Killer, all-state senior in three sports when I was a fresh-man. They made baseball cards of the team that year, and Ben actu-ally asked Kasen to sign his, like Ben was seven and Kasen played for the Red Sox or something.

No wonder Ben spilled his guts. I'm surprised he didn't offer to bring his hero right over.

"Good morning, miss." So he doesn't remember sitting next to me in beginning ceramics, way back when. "Can I ask you a few questions?"

"Of course," I say, coming out and closing the door behind me. "Have a seat." I gesture to the chairs on the porch, hoping this little bit of hospitality will make up for the fact that I'm definitely not inviting him in.

Stay inside, Ash, I plead silently, imagining her huddled in the closet. *Stay quiet.*

It's weird to see Kasen in a sheriff's uniform instead of Har-mony High green and gold. He tugs at the collar; maybe it's still weird for him too.

"I'm sorry about your dad," he says, because even if he doesn't remember me, of course he would know my dad. "We had to put our dog to sleep a few years back, and he was real nice to us that day." I'd forgotten about his accent, soft and subtle and just enough to remind you that he didn't grow up around here.

"Thanks," I say. "Those were his hardest days, when he knew doing the right thing would still break kids' hearts."

I wait, hoping the silence will help him get to the point. Lucky for me, he takes the hint and jumps right back in. "I'm investigating a missing persons case," he says. "A girl disappeared from Ash Creek."

"That's really sad," I say, and I mean it. Maybe there's a way to get through this without lying outright.

"Have you seen anybody like that?" he asks. "Red hair, thin, kind of scrappy."

"I'm not sure," I tell him. "This week has been . . . a lot."

"Of course," he says. He pulls up a picture on his phone. "This is her," he says, turning the screen so I can see.

The photo is blurry and taken from a distance. It shows four little girls lined up in pastel dresses, violins tucked under their right arms, matching bows in their hair, matching bows of another kind in their hands. "The one on the far right," he says, before I can even ask the question.

The girl on the far right wears a pink dress; she's the only one not smiling at the camera. She's so much younger than Ash that it couldn't be her, and I can't quite decide how I feel about that. "I haven't seen anybody like that," I say, grateful it's true.

"She's older now," Kasen adds quickly. "Thirteen. But they don't take many photographs there. They play by their own rules down in Ash Creek." He pulls a piece of paper from his back pocket and unfolds it. "This is her too. Her little sister drew it."

This I study more closely. It's definitely a kid's drawing. But I can't help studying the details that seem to match Ash. Is that a stray pencil mark or a freckle by her eye? Is it more common than I think it is to have orange hair and bright green eyes?

63

"I hope she's okay," I say. "They must be so worried."

"So you haven't seen her?"

"I don't think so," I say, which is still true enough. "Do they think she ran away?"

"That's what we're trying to find out."

I can't stop myself. "Do you think if she did run away, she had a good reason?"

"Maybe," he says, looking so sadly at the picture, I swear it seems like he might cry. "That's certainly something I'd want to ask her, if I could talk to her."

But then his gaze flickers back toward the door. And that's when I see it: the easy grace he would shed at just the right moment on the basketball court. Draw the defender out so you can drive past them to the hoop. It was Dad who pointed it out to me during Kasen's senior season. (I'd always sit by Dad for the first half—he seemed so lonely otherwise.)

Watch him, Calli. He knows exactly what he's doing.

And he does. I see it now. He doesn't care about her; this is just strategy. Draw out your opponent, then go in for the kill.

"Well, good luck with that," I say, standing up and brushing absolutely nothing off my thighs. "Thanks for stopping by."

"Mind if I come in?" he asks, reaching for the door in almost exactly the same way Dylan did last night—only he doesn't drop his hand.

"Why?" I ask, stepping between him and the house in what I hope is a natural way. "Did you need something else?"

"A drink of water would be nice," he says.

I squint past him. "Is that a water bottle in your console?"

He clenches his jaw, only for an instant. "Ah, yeah. Of course. Forgot I had that today."

"Glad I could help."

The lie sticks in my throat as I say goodbye and slip back into the house. Will every half-truth make me less like my dad? And why does this lie feel like what he would have wanted?

Once Kasen's cruiser disappears around the corner, I find Ash—still in the closet with her knees clutched to her chest. "He's gone," I say, sitting down beside her. She lets out a long breath and rests her head on my shoulder, holding on to the hem of my shorts as an additional anchor.

After a few seconds, wet seeps from the carpet through my shorts. *Oh, Ash.* I wonder how I didn't notice the smell the second I opened the door.

But I don't move. If she was that afraid, the least I can do is sit here with her a little longer. I try my best to tamp down my irritation at yet another mess to clean up. "He's gone," I say again, stroking her hair and wondering how many more times those words will define our hardest moments.

When Ash is ready, I help her up. "I think it's time for you to shower on your own, then we'll eat our lunch," I say, and immediately I hear his voice again.

Good, he tells me. *Give her a little independence.*

Ash watches as I gather soap, shampoo, and conditioner. If she really is from Ash Creek, are all these products in plastic bottles foreign to her or completely familiar? How do I know so little about a community so close to mine?

I've been told to love my neighbor all my life, but now that I think about it, there was almost an unspoken understanding that the commandment didn't really apply to people from Ash Creek. We tolerated them. We took their money when they came into the Dairy Freeze. But I'm not sure I ever saw anybody demonstrate anything I'd describe as love.

Anybody, including me.

I try to make up for it now, lining things up in the order she'll need them, giving little explanations that hopefully don't seem condescending. "These two are for your hair. White bottle first, rinse it out, then blue bottle. I'll set out some clean clothes I think will fit you. Holler if you need me," I say, shutting the door softly and heading to my room to change my clothes, then to the kitchen to find the carpet cleaner.

My phone buzzes as I'm scrubbing. Ben.

Please don't be mad

I am mad. I won't be forever, but he doesn't get to tell me I can't feel it now.

Another buzz.

Greg says he can put you back on the schedule whenever you're ready but take your time

I set my feelings toward Ben aside and try to absorb the fact that our manager is ready for me to come back to work. But am I ready to spend hours pulling a soft-serve lever with the grind and groan of shake motors and smoothie blenders in the background? Can I chat with coworkers and customers when I know I'll never see Dad walk through the door and order a CocoNutella shake again? And is any of that worth leaving Ash for?

But what's the alternative? Stay here, I guess. Hide here. Let Dad's death and Ash's arrival reduce the setting of my life to this house and yard.

I'm not ready to forgive Ben yet, though, so I don't answer him.

How am I supposed to have any answers right now anyway?

After lunch, Ash and I stay inside with the blinds down. I tell myself it's to keep out the sun, not because we have anything to hide. I plant myself on the couch, flipping through channels for whatever won't upset Ash. She comes to sit next to me, intrigued by the TV. But it doesn't last long; pretty soon, she's up and peeking through the blinds, then back to the couch, again and again. It's a little annoying, to be honest, even if she's feeling the same way I am: caged

66

in, but too scared to go out. And I've never in all my life been scared of anything or anybody in this town.

Or maybe I'm not scared so much as nervous. It's definitely a nervous twist in my gut when I hear an engine rev up the driveway, then fall silent right in the spot Dad used to park next to the house. The way it shudders into silence even sounds like his old Chevy Silverado.

Then three hard knocks—not at the front door, but at the kitchen door out to the carport. I stand up to answer it.

"No," Ash whimpers beside me.

"Yes," I say, crossing the kitchen. "If I don't answer the door, they might just come in. And this is still my house, believe it or not."

I feel guilty for snapping at her, but only a little. I'm not some aspiring saint like Dad was, and her freak-outs are starting to get on my nerves. That, and the mess in the closet that might need another round of scrubbing.

Still, I give Ash time to hide in my bedroom before I peek between the blinds to get a look at the driveway. When I do, I have to hold on to the counter to steady myself.

It sounded like the Silverado because it *was* the Silverado, parked in its usual spot like Dad is about to walk in, eyes tired but smiling when he catches sight of me. I yank the door open, hoping to see a miracle standing on the other side, even though I've never believed in miracles.

But it isn't. Of course it isn't. The rest of my life will be scanning crowds and opening doors and always this pang of disappointment because it will never be, could never be, the right face looking back at me.

In this case, the wrong face is well past sixty and badly in need of a shave. The man at the door is Fluffy, the mechanic from three blocks down who has a cabin near ours up the mountain.

"LuEllen made these for you," Fluffy growls, shoving a plate of brownies into my hands, then shoving his hands (with all nine fingers) into the pockets of his coveralls. Fluffy's wife is an actual saint who showed up the day before Mom's funeral to take me shopping for a new dress, "Because even on hard days, something pretty can help a little."

Dad told me later that she knew a thing or two about hard days. That she forgave Fluffy for an affair years ago that had the whole town talking for a while. That she'd never given up hope that their estranged kid would come home. In both cases, she'd learned to let her grief soften her somehow, when it does the opposite for so many.

Fluffy, on the other hand, is the opposite of both his name and his wife. Fluffy is done with this conversation, such as it was. He's brought the truck back, I guess from the scene of the fire.

He fishes the keys from his pocket and hands them to me. "It's ready to go, up the mountain or just around town. Washed and waxed it, changed the oil, rotated the tires, new brake pads . . ." He trails off and walks off at the same time, clearing his throat in a way that makes me wonder if I came dangerously close to seeing a softer side of Fluffy. I'm amazed all over again at the effect Dad had on people that I didn't even realize.

"Thank you," I call after him as he starts down the sidewalk toward his shop. *Thank you for the brownies and the truck*, I think. *For bringing a piece of him home.*

pacemaker

To the old mechanic,
machines make more sense than people.
Always have.

His wife has learned to live with it,
but their daughter never did.
From the time she was tiny,
the mechanic and his daughter
were like misaligned gears,
grating against each other
even as they tried to work together.

Machines make more sense than people,
especially his own daughter,
who left for Ash Creek years ago
to join that cult
or whatever it is.

They weren't welcome to visit her there.
He was secretly relieved.
Ash Creek was the kind of place people tried to escape,
not the kind of place you'd want to visit.
Not the kind of place any sane person would join.

He thinks of his daughter
as he walks away from Calli's,

the Silverado all tuned up
and restored to its rightful owner.

He thinks of his daughter
because he sees a girl,
her face framed by the window,
half hidden by the glare on the glass
and for a moment
his heart stops

> *which is not a metaphor for the old mechanic—*
> *he actually feels his pacemaker kick in—*

because
for a moment
he could swear the girl in the window
is his daughter.

But he shakes his head,
tries to shed the thought like a skin,
like he does all thoughts of his daughter.
He will never understand her,
and it hurts too much to try.

But he can't stop himself
from glancing back at the window.

And when he does,
the girl who is not his daughter
is still there.
Watching.

8

After Fluffy leaves, I sit down at the counter and treat myself to a brownie. It's dense and decadent, and I wonder for half a second if I can hide them from Ash. LuEllen really is the best baker I know. It's LuEllen who brings the sacrament bread, hot and fresh, to the church each week.

I still remember the day I learned that fact. One morning, some Sunday just before I turned twelve, I watched the boys my age line up in neat rows to pass the sacrament trays of bread and water to the congregation. It had never occurred to me before, but I was suddenly, deeply hurt to realize I would never get to be part of what had always seemed a very solemn and sacred job, just because I was a girl.

"It's not fair," I whispered, and a moment later, I felt my mom's hand in mine, her fingers thin but her grip still strong. By then, I knew hers wasn't the kind of cancer where there was any real shot of coming out on top, but I didn't know that I'd have only a couple more years with her.

When I turned to face her, tears in my eyes at knowing I'd never have what the boys had, I saw in an instant how small the injustice of not passing the sacrament seemed in comparison to the injustice of losing your mother, of losing your life.

But she still saw my small heartbreak. It mattered to her. She leaned over and whispered in my ear. "It's LuEllen who bakes the bread each week, you know. So really, she's a bigger part of this than anybody."

"And see their straight lines?" she asked. I saw them everywhere then: the rows of sacrament cups, the stiff collars and silk ties tight around their necks, the order and precision of it all. "And look at us, here," she said. "Filling in all the curves and soft spaces however we like." When one of the boys reached our row, she took a small piece of bread for herself before taking the tray. "Tell me, Calli: Who really passes you the sacrament each week?"

I looked down at the tray she held out to me. "It's you," I realized, and she nodded with a soft smile.

Later, I took a small cup of water from another tray, the tiny swallow of water seeming to quench more inside me than it should have been capable of. Because even though the boys were the ones to bless and sanctify the bread and water, we were part of it too. Rising and fluid in ways they weren't allowed to be. Would I trade that freedom for the chance to line up with them? To be in charge? I wasn't sure, but I also knew it wasn't my choice.

LuEllen's bread is still as good as it ever was, but it's no match for her brownies. I've eaten three before I make a reluctant deal with myself to save the rest—and admit even more reluctantly that I should go check on Ash, who is making frustrated sounds from down the hall.

I expect her to be in my bedroom, but it's empty. I'm about to call for her when I look through the doorway of my parents' room, and there she is, pulling all of Dad's shirts out of the drawer and pawing through the pockets.

"No," I say, hurling her own word back at her.

She ignores me, picks up another shirt, tears the pocket as she shoves her hand inside.

"Stop," I say, starting toward her. "Don't touch those."

She doesn't notice me—or pretends not to, anyway—until I'm on my knees across from her, pulling the rest of the pile away. "Get out of here," I snap. "You don't get to be in here. You don't get to mess with his stuff. He hates that. *Hated* that." I clutch an armful of shirts close to my chest. "My dad is dead, Ash. You understand that, right?"

At the word *dead*, Ash throws the shirt she's been holding like it's on fire. But I don't care, and I'm not done. "New rule: You're not allowed in this room. Never come in here again. Never touch anything of his, in any room. Do you understand me?"

She nods, even though it's an impossible rule to follow. She doesn't know his stuff from mine, and the house itself would qualify as his anyway.

Except it's not his house anymore. All he gets is a tiny hole in the ground, and I haven't even gone back to see whether Dylan Rigby has laid the sod yet. Suddenly, I'm sick at how profoundly I've failed him by not even doing this one simple thing.

I'm losing him even more because of her.

"I have to go," I say, the weight of his keys in my pocket guiding me to my next move. "I have to check on something. Stay here, keep the blinds down, lock the door. Hell, his shotgun's around here somewhere, if that makes you feel better. Do you know how to shoot?"

Her eyes go wide. She shakes her head. "No," she says. "No, no, no." She moves to hide in my parents' bed, but I block her path. I might be overreacting, but I'm so sick of *No*. So sick of her.

"I'll be back," I tell her, then go straight out the kitchen door and climb into his truck. I take my first big breath, and the smell of him cuts me deep.

I try to fit my fingers into the grooves on the back of the steering wheel exactly where his would have been. Instead of pulling the seat forward, I leave it where he liked it, stretching my toes out to reach the pedals. I reach for the broken radio knob to listen to whatever he was listening to last, to keep at least that small thing from changing.

But the knob's not broken anymore. Fluffy has replaced it. And when I turn it on to find some ranting talk radio host when all Dad listened to was oldies, I realize my mistake.

This is what Fluffy would listen to, where he would want the seat, how he would angle the mirrors. The scent is still Dad's, but the rest of him is gone already.

Everyone is erasing him, even when they don't mean to. I have to get to the one place where I know he'll still be. Forever.

⌒

The cemetery is empty, the backhoe parked in its place behind the shed. The funeral flowers are mostly still here, though the deer have eaten some of them. That would have made him smile.

I close my eyes for a moment, letting the world drift away with a few deep breaths.

"You've missed so much already," I say, relieved that in this quiet place, I can feel his presence again—not so much beneath the ground, but in the sparrow's song in the distance, the sagebrush on the breeze. In my own mind and heart.

"About the girl," I begin, opening my eyes. "I know you would want me to help her, but today I wanted to kill her myself."

He would have laughed at that. And then, without saying anything, he would have guided me back to being good, or at least not being horrible to her. He's doing it still.

When we're stressed or overwhelmed, we revert to what's familiar, or what's helped us cope in the past. That may be what you're seeing in her now.

I sigh. He's right, but I still don't want to let go quite yet. "It's just . . . she freaks out so freaking much. And it feels like *I've* earned the right to be the one freaking out right now. You know?"

Looks like maybe you exercised that right by coming here. Somehow that gentle guilt cuts me deep. Dad was tough on me, but that's only because he saw beyond who I was to who I could become.

Maybe it's morbid and maybe it's weird and maybe it's a

manifestation that I really am losing it, but I lie down then, in the spot between my parents, hoping to feel relief at having them a little closer.

But the moment I feel the earth against my back, I'm buried by a grief so sudden and consuming that all I can do is curl up on my side, not even caring who might see. For a long time, there are no words in my mind. No colors, no sounds. Maggie is right: Grief isn't linear. Sometimes it's three-dimensional, and it swallows you whole. Finally, one thought comes to me through the void.

"Maybe it wouldn't be so bad to die," I whisper. "Then I could be buried right here between you."

No, my love. In this darkest moment, it's her presence I feel. *You'll meet someone and fall in love and have babies of your own. Your life is still just beginning. Your first chapter has been full of sorrow, but that doesn't have to define your story. Your dad and I are both proof of that.*

There is no next chapter I can imagine where I don't have this gaping hole inside me. It's a tragedy, losing both my parents. Everybody has told me so. But isn't that everybody's story, one way or another? Whether it's death or divorce or addiction or abuse or a hundred other kinds of heartache, isn't tragedy what life gives everybody in the end?

There is tragedy, yes. But there is beauty too. And often, they're a bittersweet duet.

The funeral flowers are all for Dad, but I want to leave something for both of them. So I walk to the edge of the cemetery and find a smooth rock that sort of looks like a heart if you angle it right. I place it at the base of their headstone, right between them, right where I belonged, all those years ago. Where I belong still.

My eyes roam the cemetery, wondering about all the lives whose last chapters ended here.

Everyone has a story, my love, Mom seems to whisper. *People are telling them to us all the time, if only we'll stop to listen.*

75

survival guide

As the boy from the cottonwood grew,
he was determined to be
another kind of person,
and the main criterion was
not like his father.

And he did it.
He met a woman
who made him a better man.
Married her,
had a baby,
loved them more than life itself.

Built a beautiful life
in a beautiful place
where both had once been bitter.

Became known by other names:
    Doctor,
    Bishop,
    Daddy,
and those roles
and those names
made him feel
helpful,

good,
and loved.

But then his wife died,
and nothing
was beautiful
anymore.

Not even his daughter,
who reminded him
so much of her mother,
it hurt to look at her.

His wife died
and everything changed,
including the ways he saw himself:
    No longer a doctor who believed
    healing most *of his patients was enough.*
    No longer a daddy who believed
    he could keep his daughter safe.
    No longer a bishop at all,
    because he was so easily replaced
    before his time was even up.
    No longer a better man.

What choice did he have
but to find a way,
any way,
to carry on?

So he expanded his veterinary practice
with new patients,

late hours,
extended service area,
riskier procedures,
and experimental medications.

Whatever it took
to know he had done all he could
to save every one,
to numb his pain enough
to survive his own life
and regain some semblance of control
for his own sake
and for his daughter's.

Didn't they both deserve another chance at happiness?
Didn't they both deserve a fresh start?

She certainly deserved a better childhood than he'd had.
And she'd almost had it.
But even a dad who doesn't hurt you
can't always protect you from pain.

He hated himself
more than a little
for that.

9

On my way home from the cemetery, Maggie calls, but I cut her off before she can say anything. Now that I've cooled down, I'm curious again.

"Do you still have that old violin?"

"The one LuEllen passed along? I'm sure it's somewhere," she says, barely thrown by the random question. "Why?"

"Can you bring it tonight?"

"Who says I'm coming tonight?"

"It's been almost twenty-four hours. If I know you at all, Maggie, you were calling to say you're coming over tonight."

"Seven o'clock," she admits. "Let me know if you have any dinner requests."

"We don't. Just bring the violin. And thanks."

Maggie ends up bringing a take-and-bake pizza with a side of unnecessary apology. "It was a long day," she explains.

"You're off duty now," I say, taking the pizza and turning on the oven. "I can at least handle this."

"I saw that your dad's truck is back," Maggie says. "Fluffy took that little project very seriously."

Before she lets herself relax, Maggie returns to her car and brings in a battered violin case.

"I'll trade you," I say, handing her the stack of bills I've assembled for her to take to Bishop Carver as she hands me the violin.

"You planning on picking up a new hobby?" she asks. "I'm sure it's out of tune, and I haven't the first idea how to fix that."

"I . . . have a theory," I say, reaching for the handle.

Maggie scans the kitchen, her gaze resting on the corner of the floor where she first saw Ash. "Where's our new friend?"

"In my room. She's been there awhile. We had a visitor earlier she wasn't too excited about, and she got a little upset." (I don't mention the part I played in upsetting her.)

Once the pizza is in the oven, I join Maggie on the couch so I can tell her about our day in soft tones without the danger of Ash overhearing.

"I know we said forty-eight hours, but you have to cooperate with the police, Calli," she says.

"I will. That's why I asked you to bring the violin. I watched the interview with the parents online. It sounds like this kid—Charity Trager—loved to play. Like music was her life. If it turns out this girl plays, well, we're onto something. But if she doesn't even react to the violin, then maybe we can still keep the promise *you* made her and let her decide what happens next."

Maggie purses her lips. "At some point, we've got to let folks know she's here, whether she's Charity Trager or not. I can only stretch the rules so far. You understand that, right?"

Luckily, the oven timer goes off before I have to answer. "Ash," I call. "You ready for dinner?"

I say it like I'm expecting an answer. But she hasn't even been willing to look at me since I got home. Since I abandoned her.

"I went to the cemetery today," I confess to Maggie, "even though she didn't want me to. I know I shouldn't have. He would want me to do what's right."

Maggie rolls her eyes at this. "Where did you get the idea that doing what's right means doing what's best for other people, no matter the cost to you? If you needed space to grieve and remember, well, she can grant you that." Maggie follows my gaze down the hall to where my bedroom door is still shut. "Let me guess: She's not talking to you?" she asks.

"Even less than before," I say. "Which I wouldn't have thought possible."

"She will," Maggie says. "I have a feeling she's going to tell you her whole story one of these days. And when she does, you do two things for me: You listen. And you believe her. Can you promise me that?"

Something warm surges through me, even as chills prickle my arms. Maggie's words are nearly the same as the ones I imagined Mom saying back in the cemetery. "I will."

Maggie takes my hands and holds them to her. "That was the gift your mom gave me when I came here. Maybe the single greatest gift of my life, because it gave me the courage to stay gone and start over. And don't worry," she adds. "A little scuffle like this can mean Ash is getting more comfortable with you. Only makes you two seem like sisters to me."

The idea makes me soften a little, so I slice up the pizza and slide a piece onto each of our plates, then take Ash's to my room along with a big glass of water. "Hey." I gently kick the door with my toes since my hands are full. "Could you open up?"

She does, eyes still down.

"Maggie just said we seem like sisters," I say as I set the plate on the nightstand. I try to lean casually against the doorframe as I ask the next question. "Do you have a sister?"

She looks up at me and gives a single, sharp shake of her head.

"Right. Me neither. Well, I hope you like pizza." I'm suddenly unsure whether they eat pizza in Ash Creek. They must, right? Doesn't everybody?

Maybe not. Ash angles the point away from her and takes a bite, crust first.

"Do you want me to come eat in here with you?" I ask. She shrugs, her head still down.

"No worries." The sister question might not have told me

anything, but I've got another card to play. "One more delivery, and then I'll leave you alone."

When I come back, Ash watches as I set the violin case in the corner. "Can I leave this in here for a bit?" She keeps staring as she takes another bite of her crust, but eventually, she nods.

"Thanks," I say, like she's doing me a favor. I summon the courage of all the people who seem to think I'm capable of doing the right thing and add, "I'm sorry I got mad earlier. You didn't deserve that. It's just . . . I miss my dad. My parents. And I want to preserve what's left. You know?"

I'm not sure if she does know or if she even could, but she nods. Finally meets my eyes.

"Thanks for understanding," I say. "Maggie and I will be out in the kitchen, if you want to talk. She says to make sure you drink all that water. I know you've been drinking all day, but it's easier not to argue with Maggie."

Ash gives me a small smile, which makes me wonder if we're headed back toward okay.

When I sit down across from Maggie, I suddenly realize how starving I am. I've downed three pieces of pizza by the time she's finished telling me about her day and passing on the best wishes of pretty much everybody who crossed her path. "Everybody is thinking of you. Just know that."

"I know," I say. "That's sweet." Which is not a word I normally use, but that's how it feels to hear that people I barely know are asking about me. Sweet. Not the real, nourishing care of somebody like Maggie.

But sweet can be good, in small doses. So I offer Maggie one of LuEllen's brownies, then take the plate down the hall to Ash.

This time, I have a free hand, so I open the door myself. Ash is so startled, she nearly drops what she's holding—the old violin.

"Oh," I say, doing my best to act casual again. "Do you play?" I ask, unsure what I want the answer to be.

She shakes her head, and I can't tell whether I'm relieved or disappointed. But when I see the way she twists the end of the bow and the horsehair goes slack, suspicion pricks the back of my neck. It seems like the kind of small thing you wouldn't know to do unless you played.

I shouldn't let it go. This is exactly why I had Maggie bring the violin in the first place. But if Ash can play, and if Maggie hears it, she might change her mind about letting Ash choose.

"Maybe when Maggie goes home, you could give it a try. See if you can figure it out." Ash studies me, then nods, like she's picking up exactly what I'm putting down. Like we're united—not exactly against Maggie, but against the outside world.

Speak of the devil, Maggie walks in right then. "How are you feeling?" she asks.

Ash surprises me by looking straight at Maggie and saying, "Better," clear as anything. Then she comes and stands next to me and even laces her fingers through mine.

She's barely spoken all day, and there's something almost calculated in the fact that she's speaking now. Can she tell on some level that it's me who's keeping her safe, not only from the wind and the weather but from outsiders and authorities and whatever made her run?

"Well, then." Maggie turns back to me. "I'd say you're doing okay here. And you're changing the bandages? She's drinking plenty of water?" I reassure her about the bandages, and Ash gestures at the empty tumbler on the nightstand. I don't point out to Maggie that the dirt is wet around the scraggly spider plant on the windowsill that I haven't watered in weeks.

"I suppose you ladies do seem to be taking good care of each other," Maggie admits. "Holler if you need me." Then she drops a kiss on each of our foreheads (with no hint of a flinch from Ash) and disappears out the front door.

Now that we don't need a united front for Maggie, Ash and I turn awkward again.

"I'm going to watch TV," I say at last.

Ash doesn't follow me down the hall, which is lucky, because when I turn on the TV, we've left it on a local station that's currently showing the news. The photo of the little girl with the violin, to be exact. I hurry to turn the volume way down, then sit a foot from the screen, straining to hear.

"Still no developments in the search for Charity Trager, who has been missing from her home since Friday evening. Official representatives from Ash Creek have denied allegations that wedding plans were underway for the thirteen-year-old, but one community source claiming to be close to Charity says the Brethren had been telling her the time had come for her to sanctify herself through marriage. Ash Creek residents who have left the community say the Brethren are almost all-powerful within the faith, having the final word on everything from marriages to property ownership and even law enforcement."

I can't help but picture some creepy old guy deciding what's best for Ash without her input—or deciding to marry her himself. The image makes me shiver. I change the channel, more determined than ever to keep Ash safe, whether she's Charity Trager or not. There are way too many gross men in the world.

I flip through channels, settling on the safest thing I can find—Animal Planet—and curl back into the couch as monarch butterflies migrate across the screen, flashes of orange against the green of a forest and the impossible blue of a Central American sky. My eyelids are growing heavy when the unmistakable twang of a violin string sounds from down the hall.

One plucked note, then another, each sliding slightly higher than the last.

I don't know much about violins, but I'm pretty sure she's tuning it.

I'm pretty sure she knows exactly what she's doing.

I turn down the volume and wait as the pattern repeats until Ash is satisfied.

Then a melody floats down the hall, clear and true. It takes me a moment to place it, since I'm used to hearing it in four-part harmony from the mouths of the congregation and the pipes of the organ on Sunday. It's a hymn, one of my favorites. "Nearer, My God, to Thee."

It's Dad's favorite too. Not his voice, this time, but a message from him all the same. A message from him, through her. Or from God, who does feel near in this moment.

I mute the TV and just listen, a tear slipping down my cheek that I don't even bother to brush away as the next generation of butterflies are reborn, wet and wrinkled but finally ready to fly. I remember the butterflies we saw pinned in shadow boxes in biology, preserved forever at the height of their beauty. Even then, I ached a little knowing that their lives had been cut short, that they'd lost any chance to grow or change, all because of one fateful, defining moment. Now the whole idea makes me unspeakably sad.

Ash plays two verses, then moves on. "Be Still, My Soul" and "Brightly Beams Our Father's Mercy" and "How Great Thou Art," all the songs I love best. All the songs I need right now.

I have to admit, she's good. But does it have to mean anything at all? Don't like ninety-nine percent of kids play the violin at some point? And aren't most of these hymns sung by all sorts of churches anyway? It doesn't necessarily mean she's Charity Trager. It doesn't mean we should turn her over to the authorities.

This time, it's Ben's voice that cuts through my thoughts. *What's your endgame here? How do you see this all going down if you keep lying, even to yourself?*

The truth is, I don't know. But I do know I made a promise to

Ash. I can't turn her over to strangers, even if they wear badges or have medical degrees. What if the people everyone keeps saying will help her are the very people she's afraid of? And what if she's got a good reason for it?

By the time the voices and questions fade, the music has stopped. When I go to my room, Ash is already asleep, the violin resting on top of the bookshelf. So I brush my teeth and change into an old T-shirt and soft shorts and climb in beside her. I slow my breathing to match hers, and then I whisper my promise once again.

"This will heal. God will help."

I drift to sleep with those words in my head, willing the voice behind them to become his.

Then:

A terrible screeching sound.

A violin being ripped out of the hands of someone I can't quite see.

And then I realize I'm dreaming.

And then I realize it's not screeching but screaming.

And Ash is no longer beside me.

melody, part 1

The girl's first violin was made of
a paper towel tube and a cracker box,
her first bow a whittled aspen branch.

Her mama showed her how to hold it:
the box tucked beneath her chin,
the branch held by the arc of her fingers.

Stand up straight, Mama said,
placing a small, flat rock on the girl's head
to keep her posture
tall and true.

But also

Relax, Mama said,
and everywhere she touched—
knuckles, shoulder, chin—
the girl relaxed,
and then
it felt right.

Afterward,
Mama tapped the small stone on the girl's head again,
then replaced it with a kiss.

You can do beautiful things,
she said,
with the right instrument in your hands.
Just wait.

cutworm, part 1

Mama taught her other things too:
How to let the sink drip in the winter
to keep the pipes from freezing.
How to plant and tend a garden,
from spring to summer to autumn harvest.

One morning, they pulled back
the tender new leaves of a potato plant
to find a cutworm curled around the stem,
feeding on the slim stalk
that gave life to the rest.

Her mother grabbed it in an instant,
dropped it to the dirt,
ground it under the bare skin of her heel.

They fell to their knees together,
searching the other stems
and just below the soil
for any other cutworms.
But somehow, it seemed,
they'd caught the first and only one.

Thank goodness,
Mama said.

She looked at the girl, serious as anything.
You see a problem,
you take care of it
right then and there.
Don't wait for it to get worse.
That one little worm could have ruined everything.

It's
just
what
they
do.

The girl looked from the one ruined plant
to the rest of the garden,
still healthy and growing,
knowing it would keep them alive
for another year.

She ground the remains of the cutworm
under her own heel
for good measure.

She nodded.
She promised.
She wouldn't forget.

10

I stumble through the darkness, trying to fight through the twin fogs of sleep and terror and figure out where the sound is coming from.

Ash isn't in my room. Not in my parents' room. Not in the house. When I finally pause to think, I can tell that the scream is coming from outside, and I'm not sure it's human.

I rip open the back door, grabbing my old running shoes from the steps and pulling them on as I cross the patchy lawn. The sound's retreating, heading northeast, and I get a glimpse of movement too—someone or something catching the light of the nearly full moon, crashing through the sagebrush toward the creek.

"Ash," I call, then immediately regret it. We're not exactly lying low if she's out here screaming and running and I'm yelling her name. Or her name for now, anyway. But maybe, if someone or something is chasing her, I've just let them know that she's not alone.

By the time I've caught up with Ash, she's closing in on the fence, and I finally get a good look at what's been making the terrible sound.

It wasn't Ash screaming after all. As my eyes adjust to the night, I see the huddled form of a jackrabbit, backed up against a boulder at the edge of our property.

I've never heard a jackrabbit make any sound other than the shifting of dirt, the soft rustle of grass. But this one is wailing. Shrieking. I squat down to see why and immediately wish I hadn't.

One of the hare's hind legs is barely hanging on by some thin string of tendons. No wonder it's making that noise. No wonder we could outrun it.

I look over at Ash. Her eyes are lit with an animal energy of their own. She couldn't have done this, could she?

"Coyote," she whispers, as if she's read my mind. She must have woken up and gone out to break up the attack. Was she watching out the window—in the middle of the night—and just happened to see it? What was she watching for?

Ash turns from me to the hare and whispers, "Sorry." Then she grabs my arm and pulls me back, away from the animal. The hare paws at its own leg, screaming into the night. Ash closes her eyes so tight, the pain shows in her face, and then, loud enough for her voice to drown out the hare, she speaks her demand into the night.

"Shoot her."

I'm about to tell her I don't have a gun when, from behind me, I hear the click of a safety coming off, the metallic clink of a shell entering the chamber. I'm petrified, incapable of defending myself or Ash or even turning my head to see who's there.

Then the roar of the gun, from behind and beside and all around us, and the hare falls, dead, to the desert floor.

"Thank you," Ash whispers, and I turn to see who's behind us.

Dylan.

What. The. Hell.

"What are you doing on my property in the middle of the night? With a *gun*? Do I need to call the police?" The questions tumble from my mouth in a tone so fierce, I don't blame him for backing up, even though he's the one holding the gun. I hope he doesn't hear the bluff in the last one, because I'm still not ready to get the cops back over here.

"Technically," he says from the other side of the fence, "I'm not on your property. And for the record, this isn't my gun."

"The hell it isn't. I don't care if that's your dad's gun and you're *technically* two feet off my property. Is that what the creepy note meant? 'I'll always be here.' Yeah, that's the problem. You've always been overprotective, but this is getting ridiculous. Do I need to get a restraining order?"

"It's not . . . I don't . . . ," he sputters before finally landing on "No. I was walking by the creek, and it's barely eleven. I went up by the canyon to call coyotes. Not to hunt them or anything, just to hear them call back."

"You weren't hunting. And that's why you brought your gun."

"I told you, it's not my gun. I almost tripped over it, right here, when I heard the noise and ran to see what was going on." Dylan bites his lip. "Cal, I think this is your dad's gun."

I'm about to tell him that's ridiculous, there's no way he'd know that. But then I think back to when we first got together, remembering how Dylan tried to impress my dad by taking him coyote hunting.

"Let me see it," I say, holding out my hand. When he doesn't give it up right away, Ash steps forward and takes it from him. The sight of her with the gun sends a shiver up my spine.

"Can I have that?" I ask her, as gently as I can.

Ash hugs the gun closer to her, but I wait, trying to keep steady in spite of my nerves. But eventually, she turns to me and hands it over.

Of all the guns in the world, this is the only one I'd recognize, because he carved Mom's initials into the handle. Tonight, the curve of the letters catches the moonlight just enough for me to be sure.

"You're right. It's his. Why is it out here?"

"I don't know," Dylan says, "but the authorities might want a look."

Now I almost laugh. "They might want a look why, exactly?"

He seems uncomfortable, and I'm secretly glad until I hear his reason. "There are still . . . questions about the fire. It's looking like it might not have been an accident."

The world spins for a second, but then I feel the weight of my own two feet on solid ground. *Our ground*, Dad's voice reminds me. "What do you mean, questions? And how would you possibly know that?"

"I overheard a conversation at work that I wasn't supposed to. But that's the other reason I've been worried about you."

This is a stretch, even for conspiracy-minded Dylan. "Because the fire wasn't an accident and I'm the next target? Dylan, I promise there isn't a person alive who would want to murder me or my dad."

At the word *murder*, Ash gives a little whimper behind me. She's had enough.

"It's time for us to go home," I say. "And you should too."

"Okay." Dylan leaves the gun with me and gathers up the hand-held coyote call he must have dropped in the brush. "I'm glad to know there aren't any raccoons in your house."

Of course he can't let my lie from his first visit slide.

"This is my cousin," I say, surprising even myself at how easily another lie comes out. I don't dare look over at Ash to see her reaction. "She's only here for a few days. Not really worth mentioning to anybody."

The way Dylan catches my eye, I know he catches my meaning too. "Okay, Cal." There's still something so intimate about the nickname that I feel myself blush. "Whatever you say.

"Nice to meet you," he says to Ash in the patient-yet-playful voice he uses when he coaches kids at summer day camps. "You'll be much better company for Calli than a raccoon. You won't poop in the kitchen and eat the trash, right?"

Ash can't help but match his charming half smile with one of her own. He crouches down to look her straight in the eye, and even though she flinches a little, she stands her ground like maybe she's not afraid of him after all.

"Stay safe out here, okay?" Then he gives one last glance toward the rabbit's body and walks off into the night.

⁓

Back in the kitchen, Ash heats up a glass of milk in the microwave—then heads for the back door.

"Hey," I call. Gently at first, then with a sharp edge. *"Hey."*

But she doesn't turn back. What choice do I have but to follow her?

Ash marches across the backyard and out into the brush. She's acting weird, even for Ash. I'm about to insist we go back inside when she sets the milk in the dirt, twisting the glass until it's secure. She kneels down near a big, scraggly sagebrush and reaches her hand into a hole.

"Um, I wouldn't, actually," I say. "There could be a fox or a badger or a rattlesnake in there."

But of course there isn't. When she draws her hand back out, she's holding a baby jackrabbit, small and wriggling. She must have run out here the second she saw the attack. She's probably the reason any of the jackrabbits survived at all.

Ash hands it to me wordlessly and reaches her hand back into the hole, frowning and maneuvering until she's shoulder deep. Finally, she pulls out another.

"Are there any more?" I ask at this sad, sick version of a magic trick. But Ash just shakes her head and cradles the second hare as she settles herself cross-legged in the dirt.

I can't help glancing around us, wondering how many there were before the coyote came. How much of the mother's wailing as she left this place was so all of us—coyote and humans alike—would stay far away from these little ones. I try not to picture the mother, splayed out in the sandy soil, as I stroke the soft fur of the small life in my hand.

Ash dips her finger into the glass and presents it, a drop of milk ripe on the tip, to the little hare. At first the hare shies away, but then its nose starts working and wiggling. Soon it's taking the drop right from her finger.

"Hang on," I say, handing my hare to Ash. "I've got something better. Are you okay if I go to the barn? I'll be right back."

Ash nods, and I run to the barn. Luckily, I know where the basic supplies are, and the key too. I unlock the door and click on the light, focusing intently on the task at hand so the memories of Dad in this room, healing and helping at all hours, won't swallow me whole.

Minutes later, I'm back with a jar of formula and two small syringes. I carefully draw up a few milliliters of warm liquid into each syringe, then pass one over to Ash and take my hare back. (At least I think it's mine. It's hard to tell in the dark.)

"Vet supplies," I say. "Thanks to my dad."

She nods.

"He died in a fire," I say, and, as though it will prove Dylan wrong, "Only a fire. Nothing more for us to worry about."

"Nothing to worry about," she says, in such a calm, reassuring way that it makes me wonder if she's listening to me at all or just talking to the jackrabbit.

The hares don't drink much, but that could be because their mother fed them recently. Cow's milk isn't the best thing for them anyway, although I don't blame Ash for trying.

"Did you have pets, back in Ash Creek?"

I nearly bite my own tongue. I didn't mean to say that. Ash shakes her head, but whether it's in answer to the pet part or Ash Creek I couldn't say.

"Did you ever want one? Because jackrabbits would be terrible pets. I just want to warn you now. We'll feed them for a while, but they'll be miserable penned up. We'll have to let them go, and then we'll probably never see them again."

I'm rambling again, I know. Overcorrecting for my mistake in mentioning Ash Creek. I wanted to show Ash that *she* has a future here, that I'm not going to send *her* back—but my awkwardness means I might have done the opposite.

Then, in the distance, the mournful howl of a coyote. I half wonder if it's real, or if maybe Dylan headed back up the canyon with his handheld coyote call after he was sure we were gone.

But no, I hear the howl again. Closer.

The coyote's coming back to finish what it started. We're downwind, so it can't smell us. Somehow, it hasn't seen us either as it inches forward through the brush.

"Go on," I shout, standing up and clutching my tiny jackrabbit against my chest. "Get out of here." The animal startles at my voice. Through the darkness, I see one snarling flash of teeth before it turns and disappears into the night.

"Let's get inside," I tell Ash. But when I turn around, she's already through the door.

I can't blame her. Because even though I watched the coyote run away, I can't shake the feeling that there's something else out there. Somebody, maybe. I think of Dylan's warning, and then my own words echo in my mind.

Coming back to finish what it started.

I bolt the door and check all the blinds again before I go to bed.

coyote call

Most North American predators,
    wolves,
    bears,
    mountain lions,
have seen
a drastic drop in population
in the last century.

But not coyotes.

Coyotes are surviving,
thriving,
driving their prey
into burrows and nests and beyond,

because

for a hungry coyote
almost anything can be the next meal.

Coyotes are the ultimate survivors,
willing to eat
watermelon
grasshoppers

mice
lamb
pizza
even the carcasses of others' kills.

If it's edible, coyotes will eat it.

If there's land, coyotes will claim it.

If it's there, they consider it theirs.

Some humans admire this.
Emulate it.

Others put a tan coat in their crosshairs
because of the bounty:
fifty bucks for every kill,
and all you have to do
is turn in the jaw and the ears.

There are those who fear coyotes too.
In some cultures, if you see one,
you turn around and walk the other way
because terrible things
will happen
if you dare to cross its path.

The young hunter
is some combination of all of these things:
admirer,
emulator,
bounty collector,
believer.

He loads the coyote call into his truck,
congratulating himself on keeping his cool
back by the fence.

He didn't lie—
    he did call coyotes tonight.
But that wasn't why he came.

He knows more than he's saying.

But what he knows
is more than she needs to know right now.

11

When morning comes, Ash is gone again—but this time, she's only in the kitchen.

"Morning," I say. I'm so tired that it comes out sounding more like a not-so-observant observation than a greeting. Ash has already mixed more formula for the hares, and whether it tastes better or they're just hungrier, the hare she's holding is much more enthusiastic about eating now.

"You're so good with them." Ash smiles at me as she soaks in the praise. The hares seem to have released the tension that built between us yesterday, and I want this feeling to last. So I take the little cup of formula and draw some into the other syringe, then scoop up the second hare from the plastic bin they slept in.

So many things about this tiny animal are like magic to me: the flutter of her heart under the soft fur, the bright spark in her black eyes, the impossibly quick wiggle of her nose as she gulps down one drop after another.

I keep thinking of them as bunnies, but Dad would remind me that jackrabbits are hares, and a baby hare is called a leveret. Bunnies are born undeveloped—closed eyes, no fur, unregulated body temperature. But these little ones are born fully developed, ready to live on their own soon after they're born—if they had to.

Looking at Ash now, I wonder whether she could make it on her own. I wouldn't bet against her. As helpless as she can seem at times, there's something scrappy about her.

Maybe she's had practice getting by. I decide to prod at the mystery of her past, but gently.

"My dad taught me how to do this," I say. "Who taught you?"

"Dad," says Ash, without looking up. I add it to the word list, even though I'm willing to bet she's just copying me. Then a new thought hits me, and the question comes out before I have time to even wonder if I should ease into it.

"You mean *my* dad?" He did house calls all over the county and beyond, including Ash Creek, so he certainly could have known her. And if I'm finally getting a clue—

"No," she says, her face darkening. "*My* dad." Then she shuts her mouth into a line so tight, I back the heck off. Mom taught me that it's better to turn around at the first sign of a storm than to plow ahead and pretend you don't see the clouds.

Luckily, we get a distraction that clears the clouds before I even have to retreat. A triple distraction in scrubs. Maggie barely knocks before she, Sofia, and Trish barrel through the door.

"Calli!" Maggie takes in the scene in the kitchen, eyes wide. "And to think I was worried about you living alone."

"Right?" Trish says. "Meanwhile, the inhabitants of this house are multiplying somehow, like, well . . ." She shrugs and gestures toward the jackrabbits in our laps.

"We're all female, genius," I say, because I've checked the hares. "And different species."

Trish elbows me playfully and smiles at Ash. Even though it was a bad joke and she made it herself, I feel awful when I realize I might have implied she and Sofia couldn't be parents. I remember them having a heartbreaking close call with an adoption not long after Mom died, but I've never dared ask them whether they're still hoping to adopt. *I* hope they are. Any kid would be lucky to join their family.

Thankfully, Trish doesn't seem offended at all. (She never does, really.) She whips something from behind her back so she and Sofia can hand it to Ash together. When Ash pulls back the wrapping to find a new pair of shorts and a T-shirt, her face lights up, and she takes off to try them on.

"Be careful with your bandages . . . ," I say, trailing off because Ash is totally ignoring me and it's too late anyway.

A minute later, there's a soft click as my bedroom door opens. Ash comes out, a shy smile on her face. It's amazing how much stronger she looks in her new Nike soccer shorts and jersey (which tells me Trish picked the outfit). The clothes fit her perfectly, and the green brings out her eyes (which tells me Sofia helped).

The way she's looking at herself in the mirror, though, I wonder if it's more than just wearing something new. I picture the Ash Creek women in their long sleeves and dresses, even in the summer. Maybe it's the first time she's ever worn something bought brand-new, just for her, that lets her move so freely.

Trish and Sofia look at each other and smile, then fawn over Ash, which makes her smile too.

"Well, don't you look like a million bucks!" Maggie gushes, coming in from the kitchen, where she's been folding the load of laundry I forgot about in the dryer. "Tell me this, honey: Would you like me to braid that beautiful hair of yours?"

Ash says "Yes" with the force of a footballer, and we all laugh in surprise. But something about her enthusiasm makes me a little sad, imagining that she may never have had anyone taking care of her like we are now.

Maybe that's not fair. Maybe even a life you run from isn't *all* bad. Girls from Ash Creek always have their hair in neat braids. So maybe this is a way to connect with who she was, not distance herself.

Maggie and Ash head for the bathroom and Sofia goes outside to water the flowers, leaving Trish and me alone in the kitchen. "Ben says you might be going back to work," she says, once we're alone. "Are you sure you're ready?"

"Nope. That's all Ben. *I* didn't say I was going. I haven't even told Ash yet. She might not like that."

"Ash, honey." Maggie's voice carries from the bathroom, loud enough that I know we're supposed to be listening in. "Would it be okay if Calli went to work for a bit if one of us stays with you?"

There's a pause, then Maggie's voice again. "She says that's fine. Or she nodded, I guess. But she's going to hold her head still now unless she wants her braid to be crooked."

Trish rolls her eyes in Maggie's general direction, but it's an affectionate eye roll.

"You don't have to do anything until you're ready," Maggie says, as loud and in charge as ever. "And don't you dare do it for the money. We can tide you over until the life insurance comes through. On the other hand, if you're wanting to get out, we can certainly stay with Ash. That's the advantage of being the one who sets the schedule for the med/surg floor."

"I'll stay with her," Trish says. "Especially if you bring me a peanut butter shake, Calli."

I still haven't forgiven Ben for talking to Kasen Keller, but getting out of the house for a couple of hours does seem like it might be a good idea. I think I need a break from Ash.

"I bet they could use me during the lunch rush," I say, which would still give me the rest of the morning to back out if I need to.

"Perfect," Trish says, handing me ten dollars. "In that case, you can bring me a chicken deluxe combo with that shake when you come home. Crinkle fries, please." Trish is always planning her next meal, and she doesn't care who knows it. With metabolism like hers, maybe you have to be.

"You're welcome to eat here," I say, typing a quick text to my manager but not taking the money. "That fridge is full of food."

"Thanks, but no thanks." She drops her money on the table. "That was a lot of lasagna in there. Sometimes it's best to get a fresh start, you know?"

"I know," I say. "And I'd be happy to get you lunch." I almost want to thank her for asking, because it feels so good to have somebody besides Ash ask something of me again. Like maybe I'm still capable of contributing to the outside world.

I pick up the hares in their bin and take them out back for some fresh air, then sit by Sofia on the porch swing. "How's it going?" I hadn't even noticed until now, but she looks so tired, she must be coming off a shift.

"I had to give a new patient the deluxe package last night," she says with a little sigh. "Lab draws, catheter placement, IV infiltration, stool sample, the works."

"That sounds . . . important," I say, proud of my last-minute replacement for "unpleasant" and wondering again whether nursing is really what I want to do with my life.

"Thank you," she says. "It is, actually. And people don't necessarily appreciate it." She leans back and closes her eyes. "So," she says, "Kasen Keller came by, huh?"

"Yeah."

"And he said Ash could stay here?"

I pick my words carefully. "He didn't take her, did he?"

"You know," she says, "when I have to give a deluxe package, I always tell the patient, 'This will be a lot less miserable for both of us if you let me do my job.'"

I pretend not to see what her story has to do with my current situation. "Thankfully, nobody around here is giving anybody a stool sample," I say, trying to dodge the serious conversation. "Well, except maybe the jackrabbits."

Sofia gives me a courtesy smile, but she's looking back at Ash through the window. "She's healing nicely," she says. "Physically, and I think emotionally too. It's an incredible difference for just two days. But she can't stay here forever."

I know that. Of course I do. But I also wonder why we can't take this one step at a time. Every hour that we're here together feels like it's giving her a better chance at safety. At survival in the long run.

Which, I guess, is what we're doing with the hares. Once the thought hits me, I scan the sagebrush for signs of the coyote, even though it's not likely to be out this time of the day. Whether it's a trick of the light or some other animal, I can almost convince myself I see a dark shape in the distance.

"Is she talking any more?" Sofia asks.

"A little," I say. "When she feels like it."

"That's good." Sofia lays a soft hand over mine. "And you're doing a great job here. We aren't trying to come in and second-guess your decisions."

I almost laugh at that. "If you say so."

Sofia squeezes my hand. "I mean it. I was afraid I was going to find signs of abuse when I cleaned her up. Characteristic bruising patterns, things like that. My cousin works with at-risk kids in the city, and he taught me what to look for a few years back when I was concerned about a patient of mine. I came here yesterday thinking I'd try to talk you into taking her in for a full workup, but Ash's injuries seem consistent with somebody who was out in the elements for a few days. Very little bruising at all, in fact." Her eyes dart to the kitchen, where Ash is showing Trish how her fancy new braid wraps from one side of her head to the other. "That's not to say that she wasn't ever abused in the past or running from the threat of future abuse. And she certainly may have been neglected."

I shiver at all of that. "So what do we do now?"

"I think the best thing is to make her feel safe enough that she starts talking. And you're doing a beautiful job of that already."

"Wait," I say, realizing I've skipped over something important. "You have a cousin in the city?" I don't know why I always assumed Sofia was the only member of her family in America. Why didn't I ever ask?

"I have two cousins in the city. Brothers." Sofia stands and stretches, then heads for the back door. But when I reach out and touch her elbow, she turns, eyes warm and waiting.

"I would like to hear more about your family someday," I say.

"And I would be happy to tell you."

⁓

Before long, Maggie, Trish, and Sofia say goodbye, promising Ash that they'll be back—and they'll bring her more clothes.

"Drive carefully," I call to them all, but mostly to Sofia, remembering the fatigue in her face earlier. It's too easy, now, for me to imagine losing the people I love.

Meanwhile, Ash has brought the hares back inside. The three of them seem to be waiting for me—but so is a text from Greg, my manager.

Good to hear from you. We could use you 12–2 today if you're free

When I look up, Ash is watching me in a way that makes me wonder if she's already seen the message. If she saw the text come in.

"You like them, right? Maggie and Trish and Sofia? And you're really okay if Trish comes back for a couple of hours while I go to work?"

She nods, and we stand there together in silence, watching the hares bound around the bin in tiny, tentative hops, then finally settle next to each other in a sort of yin-yang shape in the corner and fall asleep. They look exactly the same today as they did last night, and no doubt they'll look the same tomorrow. But if we can keep them alive, they'll change, little by little, from small and soft to lithe and lean. From something to save to something to shoot.

Most of the boys I grew up with hunt hares. Not to eat—jackrabbit is tough as hell, apparently. Just for the fun of hitting what you aim at and watching it go down, whenever you want, because there's no limit on jackrabbits around here. The Rigby boys shoot them as a Thanksgiving tradition, whether they're full-grown or not, and the idea of it has always made me a little sick inside. The entitlement, I guess, of feeling totally justified in causing suffering if it makes you feel excited or empowered. And the fact that the boys around here learn it so thoroughly, and so young.

As I look over to watch Ash tracing the edge of the hare's ear with her finger, something prickles at the back of my neck.

And what destructive behaviors did she learn, growing up? Keep your guard up, Calli. I can't let anything happen to my girl.

The voice is clearly his again, but the message isn't. Wasn't he the one who told me to take care of her in the first place? Shouldn't he be quoting 2 Timothy 1:7 at me instead? *For God hath not given us the spirit of fear; but of power, and of love, and of a sound mind.*

Maybe I no longer have God with me because I no longer have a sound mind. It's one thing to hear Dad's voice, but this paranoid, possessive version doesn't feel like him at all.

I shake it off, shower, and get ready for my shift at the Dairy Freeze.

Except not really. Even the shower doesn't wash it from me. Even walking out the door with somewhere I need to be for the first time since the funeral doesn't feel so much like stepping away as being followed.

Followed by what, I couldn't say.

good cop, bad cop

There are good cops
and there are bad cops,
and the young deputy knows
which kind he intends to be.

He built himself the armor
of being exceptional
even before he wore the armor
of the law,
and he doesn't intend
to take off either one
for even a moment.

It's not about following the rules,
because some of the rules
are corrupt as hell
and so are some of the rule followers.

No, it's about right and wrong,
powerful and the powerless,
us and them.

But above all, it's about
her.

He doesn't mind if the girl stays where she's at.
It's an easy enough place to keep an eye on,
and the vet's daughter is probably every bit
as predictably righteous as her dad.

Creepy, though,
how the girl keeps watching out the window
whenever he drives by.
Like she sees him,
sees right through him,
when he can barely see her at all.

It may be time for a closer look
or maybe even a few words
next time she comes outside.

He's a patient man,
but this can't wait forever,
and he'd hate for her to fall into
the wrong hands.

The thing the young deputy can't admit,
even to himself,
is that, in his mind,
the wrong hands
are any hands but his.

12

The defining design element of the Dairy Freeze exterior is the life-size Holstein cow on the roof. The cow has been there longer than I've been alive, and she's been stolen at least a dozen times: left in farmers' fields, tied to the hitching post at the livestock auction, painted the rival high school's red and white and left in the middle of the football field.

"I guess there are worse things these pranksters could be up to," Greg would always say, laughing it off. But later, when he'd mess up his back hauling the cow back onto the roof or slice his finger bolting it in place, I'd wonder whether the harmless pranks were really so harmless after all—or whether it was another example of the entitlement of doing whatever gave you that high, that feeling of power and control, regardless of how it impacted anybody else.

The lunch rush has already started when I get inside, and it's clear Greg didn't call me in today out of charity, but out of actual necessity. Today's primary demographic is post–pool party kids. The dress code at the Freeze is nonexistent, so everybody under the age of ten is sporting swimsuits. Some strut around in their Paw Patrol surfer shorts like they own the place; others shiver, wet-haired and wrapped in their towels (and their parents' arms), waiting eagerly for their ice cream even though their lips are blue.

"Hallelujah," Ben says when he sees me, his fingers splayed, octopus-like, around four Kid Kones in each hand, the Dairy Freeze hat covering his hair situation. "Hey, I'm sorry about Keller. All I told him was that there might be somebody at your house who matched Charity Trager's description. I just—"

"You're dripping ice cream," I say, because I'm here to help, even if I haven't totally forgiven him. "What do you need me to do?"

Ben gives me an elbow bump that I think is supposed to show how grateful he is. "Can you take over the register?"

I'd hoped I could work in the back, making sandwiches and running the fryer. I'm guessing that the fewer sympathetic looks I get, the easier the next two hours will be. But I'm a team player, so I wash my hands and step to the register with a smile pasted on my face.

"Welcome to Dairy Freeze. How can I make your day sweeter?"

As it turns out, I didn't need to worry about sympathy. Somehow, the world has kept turning in spite of all that's happened in my life over the last nine days. Even Jane Carver barely makes time for a "Hey, Calli" before diving in on her order.

The next hour passes in a blur, especially since Elliott, the employee out front with us today, decides to take his lunch break during a rush and leaves me to run the drive-through too. By the time I finally have a chance to look up from my sticky touchscreen, most of the swimmers have gone—except for Jane and her kids, who are still sitting in the corner and have been joined by Bishop Carver in his uniform: cargo pants, work boots, forest district T-shirt, and a radio at his hip. The little ones are enthralled by the windup toys that came in their kids' meals, which is good because the parents are absolutely wrapped up in their conversation. The gossip in me wonders what they're talking about so intently—until Jane glances up, sees me looking, and drops her gaze quickly enough that I don't have to wonder anymore.

"I'm taking my break," I say to Ben.

Elliott scoffs from behind me. "You don't get a break when you're working a two-hour shift after two weeks off."

"Watch me," I say. "Better yet, tell Greg."

I scoop myself a medium fry, snag a mistake shake that was destined for the garbage, and hurry out to the lobby. Jane and the kids have disappeared, leaving Bishop Carver to clean up in their wake.

"I can get that," I say, knowing he won't take me up on it.

"Nah." He sweeps stray crumbs and salt crystals into one hand with the edge of the other. "You already made the food, and we made the mess. Least I can do."

But he doesn't look up at me.

I clear my throat. "Could I talk to you for a minute?"

"Of course, of course," he says, gesturing to the other side of the booth. I slide in, grabbing some napkins to sop up the puddle of melted vanilla where his daughter was sitting.

"We've been putting together a care package for you," he says. "Stuff for the pantry, and a bunch of gift cards so you can buy things you'll actually like and use. Feels like almost everybody in the ward contributed something." He stops. Looks stricken for a second. "I probably wasn't supposed to tell you that. I think I ruined the surprise."

"I'll act surprised," I say. "And thank you." When I picture my congregation doing this for me, it's so thoughtful I have to blink back tears. Remind myself of the reason I came out here.

It wasn't to talk to Bishop Carver, who has grown into a genuinely good listener.

And not even Travis Carver, the younger cousin who was more like a brother to Dad and looked up to him all his life.

Today, for the first time, it's Chief Carver I need. The wildland firefighter who first broke the news of Dad's death to me.

"Was the fire an accident?" The words burst from me like fire itself.

"Oh, Calli," he says, sounding almost like Dad for a second.

"Please," I say. "Be honest with me."

He stops cleaning and glances up. "I didn't want to burden

you with any of this until we knew for sure. Or ever, if I'm being honest."

"I know. But it's not a burden, I promise. Not knowing is a heavier weight to carry."

He sinks to the seat and kneads his fingers together, but his eyes are steady on me now, and I appreciate that. "The fire started with an explosion. That much we knew already. That much you knew too. It all happened so quickly, there's no way he could have gotten out."

And I did know this, even if it's only coming back to me now. This same man, speaking nearly the same words, telling me that there had been an accident over in Aspen Grove and my dad was gone. The details didn't matter when he first told me, but somehow, here in this booth, they do.

"Okay, the explosion, then," I say. "But that doesn't really answer the question. Was it an accident?"

Bishop Carver lets out a long breath, like maybe he was expecting this. "We originally thought it was started by some old, unstable chemicals stored in the barn. One of those terrible coincidences or perfect storms or whatever, all started by one stray spark. But forensics found remnants of a shotgun shell outside the barn."

"That doesn't seem like such a weird thing to me," I say, because it's true. Most of the land around here, public or private, is littered with them. It's not even outside the realm of possibility that there are shells in the Dairy Freeze parking lot right now.

"That's what I said. Plus, there were no guns of any kind on the property, and no tire tracks going in or out except your dad's. Nobody but the property owner was there with him when it happened."

"And whose property was it again?" I ask, trying to make it all add up.

"Her name was Miranda Tuttle. One of those off-the-grid folks, middle-aged and prickly, living up there by herself with a few animals. That's what your dad was doing there, I'm sure. The response team found a goat on the property with an infected leg. That's where they found his bag—just outside the goat pen. Must have needed something in the barn, and then . . . well . . ."

In all my grief, I'd forgotten that there was a second victim. Maybe it's some small blessing that she didn't leave anyone behind to mourn her. Or maybe that job falls to me now too.

Bishop Carver starts kneading his knuckles again, and I want to tell him it's not his fault, even though we both know that and it wouldn't help.

"Whatever it is you're holding back, I promise I can take it."

"I'm no expert on the forensics," he admits. "I'm only good at the part where we put the fires out. But I don't know what we gain by dragging this one out. Neither your dad nor this woman could have shot the gun. They were both in the barn, and the shell fell outside. Neither body had any evidence of gunshot wounds, and a shotgun blast isn't typically enough to ignite the chemicals that caused the explosion anyway. So what's an old shotgun shell but a scrap of garbage we're reading way too much into? That's why I didn't want to tell you. In my opinion, it's best to just let them both rest in peace."

Still, a part of me—one I'm not proud of—wants to blame this woman for my loss. Maybe then I could stop blaming everyone else: God, myself, my dad.

"Are you sure there wasn't anybody else there? Did she have any enemies?" I ask, knowing (but not caring) that I sound like I'm trying to play a cop on TV.

"Far as I know, she didn't have any anything. Enemies, friends. She had No Trespassing signs on every other fencepost—that kind of place. Not sure she let anybody in but your dad."

"Why would she have explosive chemicals?"

"None of it was illegal, or even suspicious, if that's what you're wondering. A couple of gas cans, some old fertilizer, low-risk explosives for target practice, that kind of thing. None of it would have been dangerous under normal circumstances." He stops. Sighs. "In the end, I really do believe it was an accident. An accident—and a tragedy. Trust me, I feel that part too."

His voice shakes when he says it, and I know he's telling the truth. He's lost somebody he loved, even if they weren't as close as they used to be. Even if they never in a million years would have used the word. "Don't let those questions keep you awake at night," he says. "I know I won't."

Except everything about his face tells me that, for this part, he only wants it to be the truth. That, in spite of all his assurances, he can't stop thinking about it either.

⁓

After Bishop Carver leaves, I curl my legs up onto the booth and use my phone to pull up Dad's QuickBooks to see if I can find anything at all about Miranda Tuttle. I was supposed to help him with billing this summer, but we never quite got around to finishing the training. Still, it's easy enough to search the records, so I try her name: first name, last name, every variation on the spelling I can think of.

Nothing.

"Oh, Dad," I whisper.

He never charged her a dime.

Of course he didn't. Because what money would she have had? I love him so much in that moment. But underneath it, I feel a spark of anger. This is how the universe rewards something like that—with a freak accident. This is the price of kindness in this world—you pay for it with your life.

I'm not angry at just the universe, though. The spark is spreading, and now I'm angry at him too. Because if he hadn't felt compelled to help every damn person in every way he could, he'd be here with me now. I lost my dad because he lost himself in his own quest to be everything to everyone, as if it could bring my mom back. Couldn't our life together have been enough?

Back behind the counter, I throw away my fries and my mistake shake, wondering how I thought I'd be able to eat them in the first place. The lunch rush has passed and it's pushing two o'clock, so I could leave anytime I want. But now that things have slowed down, I could finally have a chance to talk to Ben, and as I watch him chatting with a group of ten-year-olds, I realize how much I want that.

"Hey," he says, once the ten-year-olds have gone. "Seriously, about Kasen Keller, I—"

"It's okay." I sigh, then look him in the eye so he'll know I mean it. "You thought you were doing the right thing. Maybe you were. I'm not sure about any of it anymore."

Then I'm about to cry and his arms are around me. He rests his chin on the top of my head and whispers, "You will be. That's one thing I know about you, Calli. You'll figure it all out. You always do."

Elliott walks by, dropping a stack of trays on the counter with a crash so loud, I feel myself tense up. "Sorry if I scared you," he says. "But Greg isn't paying you guys to get in each other's pants."

I feel one of Ben's hands leave my back, probably to flip him off. "Hey, Elliott," he says. "Greg isn't paying you to be an ass. Go wipe the counters." I never would have thought Dairy Freeze shift manager would be a position with a sexy amount of power, but here we are.

Hang on. Did I just think *sexy* in reference to Ben? I'm not sure how to feel about that, but I don't pull back.

Ben's the one who pulls back, eventually. "Do you want to talk about any of it?" he asks gently.

"Yes," I say. "But probably not with Elliott listening in." Elliott, for his part, looks down intently and starts wiping the counter faster.

"Good call," Ben says. "I'm off at eight. Should I come over?"

"It would be great to talk to you," I say. "If you're not too tired."

"Yup. Absolutely. I'll save my energy by making Elliott do everything."

"Good strategy," I say, taking off my apron and hanging it on the rack in back. "See you tonight."

"See you tonight," he says to me, then turns to Elliott. "Somebody's pulling up to the drive-through. And after that, it looks like the garbage cans in the dining room need to be emptied." He taps the side of his head, mouthing the word *genius* with a half smile.

I feel myself smiling back, amazed at how even a few minutes with Ben can make it feel like things are right in the world again. Or like they might be, someday. I'm still marveling at it as I cross the parking lot, pulling out my phone to let Trish know I've got her lunch and I'm on my way.

But it's not soon enough. The screen lights up with texts.

Call us when you can.

Everything okay. Sort of.

Police will be here any second. I'm sorry.

"Shit," I whisper, and then I race home.

integrity, part 1

As the bishop opens the door to his truck,
his fingers stick, just a little,
to the handle.

Ice cream,
probably,
from trying to be a perfect dad
in the middle of a busy workday.

Perfection is impossible, he knows,
but that doesn't mean you don't try for it.

He thinks of voices
from the Young Women's class
at church each Sunday of his youth,
reciting a list of values that ends with
Good Works and
Integrity.

He is significantly better at the first.
It is easier to
wipe up spilled ice cream,
lend a listening ear,
than to live in alignment

with even your own truth
all the time.

Even when there's somebody
sitting across from you
expecting your honesty.

Maybe especially then.

He wishes she would let herself
grieve and heal
without asking so many questions
and looking at him
like he should have the answers.

They all look at him that way sometimes,
ever since he became bishop.

But he still feels like a fraud.

What if they found out how far he is from measuring up?
What if they all knew what he really believes?
And what he doesn't?

He wishes she would just call him Travis again.
Hell, he wishes he could just be Travis again
and undo,
unlearn,
unsee,
go back.

Because even though he should have
more answers and fewer questions,

there are still things
he knows
he'd rather not know.

After he turns the key,
he wipes his hands on his pants.
But they don't come clean.

Integrity.
He'll work on that one.
But not when it comes to this.

fairy tale

He wasn't always a monster—
unless maybe, part of him was.

He knows Whitman and Dylan both,
and he, too, contains multitudes.

But he's not the only one.

Read a fairy tale
and instantly
you are the prince or princess,
the chosen,
the innocent,
the noble-hearted hero.

But read again,
because you are also
the ogre,
the sage,
the trickster,
the monster,
all at once.

They are all within you,
just waiting to come out.

13

There's already a cop car sitting in front of my house when I pull up. Not Kasen Keller's sheriff truck this time, but city police. I follow the sound of voices to the backyard, and then to the barn.

"What happened?" I ask, bursting through the doorway.

I can't see Ash anywhere. Only Trish talking to a fifty-something man I almost recognize, her voice hushed and worried. They both turn to look at me, and the officer speaks up. "You must be Calli," he says, holding out his hand to shake mine. "I'm Officer Hunt. And don't worry, everybody seems to be okay here."

"Everyone's okay except this little one," Trish says, holding up one of our jackrabbits and folding the left ear toward him. "See?"

The hare is skittish, sniffing and squirming and trying to burrow into Trish's chest. If the hare is our biggest problem, Ash must be fine. So why the hell did Trish call the police?

"What exactly am I looking at?" the officer asks, peering down at the hare.

"That little notch out of her ear."

He stares at Trish, maybe trying to tell if she's serious. When she gives him a look that tells him she definitely is, he sighs and turns his focus back to the hare. He reaches out and takes her from Trish, almost tenderly, cradling her against his uniform. "Could it have been a wild animal?" he asks.

"No," she says, at the exact same moment I say, "Yes."

"What do you mean, yes?" Trish asks. "You weren't even here!"

"They were attacked by a coyote last night," I say.

Trish takes this in, but she still thinks she's right. "All I know is there wasn't a notch out of her ear this morning. And look how perfectly straight the lines are."

I study the hare's ear, its notch laced with red, then study Trish herself. She's a little more drama than Sofia or Maggie, but why would anybody call the police about something as small as this?

"Trish, there *was* a notch out of her ear this morning." I think back and I'm almost sure of it. "It's not like there are no straight lines in nature. It probably tore along the way the fur grows or something." Maybe what I'm saying doesn't make much sense, but it makes more sense than somebody doing this on purpose. What could the motive possibly be?

"Was there anything else you wanted to show me?" the officer asks, clearly done with the whole hare investigation.

I want to tell him *No, thanks for your time, sorry to have bothered you with this.*

But Trish answers with a firm "Yes," and we both follow her toward the barn door. I try to catch her attention to ask her where Ash is and what's going on, but she's locked in on her destination and not even looking at me.

Then I see what she's leading us toward: The door has been forced. It hangs limp from a single hinge, one of the boards splintered. The barn's been falling apart forever and the door wasn't that sturdy to begin with, but still. Who would do this? And why? The door to the back room is always locked, but this one's left open as often as it's closed.

"Somebody broke into the barn?" I ask, because it's the only explanation I can come up with. Inside, I'm praying, *Please tell me Ash wasn't there*, but I don't dare say it out loud because I'm not even sure whether the officer knows about her.

"Broke out, looks like," he says, pointing at the latch. "See how the impact must have come from this direction?"

Once he says it, I can see it. The barn's built so you can latch the door from either the inside or the outside. It looks like somebody latched it from the inside, then busted out. But all that only makes it more confusing.

"And you found it like this?" I ask Trish as the officer steps in for a closer look.

"Not me," she says, and gives a little jerk of her head back toward the house.

"Where is Ash?" I ask, dropping my voice so he can't hear. Getting law enforcement involved was probably the right call, but I still hope Ash can decide what happens next to some degree.

Trish matches my whisper. "Inside. I was sitting there, watching her play with the rabbits in the yard, and I must have fallen asleep. Night shift, you know?"

"You fell asleep? Are you serious?" Trish has a knack for falling asleep anywhere, anytime, but I still can't believe it.

"I've been up for almost twenty-four hours! And it couldn't have been more than a few minutes. I think."

Trish goes silent for a second. Even she realizes how bad that sounded. "Anyway," she says with false confidence, "the next thing I know, she's running back toward me, shouting about somebody in the barn. That's when I called the police. I tried to get her to talk, but she clammed up again."

I never should have left.

"You didn't see anyone?" I ask Trish, my voice tight and steely.

"No. When she ran in toward the house, I ran straight out. Rounded up the rabbits and scanned the place. I would have taken somebody down if I needed to. You know that, right? But there was nobody there. Just the door to the barn, broken in. Or out. Or whatever."

I can't decide whether I want to hug Trish or strangle her, so I leave her with the officer and head for the house, needing to see

Ash with my own eyes. Relief rushes through me when I find her curled in my bed, the covers tight around her.

"Ash." I kneel beside the bed so she can see me. "I'm home. It's okay."

She gives her head the smallest shake. I wish I could be gentle with her still, but there's no more time for that.

"The police are here," I say, glancing toward the bedroom door to make sure the officer isn't listening. "If somebody's trying to hurt you, I think we need their help."

She doesn't nod, but she doesn't shake her head again either.

"Did you see somebody today?" I ask. "Somebody who scared you?"

She nods, tears pooling in her eyes.

"Who was it?" I ask. "Somebody you've seen before?"

"Yes," she whispers. Then one of her hands emerges from the blanket and points across the room to the shotgun propped against the dresser.

My blood runs cold. Did I put it there last night? Did she?

"Dylan?" I ask, my heart dropping. "The boy from last night?"

"In the barn," she says, her eyes blank, her voice empty and distant. "He was there in the barn. He was going to hurt me. He wouldn't let me out . . ." She trails off, but I have to keep her going so she doesn't fall silent again, even if she's not entirely making sense.

"Is that who you were talking about the first day too? When you hid in the kitchen and you kept saying, 'It's him, it's him, it's him'?"

Ash looks past me, like she's expecting to see him even now.

"Help me understand," I say. "I saw you with him last night by the fence. You trusted him. It seemed like you liked him."

Her eyes go wide; she stares at me, stricken. Panicked. "Different," she says. "He looks so different sometimes." Then something flashes across her face, and the words pour out of her. "You said he

126

was gone. You said he wasn't coming back. But then he did. And you didn't stop him. You weren't even here. He's going to hurt me. He's going to find me wherever I go." She closes her eyes and starts whispering words that sound like a prayer. "Thou art my hiding place; thou shalt preserve me from trouble; thou shalt compass me about with songs of deliverance."

Ash falls silent. My head is swimming, but I try to press on anyway. "I'm not going to let anybody hurt you." I still can't believe it's Dylan who Ash is truly afraid of, especially since she didn't seem afraid of him at all last night. Could there be somebody from Ash Creek who looks like him when the light's just right?

I swallow hard and force the words out. "I think we need to tell the police. I'll go get the officer. You can tell him what you told me."

"No police," Ash hisses, scrambling backward to the corner of the room, dragging the blanket with her. "No police no police no police. They'll take me away."

"I won't let them take you, but we have to let them help," I insist. "Tell them what happened. I don't know if I can protect you by myself."

"No," she insists. "No no no no no . . ."

Her voice is growing softer now, and she's back to one word.

"Ash, please," I say. "I can't fix this on my own. I need help to keep you safe."

I pull out my phone and find the photo of Charity Trager, which is all over the internet now. "Ash, is this you? Please, you have to tell me."

"No," she says again, but there's a new fear in her eyes that makes me wonder if she means the opposite. "No no no no . . ."

There's a soft knock on the door, and Trish is back.

"Can we come in?" she asks, and I see the officer waiting behind her.

He pulls out a notebook. "I'd like to get her version of what happened out there. Anything she can tell us, any little detail, might help."

"Okay," I say. "But I don't know how much she'll tell you."

The officer steps forward, but he still leaves space between us.

"Hi there," he says, crouching down so he's in Ash's line of vision. "My name is Officer Hunt. I wondered if we could talk for a minute." After a beat, he adds, "I have a daughter too. She loved to tell stories when she was your age. Do you like to tell stories? I'd love to listen." When Ash still doesn't show any sort of response, he turns to me. "You called it. Any idea why she's afraid to talk?"

There's no truthful way to answer this question without giving her up to some degree. But this isn't Kasen Keller. This officer is quiet and thoughtful at the side of the room, not striding forward and demanding answers. And something in the way he held the hare reminded me of my dad.

"She's . . . been through a lot lately."

Officer Hunt stands and straightens his uniform. "I understand. I really do. But the more she's willing to tell me, the better I can keep her safe. What if I step out for a minute and you try to help her see that?"

"It's worth a shot," I say.

Trish nods at Officer Hunt as he leaves the room, then turns her attention to us. "Hey," she says, sitting down on the floor on Ash's other side. "I'm here for you guys. Both of you."

At that, Ash pulls the blanket around herself. When I put an arm across her shoulder, she leans into me. I look at Trish over the top of Ash's head. "I feel like I'm doing this all wrong."

"The story of my life," says Trish. "Well, nah, I mean, I have it all together," she adds with a smirk to let me know she's kidding. "But when the heavy stuff comes around? I almost always feel like I'm doing it wrong. I think that's how you know you're taking it seriously enough."

Ash has grown limp next to me. I drop my voice, hoping she's tired and not withdrawing again. "Have I messed everything up?"

Trish sighs and leans forward to look at Ash. Then she closes her eyes and rests her cheek on her hands to show me that Ash has fallen asleep. She answers me in a Trish whisper—like she's really trying to be quiet but can't quite manage it.

"We're all doing the best we can, including you. Especially you. Sofia and I were on the same page—when we saw Ash this morning, we could barely believe it. She was practically a new person. That's why I let her go outside by herself. You've done more for her than I would have thought possible. It wasn't until she went out to the barn that things went south."

Right. The barn. I chew my lip, figuring out how to phrase the next part. "Do you think it could have been Dylan out there?" I ask. "I mean, maybe he was stopping by and thought it was me in the barn or something, and she freaked out because she thought he was somebody else. Maybe somebody did hurt her, but it has to be somebody from Ash Creek, or wherever she came from. Not anybody from here. It has to be a mistake, right?"

"I don't know Dylan like you do, but I'd be surprised. I mean, I would and I wouldn't." She scratches the back of her neck, like she's working out how to say the next part. "We get trained on this stuff at the hospital. You want the bad guy to look like a bad guy. You want it to be the creepy guy in the creepy van, or the Brethren from Ash Creek. Somebody who looks or acts different who you can easily identify as not like you. But the truth is, when somebody hurts a kid, they're usually pretty good at hiding in plain sight."

I don't want her to be right, but she probably is. A memory comes back to me of a guest speaker pacing the cheap tiled floor in health class, telling us that most victims don't report their abuse until they're adults, and over ninety percent of juvenile victims know their abuser. Not just in places like Ash Creek, but everywhere. Here. So even if Ash were part of the ten percent who didn't know their abuser, he'd probably be good at concealing that part of himself.

"The odds are," the speaker said, "even if you've never been abused, you know both victims and abusers. And they're likely closer than you think. Maybe even in this room. If this is hitting close to home, please know that you don't have to speak up now— but I'll be in the counselor's office after school, if you want to talk." I kept my eyes fixed on my notebook as he talked, not wanting to "catch" anybody who was triggered by the talk. But now I wonder whether I kept my eyes down because I was afraid to know just how close I was to it all.

Ash's breathing is slower now. Peaceful. But maybe not for long. There are voices outside: low murmurs at first, but soon, things are escalating.

I transfer Ash's head from my shoulder to Trish's and stand up to take a look.

thin air

Once upon a time,
a girl from Nowhere
ran away
to live in the barn
and latched the door behind her
just to be safe.

Her mother couldn't come to find her,
because her mother was already gone.

Instead, her monster found her.

It happened so quickly—
she'd only rubbed her hand
across an old kerosene lamp
and there he was,
a terrible genie,
her worst nightmare,
out of thin air.

Not you, she said,
struggling with the latch,
finally breaking free,
breaking out,

wishing she'd killed him
when she had the chance
but no longer sure
that was possible.

14

The voices outside belong to Officer Hunt—and Kasen Keller.

Kasen's pulled up his sheriff's truck within an inch of Officer Hunt's bumper, and from the way Kasen himself is up in the cop's face, I'm thinking that was no accident.

I sneak from my room to the living room to get a better look, leaning toward the window to try to catch their conversation. When I can't, I crack the window slowly, and the words come pouring through.

". . . didn't trust my police work, so you decided to come see for yourself?" Kasen is pissed. There's no gentle drawing out his opponent this time—it's full-on attack mode.

Hunt's voice is cool and steady. "I came here because there was suspicion of criminal activity and dispatch sent me here. The second I saw the girl and realized this might be beyond our jurisdiction, I called it in. I don't know what more you want from me."

"How about an apology? How about you get the hell out of here? The only criminal activity around here is your blatant disregard for jurisdiction." He waves his arms in a pretty impressive wingspan, and something about the gesture reminds me of watching Dylan swim. It was always Ben who worshipped Kasen, but I never realized how much Dylan looks like him.

Hunt's tone is still steady, and I wonder how many hotheads he's dealt with over the years, both in and out of uniform. "With all due respect—and I'm not saying that's much—you don't have the slightest idea what happened here today. And I'm beginning to wonder if this isn't your jurisdiction either. You probably have the same guess as me, don't you? That this is the girl from Ash Creek?"

At this, I lose my balance, tipping forward and hitting my knee on the wall with a solid *thunk*. I hold my breath, hoping they didn't hear anything.

Kasen scoffs. "You haven't figured out yet that Calli and the girl are cousins? No wonder you never made detective."

For a second, I almost dare hope he knows something I don't. That maybe the lie I told Dylan by the creek somehow wasn't a lie at all. But then Kasen's eyes dart to the window. I duck, nearly hitting my head on the windowsill, but even before I've curled myself below the glass, I know he's seen me. That his lie was meant for me. The only thing I can't figure out is: Why? Is this some kind of a trap?

Kasen drops his voice, too soft for me to hear the words but loud enough that I catch the rhythm and lilt of his voice. A shiver dances up my spine as finally I place his soft accent—the one I've been listening to with a hint of a crush since freshman year.

Kasen Keller is from Ash Creek.

His name wasn't even Kasen when he moved here; it was Chasten. I know this when a sudden, distinct memory appears in my mind: one varsity cheerleader saying to another, "I'd let him chasten me," and when her friend stared at her blankly, she explained about the name change. How he and his mom had fled their old life and started over in a new place with new names. How he'd been strong enough from farming that the football coach had recruited him freshman year, and the rest was history.

How did I forget all this? And more important, does it have anything to do with Ash? Could Trish be both wrong and right— it's somebody from both their community *and* ours that Ash is afraid of? Even though he's older, there's no denying that Kasen or Chasten or whoever he is looks a lot like Dylan. Same build, same dark hair and eyes, same soft voice—except when it isn't. And didn't Ash freak out most of all when he pulled up the first time? I take the theory into my mind, stretching and molding it, shaping it to be what I need it to be.

Then his words and Maggie's come together like pieces of a puzzle snapping into place, showing me another possibility.

They play by their own rules down in Ash Creek.

I'm not saying the system's broken, although there are some who would say exactly that. I'm just saying it doesn't always work perfectly for everyone. Especially kids.

Maybe Kasen thinks Ash is Charity Trager too—and he knows how bad things could be for her if she gets sent back. He's trying to protect her and willing to bend the rules to do it, just like I am.

"Cousins?" asks Hunt. "Are you sure?"

Kasen's eyes flicker back to the window. "Ask her yourself. But I'm telling you: If Charity Trager is hiding somewhere, we won't find her." Then Kasen mutters something too soft and low to understand.

"What was that?" Hunt asks. "Speak up; I can't hear you."

"I said, 'Thou art my hiding place.' Psalm 32. It's their favorite scripture down in Ash Creek. They've been hiding from the government for years. Hell, the whole town is a hiding place. Which you'd know if *you* belonged on the Charity Trager case. Which this is not."

Thou art my hiding place. My mouth goes dry; those are the exact words Ash spoke a few minutes ago.

"What does that scripture have to do with anything?"

"That's why it's so hard to leave. You live your life under their strict watch, and even if they don't come looking for you, you lose your shit when you try to live any other way. Look at Miranda Tuttle. You call that a life? Literally shacking up in the middle of nowhere, relapsing, and then blowing up the one person who tries to help you?"

The words are a blunt pain against my belly. Miranda Tuttle was from Ash Creek. Does that figure into all of this somehow? Either way, she doesn't deserve to have anybody talking about her like this—and Dad sure as hell doesn't either.

"That's enough." Hunt's voice is sharp. He steps toward Kasen and stares him down. "Accidents happen. Chemicals are dangerous. And so is speculation."

Kasen lets out a short bark of a laugh. "Yeah, okay. I'm the dangerous one here. Maybe we should compare personnel files sometime, huh?"

A chill spreads across the back of my neck. What's in Officer Hunt's personnel file that makes him dangerous?

"That's what I thought." Kasen practically spits the words at Hunt. "Good luck with this one. It's all yours." Then he climbs into his truck and I sneak back to my bedroom, knowing that Hunt will be headed for our front door any minute.

When Hunt knocks, Trish looks up at me sleepily with a question in her eyes, but I gesture for her to stay put. Ash is still asleep, her hair splayed across Trish's lap. For a moment, I wonder if she's been pretending all this time, but then I see the widening circle of drool near Trish's knee.

"Come in," I say at the door, trying to conceal any sign of my eavesdropping.

"Is that girl your relative?" Hunt's not wasting any words. So much for me being prepared when he came back in. It's Dad's words that save me, in the end.

She's your sister.

"Yeah," I say. "We're related."

"Why didn't you tell me?"

I shrug. "You didn't ask."

"Because if she's not your family, she'll have to go to the shelter over in Cedar Falls until we can get her into foster care."

I picture Ash being taken away, broken and screaming, afraid and alone. No way in hell am I letting that happen.

"She's absolutely my family. She stayed after the funeral to help me go through stuff. And so I wouldn't be alone. I think somebody figured it would be good for both of us." It's all true enough. "But shouldn't we be focusing on the person who broke into my barn and scared her? Who's the criminal here?"

"Okay, okay," Hunt says. There's still a note of suspicion in his voice, but he leaves it. For now, anyway. "I'm going to ask around, see if any of the neighbors saw anything."

"What about Kasen? Officer Keller, I mean. Is he coming back?"

"He'd better not be."

I think of the cold edge in Kasen's voice, even as he was lying for me and Ash. How am I supposed to know whether he was keeping her out of the system to keep her safe and not for some motive of his own?

"Should we be worried if he does?"

Officer Hunt stops to think about this, which I appreciate. He's not going to defend somebody just because they wear a badge. "Worried for his career, maybe. Seems like he'll cross lines when he's sure he's in the right, but I haven't heard anything about him hurting anybody as a result."

It's not the strongest endorsement I've ever heard, but at least he's honest. Maybe honest enough to tell me what Kasen Keller was talking about.

"How about you?" I ask. "Have you ever hurt anybody?"

He chews his tongue. Furrows his brow. "Yes," he finally says.

"Is that what's in your personnel file?"

He sighs. "You heard that, huh? I broke protocol to cover for a buddy once. Thought I was doing the right thing by keeping something on the down-low. But yeah, somebody got hurt as a result. And the truth has a way of finding the light."

He's looking at me so intently that I wonder if this has taken a turn from story to advice. If he sees himself filling the role of some father figure for me. And maybe it's stupid or just a sign of the gaping absence inside me, but I let it happen. Seek it out, even.

"Would you do it again?"

"No. Don't ever sacrifice your integrity for somebody else's sake. You have to trust your gut." He rakes his hand through his hair. "Look, I know that's a little vague, but you're not telling me everything either. And that's okay. We don't have to go full disclosure in order to trust each other. But I do want us to trust each other. Okay? My goal really is to keep you and your cousin safe."

I decide to trust him. To reward his honesty with some of my own.

"Do you know Dylan Rigby?"

He nods. "He mows the strip of lawn in front of the station. Comes in to shoot the breeze with us sometimes."

So maybe that's how Dylan knew about the crap forensic evidence they found after the fire. Tempted as I am to ask him about it, I stay on track. "Before she went quiet again, Ash made it sound like she'd seen him." I swallow my hesitation so I can push the words out. "She made it sound like maybe it was him in the barn. And I'm not saying it couldn't be him, but I know him. We were together for a while." I feel the heat rising in my cheeks, but I keep going. "The other thing is, I can't help but notice how much he looks like Kasen Keller. Because wasn't it weird how quickly Keller got here? Almost like he wasn't that far away?"

Officer Hunt puts up a hand. "I'm glad you told me all this," he says. "But you can probably see how it isn't enough for me to make any accusation yet. I'd need to talk to Ash myself, for starters. And I'd like to talk to Dylan too. Officer Keller is trickier, but I might be able to have that conversation."

"Good," I say. "Because there might actually be somebody trying to hurt her, and those are the only leads we have right now."

"We?" he asks, fighting a smile.

"*We* have to protect her. I promised."

He gives my shoulder a pat that's either compassionate or patronizing—or maybe both. "I'm here to help you keep that promise," he says. I hate the way the tears pool in my eyes. I hate how much I want to help her and how helpless I feel about it. I hate how much it means to have him say those words and really seem to mean them, just like my dad would if he were here.

The radio at his hip crackles to life, releasing the emotion of the moment before I totally break down. The voice transmits a combination of words and numbers that are meaningless to me, but his jaw tightens as he listens. "I'm sorry," he says. "Small force, you know, so I should probably respond to this. You need me to stay, though?"

"No," I say. "We're fine."

"In that case," he says, replacing his radio, "I might see if I can have a word with Dylan Rigby after I'm done with this. Sit tight, okay?"

"You'll tell me if you find out anything important?"

He nods. "I will. You'll both still be on your property and in one piece?"

"We'll try," I say. I mean for it to be a joke, but it comes out high and strained and a little desperate.

"You will be," he says. "I wouldn't leave if I wasn't sure." He takes down my phone number, then pulls a card from his pocket and hands it to me. "That's my cell. Call me directly if you need anything at all, okay?"

"Okay," I say, once to his face, and once to his car as it retreats down the road. "Okay."

It will be.

It has to be.

breathing

The officer checks in with dispatch
as he pulls away from the vet's place at the edge of town.
Damn shame, what happened to him
and to his daughter.
She reminds him a little of his own kid,
who's grown and gone with a family of her own.

The vet's girl is tough,
and the officer can respect that.
He knows she's lying and can respect that too.

If those two girls are cousins,
then he's Father Freaking Christmas.

The deputy's two blocks away,
still circling the place.
It's his lies and smug superiority
that make the officer want to flip his car around
and take that asshole down a notch or two,
even though, technically,
the girl's lie and the deputy's are the same.
The vein in his neck throbs
just thinking about the way that punk talked to him,
when the kid's still so green
he probably shits shamrocks.

But he catches himself,
breathes in,
holds it,
breathes out,
holds it,
remembers the box breathing
they learned in wellness training last year.

He's taught himself to channel the anger
because he knows from experience:
It's hard to think straight when you're angry.
And the officer
has a lot of thinking to do.

It all goes back to the girl
who is nobody's cousin around here.
But surely she must be
somebody's daughter.

15

When I peek back into my bedroom, Trish and Ash are still asleep. I know Trish needs to get back to the hospital; she was supposed to head back at two, and now it's nearly three. But first, I need a few minutes. Something's drawing me out to the barn to see things for myself, by myself. So I steal outside, trusting my gut that if there was anybody here, he's long gone by now.

The barn is familiar in every way: the slant of the sunbeams coming through the gaps in the boards, the smell of soil and hay and motor oil, the sound of my own feet shuffling along the dirt floor.

Then a scuffling sound behind me. My mouth goes dry and my body tenses, but I manage to creep behind the stall divider. When I see what was making the noise, I let out a long breath.

It's just the jackrabbits in their plastic bin. A laugh bursts from me like a release; I'd forgotten they were out here. Still, I look for any hint that something isn't right. I check the exam room at the back, but it's locked, and there's no sign that the key's been moved. I move it myself, though, and unlock the door to be sure.

Everything seems to be in its place, and I stand there for a moment at the threshold of the cleaned-up, clinical part of the barn, with its neat rows of drawers and sterilized countertops. A memory comes back, then, of standing between these two realms a few months ago while Dad removed an enormous, bristling thorn from a chocolate Lab's paw. As I watched from this very doorway, I asked, "Which is the real you? The mess out here or the order in there?"

He was quiet a long time, soothing the dog and smoothing her fur as he began treating the site. I almost wondered if he'd heard me, but finally, he answered as he wrapped the injured paw without looking up. "I like to think I'm a little of both. I like to think maybe we all are, and that's okay."

I smile at the memory as I scan the area once more. The rest of the barn is still such a ramshackle scattering of stuff that it's hard to say for certain, but I can't find anything that seems off beyond the broken door latch. It all feels so familiar, such a part of who I am, that I feel my pulse slowing in spite of the circumstances.

I even lived in the barn once—for a couple of hours, anyway. When I was little, I broke Dad's fly rod pretending to fish in the backyard. Standing there with the snapped shards in my hand, I was so afraid of owning up to what I'd done that it seemed smart to get a fresh start somewhere else.

It was Mom who found me and convinced me it would be better to come home than live in the barn forever. Told me she'd talked to him and he wasn't mad anymore, just worried about me. That night, he made us strawberry crepes for dinner to apologize for getting mad. "See?" Mom asked as she loaded her plate. "We can always make it right."

The day I broke Dad's fly rod wasn't the only time I hoped he wouldn't find me here. Heat creeps up the back of my neck as I remember meeting Dylan out in the barn one night last summer. I knew I was breaking curfew, but really I wasn't, because hadn't Dad only said to be home by midnight? And wasn't I as much at home in this broken-down barn as anywhere? We'd spread a blanket on the ground and stayed out there until the light started to touch the horizon, kissing and telling whispered stories and even falling asleep for a while.

Then I remember why Dylan and I had been so desperate to spend every hour we could together that night: He was leaving in the morning for two weeks on a construction site with his dad and brothers, somewhere remote where he wasn't sure he'd even have cell service.

Wait a second.

Where was he going?

In the slanted shadows of the barn, I pull out my phone, remembering a very specific picture Dylan sent me of himself pretending to mail me a letter the first day he was away (once he realized he did have a signal). I can almost hear Officer Hunt cautioning me that, even if Dylan did go to Ash Creek, it doesn't necessarily mean anything.

I scroll backward through my photos. At first I go past it, but then I reverse my scrolling, slower, until there it is: Dylan, hair matted down from sweating in a hat all day on the job site, face smudged with dirt but fully lit up in a smile. Sliding what I can only assume is a piece of junk mail (or some other trash from the floor of his truck) into a slot at the tiny Ash Creek post office as he shows off his backside.

He turned it into a meme, with big block lettering at the top and bottom: **GREETINGS FROM YOUR FAVORITE DUMB-ASH.**

I think back, begging my brain to recall any small piece of information from that trip. Was it just the one text and picture, that whole two weeks? Was he different when he came back? Less playful, more possessive? Was that when things started to fall apart between us? Another memory surfaces then, of a gash across his cheek that he said had come from a mistake on the job site that he definitely didn't want to talk about.

I put a pin in the memory and keep scrolling, no longer sure what I'm even looking for, pulled in by my own past unspooling in front of me. The longer I scroll, the more it strikes me how few photos I have of Dad. It seemed like he was always posing for other people's pictures: serving at the soup kitchen, assembling hygiene kits with the local youth after a natural disaster, dressed in a padded suit to play Santa for the church Christmas party. So why don't I have any?

Maybe it's just that he was so busy with his practice and his church callings that there was little time for any sort of personal life. Maybe that's why my memories, like his pictures, are so often in public settings.

Finally, I find a picture from a couple of years ago. His hair is full and brown, his body strong and able. He's smiling back at me, a small V of sweat down the front of his shirt because it's August and we've just finished hiking up the ridge behind our cabin.

When I take a closer look at his face, the thing that strikes me most is how exhausted he looks, and I have to acknowledge that his fatigue was at least partly my fault. That trip was my idea, a rare chance for it to be just the two of us. He'd been tired, working overtime, doing his best to balance being a vet with being a single parent.

I was the one who'd decided we needed to get away, to bring him back to that feeling of freedom from before we lost Mom. "I'm like a new man up here," he'd said, making a show of turning off his phone as he shed all the responsibilities of his life back home.

So it was me who bought the groceries and packed the gear. I was sure I was doing the right thing and congratulated myself for being such a good daughter.

But in this photo, he's not okay. *Haunted*, something in me whispers.

"No," I say, the sound of it floating to the far corners of the barn. I won't let my own exhaustion and grief color the memory of the very best person I ever knew.

But could he have been afraid of something? Even if I can't fathom a reason, could there have been somebody after him? Could Kasen actually be right about Miranda Tuttle causing the explosion?

Probably not. The people I actually trust are telling me it was an accident. I've been through a lot, I remind myself, and grasping at wild theories is my brain's way of trying to make it make sense. Do I believe Bishop Carver or Kasen Keller? The choice is an easy one.

So I focus on the smile in the picture. The Dad I remember. No matter what happens, I know this is true: We loved each other. *Love* each other. And he wouldn't want me stuck in the past or chasing conspiracy; he'd want me here, in this moment, to figure out how to help Ash.

"Even if I've never been enough before, please help me be enough for her," I whisper, not quite sure whether I'm speaking to him or to God. "Please help me become who I'm supposed to become."

A vibration in my hand turns my thoughts back to earth. I expect the text to be from Trish, finally woken up and wondering where I am. But when I look down at my phone, Ben's message makes my stomach flip.

Hey. I know it's cheesy but I wanted you to know I'm still thinking about you. Can't wait to hang out tonight

It's a thoughtful, best-friend-Ben kind of message. A month ago, I wouldn't have thought anything of it. But has Ben ever said he's thinking about me? Is it a "thoughts and prayers" kind of a thing, or something else?

My mind searches for some inside joke or movie line he's referencing, but I come up empty. Maybe what he means by it is that he actually can't wait to hang out tonight. Which feels like it could mean something brand-new.

I feel the corners of my mouth curve into a smile as I text him back.

Same ♥

The second I hit Send, I get an immediate and acute case of emoji regret. Maybe if I bury it with a diversion . . .

Wait a second, are you still at work? Isn't Elliott going to report you for texting while you're on shift?

The three pulsing dots tell me Ben is texting back, and my own pulse quickens more as I wait for his response.

I'm on my break. And Elliott is currently inspecting his left nostril in his reflection on the fryer, so . . .

When I read the message, something inside me breaks open, and I tip my head back and laugh straight toward the rafters. It feels good to be out here, cracking up, connecting with my best friend, knowing that one emoji could never mess up what we have. I write a text that hopefully he can respond to either as a friend or as something more, no longer agonizing over each word.

Thank you for everything. And not just today.

Of course. I have to go back in a second, but I'll still be thinking about you. (Except when I'm thinking about Elliott)

I'm not ready to let him go quite yet. There's not much time, but luckily the perfect message comes to me in an instant, and it takes only two words.

I wish . . .

This time, it's definitely a reference—to our school musical. Because, if I'm honest about when I first wondered if there might be something more between me and Ben, it was closing night of *Into the Woods*, watching him sing "No One Is Alone." He looked right at me in the wings, the stage lights illuminating him in a whole new way as specks of dust danced around him like something truly magical.

There are so many things I wish right now. I wish I hadn't lost my parents. I wish I knew who Ash is and how to keep her safe. I wish I were sure what Ben's feeling and what should happen next.

When his text comes back, it's the next line in the song, proving he gets me more than anybody outside my family ever has or maybe ever will.

I know.

I didn't even realize how lonely I'd been feeling until I saw those words, the perfect reminder that I'm seen and known. That even though my parents are gone, I'm not alone.

I remember Ben coming to pick me up for the show that night. I was stuck in the pre-show purgatory of wearing comfy sweats—but with stage makeup already caked on my face.

Before we left, Dad pulled me close with one arm and gave Ben a solid handshake with the other. "I'm so sorry I can't come, but you'll be incredible up there, both of you." He sighed. "It's a strange and powerful feeling, to become another person for a while. Just promise me you won't forget who you really are."

"I won't forget," I whisper in the cool of the barn. In spite of all the half-truths I've been telling, the last few days seem to be bringing out some deeper, truer self within me.

The soft scufflings of the jackrabbits bring me back to the moment, and I scoop one up, feeling ridiculously like I'm in a fairy tale. The dark humor of it doesn't escape me: Of course I'm an orphan. Of course there are woodland creatures and the threat of something lurking. But that just means I'm due for a happy ending with my true love, right?

The hare tries to scramble from my arms, so I let her gently back down into the bin. As I watch her hurry to her sister, taking safety in proximity, I wonder: Why would Ash stray so far from Trish, especially when Trish had fallen asleep? Was she trying to get them all hurt? We're only paces away from where we first found the hares. I know coyotes don't come out much in the middle of the day, but still, returning them so close to where they were attacked in the first place, but trapping them in a plastic bin—they're practically bait. It's only a matter of time before he (yes, *he;* fairly or unfairly, I've decided that much about the coyote) comes back to finish the job.

I look toward the house, where two silhouettes move inside.

Even though I know it's Trish in there with Ash, my mind takes it another direction. Imagines it's me and Ash. Takes the perspective of whoever might be hunting her.

And what I see is this: If there is somebody out there, we are just like the jackrabbits. Trapped in a small space, in almost exactly the same spot where we were last in danger. Viewed from this angle, it's only a matter of time before our coyote comes back to finish things off—whatever that means. Whether it's Kasen or Dylan (which I still can't quite believe) or someone who's tracked her clear from Ash Creek, they know exactly where she is.

Unless I can change that. Unless I take us—me, Ash, hell, even the hares—far away from this place.

Unless.

protection, part 1

One day in Nowhere,
the girl's father brought home a tree,
dug a hole for it near the house,
dug a ditch so the water from the drainpipe
would find its way to the soft, turned soil
that had become a bed for the roots.

For protection, he said, looking upon the tree,
borrowing the culture of the man who'd sold it to him
like a neighbor might borrow a cup of sugar—
more to use than to ever give back.

The girl looked at the tag strapped around its trunk
and read the word.
(She was learning to read now.)

She looked at the trunk,
barely thicker than her arm,
and the branches,
thinner even than her fingers,
and wondered how something so frail
could provide any protection at all.

But when she looked into his eyes,
saw that he believed,
she decided to believe too.

Protection, she whispered,
marveling that such a thing could come
from a tree.

From an ash,
no matter how small.

16

I walk back toward the house, more purpose in my stride than I've felt since Dad died. Even if there isn't anybody out there, leaving still feels like the right call. Trish said it herself: Ash is a different person when she's spared all the intrusions and interruptions, when she can get outside. I should at least be able to give her that.

My eyes flash to the driveway, and there's my answer in the form of the old Chevy Silverado, perfectly equipped for the ruts and rocks on the old dirt road up to the cabin. Fluffy told me just yesterday morning that it was ready to go up the mountain.

The picture, the memory, the truck. And then, his voice.

It's time to go, Calli. To the cabin. You both belong there.

"Time to go," I whisper, and the words feel both rebellious and right as soon as I say them.

Inside, I find Ash and Trish together in the kitchen. "Time to go," I say again, and the way Ash's eyes come back to life, I know it's the right call. "We're leaving."

"Wait, what? Where? And who's *we*?" Trish asks.

"Me and Ash. And the hares. Just to the cabin," I say. "She'll be different up there, I promise. The person you saw this morning."

"Yeah, because no horror movie ever takes place at a cabin in the woods," Trish says. "Calli, you can't be serious."

"Of course I'm serious," I say. "You said it yourself: Ash does better when it's just the two of us. I can't stay here anymore. And today proved I can't leave without her."

It's a low blow, but reminding Trish of her own mistake seems to make her trust me a little more. "Maybe. But won't Officer Hunt be expecting you to stay here?"

"I don't see why. We're not under investigation or anything. And the cabin isn't the end of the earth, it just feels like it. There's a signal up there. He can still contact me if he learns anything. I told him we'd still be on our property, and we will. You can even follow us to the edge of town if you want, so you know nobody else is."

"And if they are?"

"Then call the police."

"I thought Maggie said you were supposed to turn Ash over to the professionals after forty-eight hours. I can't believe Hunt didn't take her with him, to be honest."

To be honest. I know my whole cousin act can't last forever, but I need it to last at least a little longer. So I let my own dishonesty coil safely inside me and jump on the last thing Trish said. "Turning Ash over to strangers was *never* the deal. I had forty-eight hours until we violated her boundaries, which seems like a pretty messed-up plan to begin with. The authorities know she's here," I say, my conscience grating a bit against the guilt of my half-truth. "You guys won, and we didn't even get our forty-eight hours. Let me give her what control I can before she's sucked into the system."

"I haven't been to your cabin in years," Trish says, still uncertain. "I'm not even sure I remember how to get there."

"Maggie remembers," I say. "So does Ben. And Fluffy and LuEllen—their cabin is across the pond, so you could ask them. You can come check on us tomorrow."

Trish reaches into her pocket absently and wraps her fingers around her keys. She's probably ready to get out of here, but she still doesn't quite dare. "Do you think there's really somebody out there?"

"You were the one who called the cops in the first place." Trish nods, conceding the point instead of getting defensive. I'm grateful enough I decide to go for honesty. "I guess I don't know. But this feels like the right call either way. Even if there isn't and it's all in her head somehow, don't you think that's a good reason to get her out of here too?"

Trish finally gives in. "Hurry and pack your stuff. I'll follow you to the canyon, but then I really do need to get back to work."

"I know," I say. "Thank you for staying so long. And for coming in the first place." I go in for the hug, which makes her stiffen in surprise since neither one of us is a big hugger. But it's barely a second before she's hugging me back.

As the tension between us dissolves, I think back to the Dairy Freeze today. How the world keeps turning and people move on— quickly, too quickly—so you have to thank the people who take the time to stay with you until your world starts to turn again too.

If Ash is really Charity Trager, she's thirteen—exactly how old I was when I lost my mom. When I needed so badly for people to protect me, to not give up on me.

I'll protect you.

I won't give up on you.

The words are clear in my head, but this time, I'm not sure if they're coming from Mom or Dad—or from me, to Ash.

I ask Ash to load up the hares while I pack for the two of us, grabbing an old duffel bag and piling in all the first aid gear we've been using, some matches, and enough clean clothes for a couple of days. I'm not totally naïve; I know that if there's somebody out there and they're persistent enough, they'll still be here when we get back. So maybe going up the mountain is my version of what Maggie said Ash needed—a way to show I'm in control of something. We can leave this place when we want, and we can come back when we want too.

"Ready," I say, slinging the bag over my shoulder as I start down the hall to where Trish is packing a cooler for us. "Where's Ash?"

"Out in the truck," Trish says as she picks up the cooler. "I helped her get the rabbits and their gear together."

When everything's loaded up, Trish pulls me into another hug, which simultaneously comforts me and puts me on edge.

"We'll be fine," I tell her. "But call or text or even come up and check on us anytime. And I'll let you know if we hear anything from Hunt."

"You better," she says, a tough edge in her voice.

"We will," I promise. "We're the last house in Harmony and the first cabin up the mountain. We're practically going next door."

Trish rolls her eyes at Dad's old joke, but it seems to help. She sweeps a hand toward the driver's side door of the Silverado. "Lead the way."

When I climb in, Ash is already buckled into the passenger seat, staring out the window with her feet on the dashboard. She's as inscrutable as ever, but I think I catch a hint of a smile when I turn the key and the truck rumbles to life.

"I'm taking you away from here," I tell her as I reach over to give her hand a little squeeze. "Somewhere safer." The squeeze she gives me back only makes me more sure that this is the right thing for us.

Before we back out of the driveway, I tilt the rearview mirror down for a second so I can see the jackrabbits. The plastic bin is against the back corner instead of up by the cab, but it'll work. They won't slide around, and they definitely can't get out. I shift into reverse, ready to get out of town. But as I tilt the mirror back, a glint of metal in the truck bed catches my eye, nearly in the shadow of the tailgate.

Ash brought the shotgun.

protection, part 2

The girl from Nowhere learned to shoot
when she was still small.

Pellets,
then bullets,
then shotgun shells.

She trained her aim on empty fuel cans,
knowing the full ones were like bombs
and a bullet could light the fuse.
She closed her eyes,
imagining what that might look like.

You'll need to know how to protect yourself
when I'm gone, her daddy said.

She hadn't asked
when
he'd be going,
    but the answer was
    soon.

She hadn't asked
why,
    and that answer never came.

She hadn't asked
what
she would need protection from.
 Eventually, that answer became obvious.
 Protection from the monster.

17

I blink, tilting the mirror back to make sure I haven't imagined the shotgun, butt up against the tailgate.

It's there. With a box of shells beside it.

I turn to Ash, wondering if I should say something. Remembering how straight she stood after Dylan handed it to her. How she finally said more than one word at a time when she held it in her hands—and has barely used her notebook since.

It's a good idea. One I should have thought of. At least, that's what I try to tell myself as I back out of the driveway.

"Ready?" I ask, forcing a smile. "Do we have everything we need?"

Ash nods, then reaches over and lays her hand on mine, like she's the one reassuring me now. Keeping me safe. I'm not totally sure she'd be wrong about that. In spite of growing up around guns, I've always been uneasy around them. Maybe she'd be the one protecting us, if it ever came to that.

But for now, I'm in the driver's seat. I ease the truck from reverse and watch as Trish pulls out ahead of us, apparently having decided to let us follow her for now. Something in me uncoils as I see Harmony in the rearview mirror.

The cabin is less than an hour away. Close enough that you can go there for the weekend or even just for the afternoon. Far enough that it still feels like a whole other world.

As we approach the small state road that will take us up the mountain, Trish pulls over. I give her a little wave, and Ash does the same. We meet each other's eyes and smile before I turn back to watch the road again.

For the rest of the trip, we'll be driving east, straight up the canyon as the road changes from pavement to gravel to dirt. The amazing thing about the high desert is how quickly it can stop looking like a desert at all. In just a few miles, the landscape turns from a barren expanse of sagebrush and wheatgrass to a thick forest of aspen and spruce.

Off and on, the road follows the same creek that forms the north border of our property, but once we get up into the canyon, flanked by steep limestone walls, you can only catch glimpses of it below. Still, I feel almost like the cool, clear water is washing over me. With every mile we put behind us, I actually feel my muscles—jaw, shoulders, neck—relaxing.

When I look over at Ash, though, she's braced against the seat, knuckles white as she clutches the grab bar. If she grew up in Ash Creek, it may be that the only stretch of road she's driven is the flat, bare desert between there and town.

"I'm a good driver," I assure her. She nods and tries to smile, but I still can't tell whether she's holding on for her life or getting ready to jump.

Then I realize she might be worried about something else entirely. "It's okay. I promise. The only people who know about this place are the people you trust anyway—Ben and Maggie and Sofia and Trish." I bite my lip, wondering whether I should add one last name, but I decide she deserves the truth. "And Dylan." I blush, remembering the times we'd sneak up here when we were together. "But he has no idea where we're going, and nobody's going to tell him. Once we get to the cabin, everybody will stop bothering us."

I glance down at my phone. I wasn't lying when I told Trish there's a signal at the cabin. It's a little patchy, and you have to turn on a booster we keep in the kitchen, but it's reliable enough.

On the road, though, there are dead spots—including the stretch we're on now.

"There are a few other cabins in the general area," I tell her. "But nobody actually lives up here. We probably won't see another soul."

Half a mile up, the road has washboarded out. "Are our friends okay back there?" I ask, expecting Ash to turn and check on the hares in the truck bed. But she keeps staring straight ahead, still gripping the grab bar and looking pretty, well, ashen.

"Not too much farther," I tell her as we begin the last switch-backs.

I'm not sure if it's my words or the road itself, but she relaxes a little when we turn onto the rocky, rutted driveway. "You're going to love this place. And so are they," I tell her, glancing back at the truck bed, where I hope the hares are faring well. "We might even want to let them go up here, when they're ready. They'd probably be safer. Coyotes like wide-open spaces. Forest, not so much."

I glance over, realizing she may not be on board with ever letting the hares go. But now she's looking out the window with something like wonder, and I find myself seeing the place through her eyes: the ledges of rock above us, broken and bare; the light around us, filtering through the trees and glinting off the pond.

"We can fish down there later," I say. "I can teach you how, if you don't know already."

After one last curve, the cabin appears. Ours is nothing like the fancy properties that rim Cobalt Lake, with their infinity pools and three-car garages. It's one of a kind and twice as old as Dad, an actual log cabin with a real rock chimney rising out of the rickety front porch instead of synthetic wood and stone.

"This is it," I say, shifting into park and cutting the engine. I open the door but stay in my seat for a second, letting the mountain air wash over me.

Ash isn't waiting. She hops out and circles around behind the truck. I flinch at the crash of the tailgate dropping, stark against the quiet. When I follow, she's sitting there, legs swinging off the edge of the tailgate, holding one of the hares in each hand. Closing her eyes and burying her face in their fur. My instinct is to take a picture, to capture this innocence so that I can remind myself—and Maggie, and Ben, and Kasen, and Hunt, and whoever else might need it, including Ash herself—that she's just a kid, quiet and loving and, under it all, probably scared as hell.

So I let her relax with the jackrabbits as I bring our stuff inside—including the shotgun. Eventually, Ash follows me, eyeing me as I tuck it into the closet under the stairs, as if having it here were my idea and she's not entirely sure it's a good one.

"What should we do next?" I ask, hoping to distract her from the shotgun.

"Fishing," she says, the energy in her voice a mismatch with the gentle way she's returning the hares to their bin.

I'd kind of figured we'd settle in first, but what the hell. The food will be fine in the cooler a little longer, and there will still be plenty of time to figure out dinner and make up the beds when we get back.

"I'm good with fishing," I say. "I'll get the poles if you'll grab the gear bag hanging right above those boots."

It takes me a minute to find the second pole in the little closet, but once I see it, I can't believe I missed it. *If it'd been a snake, it would have bit you.* I smile at the familiar phrase, grateful to hear his voice again in this place he loved so much.

The pond is peaceful, fed by a cool, clear stream that makes its own chattering music as it cascades down the rocks. In the distance, the rooftops of a few cabins peek through the trees, but none of the cabins themselves are visible. As I watch the rippling reflection of the forest and sky, it all feels protected somehow, like the trees are standing guard.

We set up near the inlet because that's where the fish are most likely to be this time of day. The fishing might be better if we came a few hours from now, but part of me always secretly hopes I won't get a bite. Even though we catch and release, I feel bad at the pain and fear it must cause to be yanked from your world by a hook in your mouth, gasping for breath.

"Spinner or power bait?" I ask, holding out a small, colorful lure and a yellow-lidded jar.

"Both?" she asks, picking up the spinner carefully, like she can imagine how much it would hurt to pull the barbed hook from her skin.

"Sure," I say. "Let's tie that on first so you can get some practice casting."

But it doesn't take much practice at all before she's laying the spinner onto the water like a pro and bringing it in every bit as smoothly, a silver sprite dancing through the water. A few minutes later, the end of the rod bends suddenly; Ash has her first bite. She turns to me with a smile as bright as the sun shining off the water.

"Keep reeling," I tell her. "Don't let the line go slack or it might get away."

Soon the fish is at our feet, thrashing and splashing. I kick off my shoes and wade in, hoping to unhook it and get it on its way as quickly as I can. It's a rainbow trout, iridescent pink and green and probably fourteen inches long. Judging by the scar on the left side of its mouth, it's been caught at least once before.

"Don't worry," I whisper to the fish, clamping the pliers around the hook. "This is almost over."

Then Ash's bare feet appear in the water beside mine.

"Want to hold it?" I ask, sliding the trout into her outstretched hands. Its gills fan in and out like a bellows, desperate to breathe. Ash is watching too, her fascination tinged with sorrow.

"Okay," I murmur, placing a hand on her shoulder. "Let's get it back in the water. . . ."

But Ash turns, taking the fish with her. I stand, my feet frozen in the mud, as she sets the fish on the ground and picks up a rock, then brings it down on the fish's head in one swift blow.

I gasp, then try to cover it with a cough. It's unfair of me to be horrified when I serve burgers and chicken fingers and even fish and chips at the Freeze every single shift. And Ash wasn't cruel. She took no joy in it. She knew that if you're going to keep a fish, it's more humane to end its suffering in a single blow than to let it die slowly on the shore from lack of oxygen.

"My dinner," Ash says, a note of pride in her voice as she wraps the fish in an old newspaper from the bag. "Now I'll catch yours." She goes a little farther down the shore, casting her lure back into the water before I've even picked up my pole again. And when the line pulls again a few minutes later and she lets out a whoop, I step back into the trees, suddenly interested in adjusting my shoelaces. When she brings the fish to show me, I give her a thumbs-up and force a smile, but I can't look her in the eye.

I want to ask her where she learned to fish. I want her to know it's safe to share her story with me. But the sound of stone against fish still rings in my ears, and I still feel like I'm doing it all wrong. I'm guessing there's a fine line between catharsis and torture in sharing your trauma, and the last thing I want to do is end up on the wrong side of it.

On the way back to the cabin, Ash begins to wander, and for a moment, I wonder if she's lost the trail. But her steps are full of enough purpose that I follow, and soon I realize exactly where she's headed.

Most of our forest is aspen and spruce, but there are a few ponderosa pines—including the tallest tree in the whole valley. It towers over the rest of the forest like Miss Kathryn in our kindergarten class picture. Ash must have seen it from the cabin.

Sure enough, when she gets close enough, she drops the bag of fish from her shoulder and steps up to the massive trunk, resting both palms against the brown puzzle of its bark and closing her eyes. I have to smile; I've been doing almost exactly the same thing since I was small.

I approach Ash and the tree. "Lean close," I say, resting my hands on the bark by hers and bringing my body next to the trunk. "Can you smell that?" I inhale the butterscotch scent of the sap.

Ash leans in. She closes her eyes and breathes deeply. "Vanilla," she says, and I almost laugh. Dad always thought they smelled like vanilla too, even when Mom and I insisted it was butterscotch.

Then another memory, so sudden and clear it takes my breath away: They lost a baby when I was seven. We drove up here right after Mom came home from the hospital; she stayed in bed and Dad took me fishing and hiking in between a hundred trips to the loft to check on her. There were other times, I realize, when Mom would be in bed for a few days and Dad would try way too hard to distract us both and cheer everybody up and no one really told me why.

No parent tells their child everything, I can almost hear him say. *If you were ready to know, we thought you'd figure it out. And if you weren't ready, what good would it have done to pull you into that pain? It's my job to keep you safe. To shelter you from the hard, ugly side of everything, including our own lives.*

I wasn't meant to be an only child. I look at Ash, running her fingers reverently over the bark of the old ponderosa as she gazes up through the branches, and I wonder if maybe the universe has a way of providing some kind of reparation after all it's taken away.

Ash couldn't look more different from me. I'm solid and strong, she's thin and small. I have dark hair and blue eyes, hers are vibrant red and green. We were born to different parents, in what feels like different worlds, and we're not cousins, no matter what I may have let Hunt think.

But maybe I was meant to have a sister. And maybe she was too.

Unless she does already. Unless there's a little girl in Ash Creek who drew a picture of her, hoping it would help her come home safe. Who's missing her even now.

I almost ask, but I hold the words inside. It's selfish, maybe, but I want us to belong only to each other, just for this moment. The rest of the world will be back to claim us soon enough.

At the cabin, Ash finds a fillet knife and takes it out the back door to deal with the fish. But I don't follow. Instead, I drag the cooler to the fridge, which reminds me that I haven't even turned on the generator yet. "I'll be right back," I say to Ash as she stands over a bucket on the deck. "Just going to get us some electricity."

The generator sits in a lean-to tacked onto the back of the cabin, and starting it has always been Dad's job. I'm usually inside the cabin, listening to the clicks and whirs as things come to life. It's not a hard job, though. Today, it's full of gas and only requires the flip of a switch. It's not until the hum of the motor starts up that the significance of that small fact knocks the breath out of me.

He even thought to top off the generator before he left last time. To have him still taking care of me in this small way fills me with comfort at the same time as it swallows me in grief. He worked so hard to build us a beautiful life, even after our heartbreak. And even as he taught me to work hard too, he was always doing small, thoughtful things for me: showing up at school with the assignment I'd forgotten, scraping my windshield on snowy days. Making it so I could have all that I needed with the flip of a switch.

I sink to the floor, letting the steady thrum of the motor drown out my sobs. He's gone. For good. How many times will I have to feel this simple, terrible truth like it's the first time?

Eventually, the wave of grief that took me out to sea returns me, gasping, to shore. I dry my eyes and take a slow, deep breath, then grab a few last things (including clean sheets) from the truck.

Inside, Ash has pulled most of the food out of the cooler and is making small piles of vegetables on two plates. I'm not really hungry (and not sure we have salad dressing), but it's the first time she's made anything for me, so I promise myself to at least try to eat it. But then, without a word, Ash takes the plates and kneels in the corner of the living room next to the hares.

Of course she wasn't making salad. She was making dinner for the hares. I'm about to tell her they might not be ready for solid food yet when the bigger one takes a few tentative hops forward and starts nibbling at the edge of a lettuce leaf. Ash looks up at me, eyes bright with celebration. I can't help but smile as I cross the room to kneel beside her. Soon, the smaller jackrabbit—Notch, I've started calling her in my head—inches forward and follows her sister. We both watch them, mesmerized by the slight variations in their small, flickering movements the same way the fireplace usually captures my attention in this very room.

In spite of everything cartoons have taught me, the hares don't touch the carrots, moving from the lettuce to the sunflower seeds before retreating to the corner of the room, where Ash has tipped their bin on its side and turned it into a bed for them. There's plenty of space for them to spread out, but they huddle together once again, heads resting on each other's backs, and fall asleep.

I'm so worn out, I'd like to do the same thing, but the press of my phone against my thigh reminds me that I need to keep my promise to Trish and get myself back on the grid. I flip on the cell booster and watch as it flickers to life, then pull my phone from my pocket and wait for the screen to light up with messages making sure we're okay.

Nothing. No missed calls or voicemails or even texts. I send the same text to all of them: **Arrived fine and the most exciting thing that's happened is that the hares eat solid food now. Love you**

A drip of sweat trickles down my back, and suddenly, I realize I'm roasting. "I'm going to open the windows, okay?"

Ash nods, still absorbed in the hares.

The big picture window that looks out over the pond doesn't open, but I remove the sawed-off broomsticks locking the rest of the windows in place and wrestle the panes across their dirty tracks. When I'm finished with the main floor, I climb the tight staircase to the loft.

With every step, the temperature rises, and by the time I get to the top, sweat beads along my hairline and drips down my spine. Mom made blackout curtains so we'd at least have a chance of sleeping in a little on summer mornings when the sun rose early, and it's darker by far up here than it was downstairs. I pull the curtains aside and force the window open, allowing myself a few breaths of cool mountain air before I turn back around.

When I do, the sight before me is a punch in the gut, like some sort of messed-up Goldilocks moment. Two of the three beds lie before me just as they should: quilts folded neatly at each foot, waiting for their clean sheets.

But on the third—the one nearest me—the quilt lies splayed across the bed, a pale amber stain spread from a bottle nearby.

Someone has been sleeping in this bed.

the cabin

For almost a hundred years,
people have come to the cabin
seeking a home,
a haven,
a hiding place.

The cabin has been all these things
to the girl and her family
and the families before them
and the friends they've welcomed
under this tin roof
and warmed
by this stone fireplace.

It has been all these things
to the man who left the bottles as well.

Home.
Haven.
Hiding place.
Standing peacefully among the spruce
for almost a hundred years.

But
nothing
lasts forever.

18

I creep forward, half expecting a hand to reach from under the bed and grab hold of my ankle.

My own hand shakes as I lift the corner of the quilt, and something clatters to the floor. It's only the beer bottle, but by the time I realize that, I've jumped out of the way like it's got fangs. The hairs on the back of my neck prickle, but I won't let myself panic.

Now's a time to be smart, not scared.

Because this isn't the first time we've found evidence of a squatter.

A couple years back, around the anniversary of Mom's death, Dad and I came here to get away from all the well-meaning well-wishers. The scene was similar: unmade bed without even any sheets, beer bottles on the floor.

The next week, Dylan and I brought a trail cam and set it up outside, hoping to at least get a grainy picture of the guy. But eventually we took it down, since we never got anything more than deer and marmots on the memory card.

And a coyote. Wasn't there a coyote once? A picture flashes in my mind, but I dismiss it. It's just my brain, trying to warn me to watch out for the same danger we faced down there. Coyotes usually live in open territory, I remind myself. The hares are safe inside the cabin, and so are we. There aren't many hiding places (or any, really) in a cabin this small, and I've checked them all. Plus, there's a fine layer of dust over the bottles, which means whoever he is, he's long gone. But I can't shake the shiver that runs through me. The squatter, the coyote, the fact that somebody's been here again.

Last time, Dad told me to play outside while he took care of the mess. This time, I have to clean it up alone. It's up to me to be the adult, to make this okay. But I know Dad hasn't truly left me alone, so I try to find some comfort in what he said to me back then.

If we could provide shelter for someone that desperate and broken, well, there's good in that, I think.

And when I let my disgust at the mess show—especially at the bottles:

We are all sinners, Calli. And it's not our job to judge those who choose to sin differently than we do.

We are all sinners. It's something I think I'd believe even if I hadn't been hearing it all my life.

But then I look over the loft railing and see Ash cradling one of the hares. Whoever hurt her, scared her, made her run away— surely there's greater sin in that than anything most people have done. Isn't there?

"Windows are open," I say, trying to conceal the bottles as I come down the stairs. "Now we've got fresh air, and we'll be able to hear if anybody's coming." I thought it'd make her feel better, but Ash looks up at me with alarm. So I add, "You know, in case Maggie can't resist bringing us more food."

Her face clears. "Or Ben," she says, then gives me a sneaky smile. "Can't resist."

Oh, no.

Ben.

I can't believe I forgot. He's still at work, but I need to figure out a way to explain how I could be so excited to see him one minute and totally abandon him the next. How to explain it to him—and to myself. Even if Ash and I are in danger, and even if Ben and I are destined to be just friends, he should have at least crossed my mind.

I almost send him a text, but at this point, it's probably better just to call him when his shift ends—he won't have another break. So I pull out the old box of checkers and teach Ash to play, wondering but not quite daring to ask whether games like this are allowed in Ash Creek.

She's a quick learner. After a few games, I'm barely letting her win. The hares wake up and sniff at the board, and when Notch knocks the pieces around, we give up and put it away. As I'm sliding the box back into the cupboard, I share the name with Ash.

"I'm calling that one Notch in my head now," I say. "Did you have a name for her already?"

Ash shakes her head.

"Maybe it's a mistake to name them when we'll have to let them go soon. And maybe it's not fair to name that one after her injury."

You named me Ash.

I spin, thinking she's spoken the words aloud, but she's across the room. Besides, there's no parallel. Ash came to me with sunburns, not burns. She isn't some animal I'll just release into the wild at some point. And, maybe most of all, Ash named herself.

A pang from my stomach reminds me I haven't eaten since the Freeze, and not much even then. "I'll make us some dinner," I say to Ash, scanning the fridge to see what looks good. "How about soup and grilled cheese?"

"Yes," she says. "And fish."

"That's your job," I tell her. "You hook it, you cook it." She smiles at the rhyme and goes to get the fish.

It feels good to go through the familiar motions of lighting the stove, buttering the bread, slicing the cheese. Good, and remarkably normal, in spite of the mess the squatter left. And judging by the contented way Ash sits cross-legged on the floor, the hares hopping in and out of her lap as she waits for the fish to fry, I'm not the only one who's glad we came. Maybe the simplicity of this place reminds her of the good parts of home, more than the tech of town ever could.

We eat in near silence, but it's a comfortable quiet, and trout fried in butter goes surprisingly well with soup and grilled cheese. Even though the hares have nibbled away a decent portion of the vegetables, Ash still makes their formula and feeds them patiently with the syringes. By the time they're finished, she can barely keep her eyes open.

"Give me a minute and I'll have the sheets on," I say. "Are you okay to change your own bandages tonight?"

She considers this, then gives me one quick nod. "Easy," she says, but it sounds like maybe she's trying to convince herself.

"Good. Your other job is cleaning up after the hares. Broom's in the closet if you need it." Now that they're eating solid food, I'm guessing other things might get solid too.

I climb to the loft and start with the sheets, but I'm listening carefully for any sign that she needs help. I decide to make the two beds on the left side so nobody has to sleep where the squatter slept. Ash comes up and climbs into the first bed the moment I've finished making it; she's fast asleep by the time I've finished the second.

Back downstairs, I channel my inner/future nurse and check the garbage, and when I do, I'm relieved to see that the bandages barely have any blood on them at all. I'll clean and check the wounds myself in the morning, but we may be ready to be done with bandages.

After the dinner dishes are washed, I run a hand over the soft fur of the hares' backs, then relax on the old floral sofa and just enjoy the quiet. With my eyes closed, the familiar sounds of the cabin wash over me. The rustle of the wind through the aspens outside. The evening calls of the robins and thrushes. And, okay, the hum of the generator too, a reminder that we're still not entirely part of nature right now. But still, the mountain whispers to me in a way that pulls the tension from my shoulders and slows my beating heart.

There's another sound too—one that's so much a part of this place that I almost didn't notice it: the steady tick of the old clock on the wall, probably the last souvenir of the mission Dad served in Switzerland right after high school. He was only a few months older than I am now when he left it all behind and flew across the world, sure enough of all he knew that he wanted to share it with anybody who crossed his path.

Half the people I graduated with will probably do the same thing—not to Switzerland, necessarily, but to wherever they are sent. Ben could be getting his own mission call any day now. And the other half will do things that seem equally brave and impossible: join the military, leave for college, or even stay in their parents' houses, living predictable sequels to their parents' lives. How does anybody choose any of these options? How does anybody choose at all?

Because these last few days have me questioning everything. Somehow, I'm hoping that Ash's path could follow mine from here on out. I know we're not actually sisters or cousins, and it's hard to imagine a future where we make sense as any sort of makeshift family. But if she doesn't have me, does she end up back at Ash Creek, tied to the same people she risked her life to leave?

The generator revs up again, knocking me out of my own head. I'm exhausted and still a little edgy. Probably not the best night to decide what to do for the rest of my life anyway. I'll just send one more text to tell the nurses good night, even if nobody's written back. Then I'll call Ben, close the windows and check the locks one last time, and go to sleep.

I cross to the kitchen and pick up my phone, but the alert on the screen isn't what I expect.

!Message not delivered

What the hell? I check the signal booster. The green light glows, which should mean it's working. I've got one tiny bar on my phone, but that's usually enough. I turn both the booster and my phone off and back on—the only tech fix I know for anything—and try once more. It takes a few minutes, but soon the alert pops up again. And then I notice the cord is frayed near the bottom. Did the hares do this?

"Shit," I mutter. I can't imagine dragging Ash out of bed and driving down the canyon until I get a signal, but if I don't send a message soon, they're going to think something's wrong and head up here. (Honestly, I'm surprised they haven't already.) The only other option is to hike the quarter mile to the top of the ridge behind the cabin and hope the cell-signal gods shine their favor on me. It's usually a safe bet you can get service up there—but then, so is the spot right next to the booster.

I sneak up the stairs and check on Ash, but she's still fast asleep. So I leave a simple message in her notebook, just in case, then lock the door and begin the hike. The last lingering daylight plus the flashlight on my phone are plenty to see by, and the woods draw me forward with a welcoming rustle of leaves. The night stars aren't as visible when the sky's this bright, but there's something comforting in knowing they're there—and feeling Mom's presence with them, almost as comforting as the Night Stars quilt itself.

Even my short and unimpressive theater career seems to have been enough to give me exactly the right song for the moment. "No one is alone," I sing softly, feeling the truth of the words. Even if the people you love have to leave you when you're only halfway through the wood. Even when people make mistakes and it's hard to see the light. I can almost hear Ben singing it again now, and with his voice as my soundtrack, it's easier to imagine that things might turn out right after all.

My lungs and legs burn by the time I get to the top of the ridge, but in the best possible way. The valley looms dark below me, the brightest light the glow of the full moon reflecting off the pond. Which is good; I can see the road for miles from here, and any headlights would mean I need to hurry back down, even if it just means explaining myself to Maggie.

I wander along the ridge for a minute, but I don't make it far before I feel the buzz of my phone in my back pocket.

Four missed calls.

Twelve texts.

Shit. Again.

The calls are from exactly who I'd expect: Trish, Sofia, Maggie, and Ben. Maggie's and Sofia's messages are variations on the same theme: checking in, call me, wanted to make sure you're okay. Ben sent one at eight o'clock saying he'd just locked up and he'd be over as soon as he closed out the tills. Trish's has a warning that she's headed up here if they haven't heard from me by nine.

I check my screen: 8:27. I feel awful about all of them, but especially Ben. Thank goodness I didn't wait to hike up here.

I copy the undelivered message I tried to send to the nurses and send it to all four of them. The words are still true; we're fine, and I love them all. There's too much going on in my head for me to worry what Ben might think of the last part. I add another line about the booster being down and a promise to text again in the morning. I tell them how great Ash is doing. I'm deciding whether that's enough for now when my phone starts vibrating in my hand with an incoming call.

Ben.

"Hey," I say. "I was just—"

"Calli," he interrupts. "Did the link come through? I wasn't sure how to tell you. None of us were. We thought maybe it would be best if you read it for yourself. I can come up there if you want. We all can. I don't know what it means, but I think—"

Then it's Ben who's cut off, but not by me. I stare at the screen, where the one small bar of signal flickers in and out. I try to call Ben back, but it never connects. I can picture him on the other end, dialing again and again, even more frustrated than I am.

What was he talking about? I'm pacing the ridge, my mind racing through possibilities, when my phone buzzes again. With shaking hands, I tip the screen and read the headline in Ben's link.

Ash Creek in Mourning: Charity Trager's Body Found

ash creek

is a high-desert town
where folks borrow sugar
and return favors
and sing together every Sunday
in perfect four-part harmony
just like in, well . . .
Harmony.

The two towns
and their two churches
have plenty of common ancestors
and scriptures
and songs
and history.

There's enough shared blood
and enough distance between them
that they see each other's sins in striking clarity.

The judgment goes both ways,
even if the exodus doesn't.

Because people do try to leave Ash Creek sometimes,
in spite of the sins of the outside world.
But they almost always regret it.

There's nothing but desert
in every direction,
since the actual creek dried up
nearly a hundred years ago.

And even if you make it through the desert,
the world
will suck you dry,
will remind you
again
and again
that you can never truly belong
no matter how hard you try.

It will see your weakness,
your otherness,
and it will strike
right at that tender place
every single time.

So you might as well stay,
except that
to stay can be a fate even worse.
A death sentence, even.

19

I stare at the headline, willing the words to make sense. It has to be a mistake.

The article takes forever to load. I keep pacing the ridge in search of a better signal, asking myself the same question again and again: If they found Charity Trager, then who the hell is Ash?

Finally, the rest of the article appears, and I want to cry and be sick all at once.

Last night, a coyote hunter was calling near Ash Creek when he came across a shoe in the dry creek bed. He kicked at it as he passed. It didn't move, which he thought was weird, so he tried to pick it up. When he realized it was still on the foot of a very buried, very dead body, he threw up, and then he called 911. They're not releasing any names yet, but there's already been an arrest and a confession. Not some outsider, from the sound of it, but someone who knew her well.

It usually is.

This time I'm not sure whether the voice is Dad's or Maggie's or my own, but it sends a shiver through me. Because if Ash isn't the girl from Ash Creek, she could be anyone, from anywhere, and so could the person who hurt her.

They don't name the coyote hunter either, but my mind flashes to Dylan. He's not squeamish about blood; you can't be if you're going to cut the ears and jaw off an animal to turn them in for the fifty-dollar bounty. I don't know how squeamish he is about dead people. I don't know how he felt as he scooped and smoothed the dirt in the cemetery the day he buried my dad. But I can see him doing all those things: kicking a random shoe in the dirt, throwing up, calling for help. I'm sorry and almost sick that I considered for even a second that he could have been scaring or hurting Ash. The only real connection in my mind was his trip to Ash Creek, but clearly that doesn't matter now.

Then my thoughts return to Ash. All this time, I've been trying to create a past for her based on something that's turned out to be absolutely wrong. Something that, I swear, she led me to believe, with all her initial wonder at the microwave and fascination with the TV.

I let myself imagine marching down to the cabin right now, waking her up, demanding that she tell me the truth about who she is and where she came from. I imagine her crying, apologizing, finally coming clean. And then . . . I can't imagine what comes next. Because underneath all that, I swear I do know her. She's still the scared, broken kid I found hiding under the burlap. This doesn't change anything. I didn't know who she was when I took her in, so why would it suddenly matter that I don't know who she is now?

Except maybe it does. Because now it's not just feeding her and helping heal her sunburns. Now we're hiding up here in the middle of nowhere, and it's starting to feel like there really might be somebody after us. I shiver, thinking of the beer bottles in the cabin. What if somebody has come already? There's no logic to the thought, I know, but fear doesn't always require logic.

Whatever the real story is, it's time I hear it. I send Ben a quick text to thank him for the article and reassure him that we're safe. Once I'm sure the message has gone through, I start back down the ridge toward the cabin. But the woods seem thicker now, and darker. Every sound makes my heart race. Every rock and branch seems set on tripping me, scraping me. "No one is alone," I remind myself, but the melody is gone, and the words themselves hold only menace.

Using the flashlight on my phone, I pick my way carefully back down the hillside, my mind filling with terrible possibilities of what could have happened while I was gone. Why didn't I wake up Ash and make her come with me? Why did I let myself imagine we were safer here? And why the hell didn't I call for backup—Officer Hunt or Trish or even Ben—when I had the chance?

As I near the cabin, something feels different, and it takes a moment to figure out why: The porch light is on. Did I turn it on? Maybe the light was blocked by the cabin itself when I was up on the ridge, since the front porch faces down toward the pond.

But as I step into the clearing, the sound of a shotgun shell loading into the chamber rings through the night.

I freeze at the edge of the forest, then slide myself slowly behind a tree until my mind can catch up with my racing heart. Maybe it wasn't a shotgun. Maybe it was just the bolt in the door lock.

And even if it was the sound of a shotgun, it could be Hunt or Kasen or somebody here to protect us. It could be Dylan.

Maybe I can sneak back up the ridge and call somebody. The police could be here in under an hour. Or I could make a run for it. The truck keys are still in my pocket. Either way, I could get the help I should have been asking for all along. What made me think for even one second I could save somebody? I couldn't save Mom. I couldn't save Dad. Maybe the only thing left is to try to save myself.

I slide my hand into my pocket.

Close my fingers around the keys.

Imagine the look on Dad's face if he were here to see his daughter driving away, knowing she was leaving someone smaller and more helpless behind.

Then the moonlight catches something metal, and the barrel of a shotgun appears around the corner of the cabin, leveling itself right at me. I dive for cover right as a shot shatters the silence, splintering a sapling twenty yards to my left.

"Leave us alone!" Ash yells, her voice cracking with fear and frustration. "You know I'm not afraid to shoot."

That one small word gives me hope.

Us.

Unless she means the hares, I think she's trying to protect me too.

"Ash," I call, my voice desperate. "It's me."

The barrel drops a fraction of an inch. "Calli?"

Ash steps into the porch light, shotgun cocked at her shoulder and still pointed straight at me. Her eyes are wide and wild, and I'm not sure it's safe to step out into the clearing.

"I thought I heard his voice."

"It's me," I say, but I don't step out of the shadows. "You know who I am. So now you need to tell me the truth about who you are."

Ash starts forward, one cautious step at a time. Gun still at her shoulder.

"You left me," she says, her voice angry and broken.

"I'm sorry," I say. "But I wrote you a note. The booster wasn't working, so I had to go up on the ridge to get a signal and tell everybody we were okay." I give her a minute to let that settle before I ask my next question, gently. "Are we okay?"

"No," Ash says, her face twisted and fierce. "I heard somebody coming through the trees. Were you talking to him? Are you on his side?"

"There's nobody else up here, Ash, and I'm not on anybody's side but yours." I close my eyes, trying to keep the fear out of my voice. "Who do you not want me to talk to?"

"*Him*," she hisses. "I thought he was going to leave me alone, but then he was there. Back in the barn."

"Who was in the barn? Dylan? Or just somebody who looks like him?" She shakes her head and refuses to answer, but there's no way I'm letting her shut down now.

So I try a different angle. "Why did you choose the name Ash?"

"Because of where I came from." She's crept close enough now that I can see she's barefoot but hardly noticing the rocks and pine needles underfoot.

"Ash Creek?" I ask.

"What do you think?" She spits the words at me, but I see the fear underneath.

I take a deep breath and try to keep my voice steady. "I think you let me believe that because it was easier than whatever the truth is. But you're not that girl, are you? You're not from Ash Creek."

"I am whoever I need to be," she says, "to keep me safe from him." There's steel in her voice, but there's hurt too—so much that I want to step out of the trees and hug her as she searches for me in the dark. "I came up here because you said so, and I thought I could trust you. Trish was going to make sure nobody knew where we were going. But I saw the bottles in the trash. He was always going to meet us up here, wasn't he? And you were part of the plan. It just took longer for you to get me here than you thought. Was that him you were talking to on the phone?"

Everything inside me is screaming to move deeper into the trees, but I step toward her instead, determined to trust. "The bottles are old. They've been here for weeks, I'd bet. And whoever he is, I'm not on his side. I wasn't on the phone." I don't know that she wants to hurt me, but she's not thinking clearly.

"Ash, if we're in danger, we're better off working together. I can't help you when you're pointing a gun at me."

Ash considers this. Drops the barrel a few degrees.

"I'm not communicating with him. There's nobody up here, and you can check my calls and texts."

She rests the gun against her hip and holds her other hand out. I hesitate, and she tightens her fingers around the barrel. "Let me check, then."

My hand trembles as I close the distance between us and rest the phone on her outstretched palm. For all her fascination with technology, Ash has never even looked at my phone. "It's the green and white squares at the bottom," I say. "Just touch it with your finger. . . ."

Ash drops the phone into the dirt and smashes it with the butt of the gun. The screen cracks into a spiderweb; the case splits open, but nothing spills out. A cry escapes my lungs and I drop to my knees, but when I reach for the phone, Ash only brings the butt of the gun down harder.

"Okay," I say, backing away, my mind racing as she bends to pick up the phone and tucks it into her pocket. I struggle to keep my voice steady. "Now you know I can't contact him. But I swear, I don't even know who he is. If you tell me, though, I promise I'll help you. I'll help you anyway, but I'll be better at it if I know what's going on."

"Silas," she says, dropping the gun to her side.

"What?" I ask, unsure I've heard her.

"His name is Silas," she says, clicking on the safety and withdrawing into herself.

I'm so relieved it's not Dylan or Kasen Keller or anyone else I know that I almost sigh with relief. But I catch myself. Her pain doesn't lessen because it was caused by someone who is a stranger to me. And whoever Silas is, he's still out there, which is an ominous thought with the forest dark around us and no way to contact the outside world.

"Tell me," I say. "Come inside and tell me."

And she does.

smart little girl

Silas wasn't always a monster.
In fact, she'd known him ever since she could remember.
He'd been the one her daddy called to help
when the roof needed patching
and when she got scratched by a raccoon.

After her daddy left, sometimes Silas stayed longer,
singing funny songs to cheer them up,
reading scriptures with them
so they wouldn't forget God's love.

They cheered him up too, the girl thought,
when he seemed lonely or sad.

It was nice having him around,
and he took good care of them.

But after a while,
the girl started to notice
it wasn't always nice anymore.
It started with soup one day when he was hungry.

After a while, he was always hungry.
After a while, there was always

one
last
thing
he and Mama needed to see in the barn.

Sometimes it was Mama's idea.
Sometimes
not.

The girl wasn't supposed to come with them,
but that didn't mean she didn't.

She watched once,
between the warped slats of the outer wall.
And even though what she saw
didn't seem so different
from frogs or barn cats
or even the beetles on the front porch in summertime,
once was enough.

She didn't like to think of her mama that way,
and the whole thing felt wrong somehow,
even though she was old enough now to understand
that there wouldn't be tadpoles or kittens or new beetles,
there wouldn't be her,
without that.
That was how the world worked.

You're such a smart little girl,
he said to her.
Sometimes, that made her proud.
But sometimes, she wished it weren't true.
There were so many things she'd rather not know.

dark and light, part 1

Once, when there was not much to eat
and no gas for the generator,
the lights didn't turn on for two days.
It was too dark to see the scripture on the wall,
but she had memorized every line,
and she whispered the verse into the night
again and again.

"Thou art my hiding place;
thou shalt preserve me from trouble;
thou shalt compass me about with songs of deliverance. . . ."

She heard the rumble of his engine,
saw the cut of his flashlight coming inside
and the curl of his lips when he saw her, huddled on the bed.

Deliverance is here, he said,
glancing at the words on the wall.
God will not leave you comfortless.
    (He wasn't God, was he?)

The next day,
he came back with bags of food
and a red gas can.
Let there be light, he said
with a crooked smile,

and like magic,
the lights came on.
    (So maybe he was.)

That week, he and Mama went out to the barn every night.

dark and light, part 2

After Silas told them
they were using too much gas,
the girl and her mama
started playing a new game,
seeing how long they could go each night
without turning on the lights.

At first, they gave up quickly,
flipping the switch in the kitchen
not long after the sun set.

But as time went on,
they got better at the game
and it wasn't so much a game anymore
as just the way they lived.

The light faded so gradually, after all,
that they could go a long time
before either of them realized
just how dark
things had gotten.

So every night,
they moved through the shadows,
together
but
alone.

bottles, part 1

All her life,
Mama had been the kind of mother
to braid the girl's hair
and give her violin lessons
and read stories, curled up together
in the pooled light of the lamp by her bed.

But one night,
Silas brought Mama a surprise
in a brown bottle
for the two of them to share.
My old friend, said Mama,
looking so happy
the girl couldn't help but hug them both.

But when the brown bottles kept coming,
and plastic orange ones too,
things started to change.
The braids, the lessons, the books—
Mama wasn't up for any of it anymore.

Pretty soon, when the bottles were empty,
Mama did nothing but wait,
prickly and snapping,
until he brought more.

Pretty soon, Mama only came alive
for the bottles
and the barn.

Silas never stayed long enough to see
how much the stuff in the bottles changed Mama.
He didn't know what he was doing to her.
Did he?

eyes closed

The girl didn't know where Silas came from
or anything about him, really.
Only that once,
when she thanked him for a new doll that closed its eyes,
he smiled at her
and said it belonged to another little girl he knew,
but she wouldn't mind sharing.

He handed the girl a butterscotch candy
from his shirt pocket,
said how lucky she was
to have her beautiful mama
to keep her safe.

The girl wanted to believe it.
But something about the way he said it—
eyes unfocused,
words slurred—
made her wonder if really she was
not lucky,
not
safe.

But she nodded.
Closed her own eyes.
Stayed quiet.
Waited for him to leave again.

melody, part 2

He liked it when she played her violin.
Sometimes he just sat on the couch and listened,
tears streaming down his cheeks.

Sometimes, if she played long enough,
well enough,
chose the right songs,
he would look at his watch,
swear,
hurry to his truck
before there was time for the barn.

Those were the only days he didn't say she was a good girl.
Those were the only days she knew she was.

alone

After the bottles,
Mama didn't care for the girl some days,
barely fed her,
maybe loved her.
Maybe not.

You don't even have a birth certificate,
Mama said one night,
breath sour,
words bitter.
Did I ever tell you that?
You're not even supposed to exist.

(She'd had a new man over earlier,
who came in wearing a uniform
and left wearing a smirk.)

He saw your clothes
    and those toys Silas leaves you.
    Said he could report me
    for negligence
    or some shit like that.
    I said he doesn't know what he's talking about.
    I live here alone.
    I don't have a kid.

She looked deep into the girl's eyes then.
   Since you're the problem here,
   you be the solution too.
   It's not enough for you to just disappear
   when I have company.
   You gotta make it look like you don't even live here
   until he leaves us alone.

So she did.
Took all her clothes and burned them,
shedding not a single tear,
even when the smoke got in her eyes.
Wore her mama's old shirts instead,
a string cinched around the waist.
Took all the toys and buried them.
Played with her daddy's old tools in the shed.
Shared her mama's toothbrush
when there was a toothbrush to be shared.

Disappeared from her life
for her mama's sake.
And for her own.

what love looks like

One day,
the man in the uniform
was still there
when Silas came.

The girl watched from a crack in the closet door
as the men smiled,
shook hands
like they were testing each other's strength.

Silas was still smiling when he left,
but not when he came back later that day.

What if he tells someone I was here?
he demanded.
Are you trying to ruin me?
You promised this would all be our secret,
but I'm not sure I can trust you anymore.
Maybe I'd better just take my things and go.

Please,
Mama said,
but her voice was weak and whimpering,
so he just pushed her away

and began grabbing things
and gathering them on the table:
colorful cans of food,
jackets and
sweaters and
all the money Mama had hidden
in the cutout pages
of Daddy's old Bible
and
all the bottles.

Please, Mama cried
when he picked up the bottles.
This time, he pushed her to the floor
hard
and she scrambled backward
across the cold, dirty floor.

The girl tried to shut
even the last slice of the closet door,
to disappear completely.

But he saw her anyway,
and the wild in his eyes
made her shudder.
Did she belong to him somehow,
like the food and clothes and money?
Would he take her away too?

NO.
Don't you lay a hand on her,
the girl's mama said,

finally looking up,
standing up,
covering up
the bruises on her body.

It's still our secret,
she said.
You can trust me,
she said.
I love you.

Silas heard the lie.
He liked it.

But the girl
had finally seen the truth.

cutworm, part 2

For the first time,
the girl saw Silas for who he truly was,
like she'd pulled back the tender new leaves
to find a cutworm,
capable of destroying everything they had.

She remembered Mama's words
from that day in the garden:
You see a problem,
you take care of it
right then and there.
Don't wait for it to get worse.
It could ruin everything.

It's
just
what
they
do.

Couldn't Mama see it?
Wasn't she going to fix it?

Or
was she the thing it was feeding on?

Because whatever was in the bottles he brought—
   potion
   or poison—
   it turned Mama into something else.

She remembered Mama's words—
and she remembered her promise too.
But this time,
it wasn't just a worm,
small and helpless,
to grind under your heel.
It was something much worse.

A monster, she thought,
and a shiver inside her
told her she was right.

Maybe he was trying to turn Mama into one too.
Maybe that's why he came here
and did the things he did.

Because even a monster
doesn't want to be alone.

(dis)appearing

You're a monster,
the girl whispered,
and he only shook his head.

You're confused,
he said.
Don't you see all that I do
to help you and your mother?
How would you even survive without me?
I'm only here to protect you.

NO

she heard again,
but this time,
it came from somewhere else.
Someone else.

Because
for every part of herself she'd cut off
as she disappeared from her own life,
something new and ugly
had grown in its place.

Somehow,
in the disappearing,
something else had appeared:

a monster of her own.

Because even a monster
doesn't like to be alone.

And neither does a girl.

Her monster spoke only to her
in a voice that sounded unnatural
but also
so
very
right.

> *He's not here to protect you,*
> *it said,*
> *but I am.*
> *In real life, the monster always wins.*
> *Haven't you learned that yet?*

(The girl nodded.
She knew.)

> *And if the monster always wins,*
> *it said,*
> *then why would you ever*
> *hold yours back?*

bottles, part 2

That night,
when Mama and Silas went out to the barn,
the girl opened all the bottles
and poured them down the sink.

It's not enough, her monster whispered.
He'll just bring more.

So she snuck out to his truck
with a handful of dirt to put in his gas tank
so his truck wouldn't be able to make it back,
at least for a while.

But even before the monster said a word,
she knew that wasn't enough either.
You didn't take the cutworm off the plant
and leave it to find its way back.

Remember what your mama said,
whispered the monster.
You see a problem,
you take care of it
right then and there.

The girl saw sunlight
glint off a barrel in the back seat
and ground her heel into the dirt.
She knew what she had to do.

waiting/watching (reprise)

The girl and her monster waited
in the clearing,
watching.
Two figures moved inside,
only silhouettes and shadows
and small, familiar sounds.
They would have to come out eventually.
Until then,
waiting,
watching.

no more time for waiting

The girl and her monster moved into the clearing,
submitting to the magnetic pull of their own purpose
and the lure of the sounds from inside.
Then another kind of noise.
A scream,
a cry—
animal enough,
desperate enough
to break even a monster's heart.
No more time for waiting.

Five fingers,
slick with sweat,
cold with regret,
closed around the barrel of the gun

as she kicked the door open

aimed right at his heart
or at least
where his heart should have been.

different

You don't want to do that,
the man said, as if he still cared about
even
one
thing
she really wanted.

He looked different now,
sounded different too—
but maybe that was because
he recognized
that he was no longer
the only monster in the room.

Slowly, she slid the safety off.
Steady, girl, she heard her daddy's voice in her ear.

But still, she could see the barrel of the gun trembling,
could feel her own heart quivering,
nothing steady at all.

Is this what her daddy would want?
Is this what he would do?
Why couldn't he have stayed?
None of this would have happened if he had stayed.

The monster always wins, she reminded herself
as she aimed carefully
and pulled
the trigger.

20

Ash and I sit in the dark of the cabin. As the story goes on, I find that I don't want to hear any more. Or at least, I want to have some control over what she tells me. Because I'm not sure I can handle it all. That I can carry all she's been carrying.

"You hurt him," I say.

Ash nods.

"You killed him?" I ask, but Ash shakes her head.

"I thought I did. But it didn't go how it was supposed to. Maybe he can't die."

"Everyone can die, Ash." I think of Mom's face, so pale at the end, it was almost blue. Of Bishop Carver on my doorstep, unsure of his words for the first time as he told me Dad was gone.

I clear the thoughts from my head. This isn't about me or my parents, and they'd expect me to be strong.

"You hurt him, so you think he might be coming to hurt you back."

Ash's eyes flash. "I didn't hurt him first. It's not my fault." There's pain and pleading in her voice, and I open my mouth to apologize for even suggesting she deserves any of this.

But she's not finished. "If he finds me," she whispers, "he'll kill me."

"I won't let that happen," I say. "But you should probably tell me the rest. What about your mom?" I ask, not sure I want to know the answer.

"She's gone," Ash says, staring into the dark mouth of the fireplace.

"Where did all this happen?"

"Back home," she says. "I told you." She gestures vaguely southwest, in the direction of Ash Creek, and I realize we haven't fully resolved that part yet.

Then it hits me: She could still be from Ash Creek. Charity Trager wasn't the first young girl rumored to have gone missing right as she reached marrying age, just the first whose parents dared go to the police. I'll protect Ash no matter what, but it might help to know her true story.

"When I asked you if you were from Ash Creek, you didn't deny it. You only hesitated when I asked you if you were Charity Trager. You're from there, aren't you? Even though you aren't her?"

"I'm from nowhere," she says.

"That's not true," I tell her. "The story you told me? It matters. Who you are matters. The fact that somebody hurt you matters. The place where it happened matters." I reel in my emotions so I can get the next part out. "The fact that you found me, that matters too. I'm here to help you, Ash. I swear to God."

Her head snaps up at that. They're not words either one of us takes lightly.

"I think that's enough for tonight," I say. "You can tell me the rest tomorrow. We should try to sleep, if we can."

Ash stands up and walks to the side of the room to grab the shotgun, and the knot inside me tightens again. But she leaves the safety on and doesn't raise it to her shoulder, just starts for the stairs as I triple-check the locks and windows. "You're right," she says. "We won't find Silas in the dark anyway. But we can be ready if he finds us."

Up in the loft, Ash props the shotgun next to her bed and climbs in, and I swear she's asleep before five minutes have passed. I pull the quilt closer and think of my mom. She left a bad situation for a fresh start, just like Ash's mom. The two of them have more in common than I would have thought, and so do the two of us. But look how differently our lives turned out. And why? What made the difference? Was it Dad? Or some inner strength in Mom? Probably it was both. But will any of it matter if there really is somebody out there determined to hurt Ash?

As the thoughts and questions swirl through my mind, I'm sure I won't be able to fall asleep. But I must, because the next thing I know, there is a blush of sunlight at the edges of the curtains, and Ash is nudging me awake.

"It's time," she says, the same steely courage back in her now that she's holding the shotgun.

"Where are we going?" I ask.

She lifts her chin and looks toward the forest. "Nowhere," she says.

When the door swings open, we surprise a buck foraging at the edge of the clearing. I take it as a good sign. No doubt he would have run off already if there'd been anybody else skulking around.

Ash leads the way. I expect her to climb into the truck, but she keeps walking, her toes straining against her thin canvas slip-ons. Could she have grown since she got here?

"There are some better shoes back at the cabin you can wear next time," I tell her.

Instead of answering, Ash turns for the trees in a place where there's hardly a path at all. Something uneasy starts inside me, waiting to unfurl itself. I reach for my phone to check for a signal before I remember with a shiver that it's not there.

Less than half a mile through the trees, Ash threads her thin body through a barbed-wire fence with a No Trespassing sign posted in the distance. This fence was always the border of my own explorations as a kid, so even now, I'm hesitant to follow. But when I call her name, Ash doesn't glance back, and finally, I duck between two of the wires and rush to catch up.

I'm about to ask her to wait when, through a gap in the trees, I see another cabin—if you could call it that. More like a shack. Dad always referred to our cabin as "rustic," which was his way of saying old and dirty and the opposite of fancy. But compared to this, ours is a palace.

Like ours, this one is made of logs—except where the logs have rotted out and been patched over with scrap lumber. The two small windows each have a broken pane that's been covered with thick plastic. If it were closer to our cabin (and not behind a No Trespassing sign), it would have made a decent hideout back when Ben and I played survival games in the forest.

But the overflowing trash bins propped against the far wall and the overgrown garden bed nearby tell me this place isn't abandoned. Whoever is thinking of survival here, it isn't a game. Could Ash have found her way here before she found me? It makes no geographical sense—but then, none of this makes sense anymore in any way at all.

"Where are we?" I whisper the words, half afraid of spooking Ash, but it's so quiet here, there's no need to speak any louder anyway. The only sounds are the rustle of the breeze through the aspens and the call of one lone lark in the distance.

Ash doesn't answer; she's wary too. When a new thought strikes me, I reach to pull her back into the trees. What if this is where the squatter lives? What if he only shows up at our cabin on nights when he can't take his place anymore and needs the feel of solid walls around him? Of a mattress beneath his tired body? As much as I want to hate him, I feel a pang of empathy. I could understand those feelings if I lived in a place like this.

But before I can even ask the question, Ash is pulling away from me, trying to approach the building.

"He could be here, right now," I hiss.

I meant the squatter, but Ash spins on me, eyes burning bright, and I realize why: She thinks I'm talking about Silas. I almost dismiss it; we're not thinking of the same person.

But then cold fingers run up my neck. What if the squatter is Silas? If Ash isn't from Ash Creek after all, she could be from anywhere.

She could be from Nowhere, her own name for this place.

"Ash," I say carefully, "is this your home?"

"No," she says, spitting the word at me.

I rest my hand on her shoulder, gently. "*Was* it your home?"

She pauses, blinking back tears, then places her hand over mine as she gives the smallest nod. I shudder, wondering if she's lived her whole life here, like this. Could she have gone through all that fear and pain just a short hike from the place that's always brought me peace?

No wonder she freaked out when we were driving up here. It wasn't because she'd never traveled through the steep canyon. It's because the last time she did, she was running away from the very place I was taking her back to. Probably running for her life.

Is it too much of a coincidence, though? What are the odds that she'd grow up this close to my cabin, then find her way to my house? Pretty high, I realize. Like I told Trish, ours is the first cabin up the road, and our house is the first property on the way back down. Dad and I used to joke that we were our own next-door neighbors, the creek a clear path from one to the other.

Fate, he whispers. *With an assist from geography.*

But still, Ash has proven she'll go along with any origin story I give her. Is this more of the same? I'm struggling to believe, even though she brought me this last stretch herself, straight to this place. Even though she knew exactly where to cast her line to catch a fish.

She needs you to trust her. Dad's voice is gentle, prodding me toward my better nature once again.

"Do you want to show it to me?" I ask.

Ash nods again, leading me out of the forest and toward the shack. The path we took isn't the only way to get here; the grass across the clearing has been worn away in two rutted tire tracks that could almost be called a road. It is possible to drive up here, then, as proven by the fresh tracks all around the place like scribbles on a kid's drawing. Big ones, from big trucks and SUVs. Which strikes me as weird, seeing as how there's not a soul around.

Before we go inside, Ash takes me to a tree, barely bigger than a sapling, that's growing near the house. There's a small ditch from the drainpipe off the roof to a sunken circle around the tree, which would make sure the tree got plenty of water anytime it rained. Still, I'm amazed it's alive. I expect to see the beginnings of fruit on the branches; it seems like if you're planting and watering a tree when there's a whole forest around you, there's got to be a reason.

"It's an ash tree," she says, answering the question I didn't ask. "They're supposed to protect you."

A broken-down generator sits just outside the door, covered with rust and a few spots of chipped paint. Inside, there's a kitchen with a narrow stove, a table with two mismatched chairs, and a sad, sagging couch. Off to the side, I can see a tiny closet and a bedroom with one patchy mattress, propped up on a metal frame supported by big bricks along the edges. And in the shadows of the space underneath, a battered old violin case. The last room is a bathroom, but I'm barely in the door before I step back out again, overwhelmed by the look of it as much as the smell.

Everything is gray and brown and rotting. Everything speaks of disease and decay. The whole place has a faint smell of mold, but there's a thread of smoke woven into it too. Ash guides me to the fireplace, where a thick layer of ash and soot coat the bottom and spill out onto the floor. There are charred remains of logs in there, but when I look closer, I see a scattering of small bones near the back. Someone here—Ash, or her mom, maybe—has been hunting to survive. Fishing too.

Trust her, he reminds me, and I try as Ash leads me back outside to an abandoned animal pen and an overgrown garden. The zucchini plants have taken over most of it, choking out the beans and tomatoes with their thick, thorny vines and broad, prickled leaves. Some of the zucchini themselves are as wide as bowling pins and every bit as long. Someone planted all this in the spring—even earlier than we planted ours, which means maybe these plants were started inside somehow, and someone took the time to clear out at least some of last year's dead remnants and grow something new.

We turn the corner to the back of the house to find more tire tracks. Still no vehicles, though, and it's hard to tell how recent the tracks are when everything's been dry for so long. I trace one set with my eyes to the edge of the clearing—and then I see where the burned-out smell has been coming from.

Down the slope, there's a blackened shell of a small barn. The trees that circle around it are blackened too—singed, but not burned. And fluttering from one branch, waving at me in the wind, is one loose piece of yellow caution tape.

My mouth goes dry. "What happened here?"

Ash won't look at me. Her face is blank. But she doesn't get to bring me here only to close up now.

"There was a fire," I say. "There was a fire, and when you came to me, you had burns. Sunburns, I thought, all over the front of you."

I'm choking back tears, choking on the words I don't want to say. But if I don't say them, I'll never know. I'll always be wondering and running and afraid.

Ash is crying now too. Tears trace down her cheeks, dripping from her jawline.

"There was a fire," I say, my voice strangled and strange. "And my dad died in a fire."

binary

Once upon a time in Nowhere,
the girl's daddy showed her
how he made the explosives
he used for target practice.

This part is the fuel, he said,
showing her what looked like gravel
but smaller, and silvery.

This part is the catalyst, he said,
pointing to the powder, dull gray like ash.

As long as you don't mix the two,
they're totally safe.

And then
he mixed the two,
fuel and catalyst,
right in front of her,
and she looked up,
shocked and sick,
because this was the first time
her daddy had made her feel
not
safe.

When he noticed,
he dropped to his knees
to look her in the eye.

I just mean
we don't mix them
until we're ready to shoot.

We never let these two touch
unless an explosion
is exactly
what we want.

Even then, he said,
it still takes a bullet.

She nodded,
closing her eyes,
trying to forget.

Not knowing
years later
her mother would mix
the whole bucket of fuel,
the whole canister of catalyst,
and leave it there
like the gaping maw of a steel trap set
for reasons
even she couldn't understand.

Sometimes
when two things mix

fuel
and catalyst

an explosion
is inevitable.

All you need
is someone
to pull the trigger.

21

My words reverberate through the clearing.

There was a fire. And my dad died in a fire.

The forest is closing in on me, dust and ash is swirling into the air and filling my lungs with every breath.

This is where they found him.

Not at a barn in a town called Aspen Grove, but at *this* barn, in *this* grove of aspens.

This is where he died.

Someone at some point—probably Bishop Carver—told me he didn't suffer, but I read once that they always say that. And in this case, I can't see how it could possibly be true. Did he cry out? Did he say my name? Mom's?

I clear my throat, push the image from my head.

"Tell me," I demand.

Ash looks down. Her chin trembles.

"You killed him," I say. Three words that change everything, forever.

"I'm sorry."

"You thought he was Silas and you killed him?" I ask, trying to understand even though I'm so angry, there's blood rushing in my ears. "You shot at someone you couldn't see clearly, just like earlier when I came back to the cabin?"

"I wasn't trying to shoot anybody. I was aiming at the wall behind him. And then . . ."

The chemicals. The explosion. The shotgun shell that everyone—including me—wanted so badly to believe meant nothing.

My dad and her mom, both gone in an instant.

And Silas, still out there.

"We're still in danger because you shot the wrong person? I lost my dad and now I'm running for my life because *you shot the wrong person?*" I pace across the gravel. "I should have listened to Maggie and Trish and everybody who told me to turn you over to the professionals. I thought I was protecting some poor girl from Ash Creek, not a murderer."

Ash doesn't argue with any of it.

"This is insane. You are insane. He came here to help your goat. Did you know that?"

Ash won't look me in the eye. She pulls my shattered phone from her pocket, and I feel a spark of hope when the screen still lights up. But she doesn't try to make a call. Instead, she pries off the case and holds out the family picture I tore from the front of one of the funeral programs. I'm about to ask her how she even knew it was in there when I remember the stack of programs on the kitchen counter the day she arrived and realize what she's trying to tell me.

"That first day. When you freaked out in my kitchen. You were saying, 'It's him, it's him, it's him,'" I say, the pieces of the puzzle beginning to click into place in my mind. "You weren't talking about Dylan. You were freaking out because you'd nearly killed yourself trying to escape your mistake, and then you walked straight back into it."

Ash still won't look at me, and maybe I should feel sorry for her. She came all that way, nearly losing her own life, then found herself faced with what she'd done.

Maybe I should feel sorry for her—but I don't.

Our mistakes have a way of catching up with us. His voice is clearer than ever in my head. Amused, almost. And that makes me angry at him too. Nothing here is the slightest bit amusing.

"That's why you didn't want me to go to the police? Because of what you did to my dad?"

She nods.

"What about your mom?" I ask. "Miranda Tuttle was your mom, right? Did you mean to kill her too?"

"No," she sobs, so broken by the question, I know she means it.

Both of us, orphaned by the same tragedy.

A tragedy she caused.

The anger flows through me, undiluted. If she weren't the one holding the gun, I can't guarantee I wouldn't try to hurt her.

But another voice inside me whispers that she's been hurt enough. She's been skittish since I've known her, and I don't think it started then. I think it started with him, with Silas, and it grew every time he took her mother away, through alcohol or pills or trips to the barn. Every time she became powerless in her own life.

So even though I can't forgive her—not now, maybe not ever—I hold back my anger. Because it's what he would have wanted. That part I know for sure.

Besides, we're still in danger.

"So Silas knows this place and could be coming back anytime. And you brought us here anyway?"

Ash nods, and I turn away in disbelief. I know sometimes people have messed-up relationships with their abusers, but how could she bring us to the location he's most likely to look for her?

"Give me the gun," I say. She's not pointing it at me right now, but that doesn't matter. She doesn't get to hold it anymore. Not ever again.

But Ash shakes her head. Grips it tighter.

"Why not? Are you going to kill me too?" I ask. "Because if you are, let's get it over with."

"No," she says, her voice thick and desperate.

"Well, I'm not going to kill you either. But that gun belongs to me, and you know exactly why I can't let you hold it anymore."

Ash relaxes her grip. Slowly, eyes down, she crosses the distance between us and gives me the gun.

"The phone too."

She hands it over without looking at me.

"Okay," I say. "Now we're calling the police."

Her head snaps up, her eyes wide and betrayed.

There's no signal here, so I use the barrel of the gun to gesture to the top of the ridge. "Up there. I'll follow you." I don't mean to make her feel like a prisoner. At least, I don't think I do. But I don't make any effort to walk beside her as she picks her way around trees and over deadfall.

The audacity of it all makes me boil inside. She saw the funeral program for the man she killed and she stayed in our house. Ate off our dishes. Pawed through his shirts. Helped herself to anything and everything. Put her dirty feet up on the dashboard of his truck, then welcomed herself into our cabin, which was always his ultimate sanctuary.

She's a kid who made a mistake, I try to remind myself, but it doesn't stick. I'm far too angry for grace right now. I hate her more with every step, and I let that hate fuel me forward, over rocky passes and through thickets, the gun growing hot and slick in my iron grip.

Finally, the forest thins and we reach the ridge.

"Good." I swing the barrel toward a flat rock. "Sit there."

Ash sits, breathing hard. Refusing to look at me.

I pull the phone from my pocket, relieved when the screen lights up again. Ready to turn her in.

But when I look up and see her small body cowering on the rock, something shifts inside me. I'm still angry, but the hate grows slippery now that I see her broken before me. I try to hold on to it, but I can't quite.

Even if she was the one to pull the trigger, it was Silas who drove her to it.

So now what?

A memory comes to me, clear as can be, of climbing this ridge with Dad when I was younger than Ash. I remember thinking, like you do when you're a kid, that surely this must be the highest place in the world, and I must be the strongest, bravest girl, seeing farther than anyone had ever seen before.

This ridge is a watershed, he tells me, in my mind and in my memory. *A raindrop that falls on this side trickles down this way and joins other drops and flows over toward Cobalt Lake. But a raindrop that falls just a few feet away flows down the other face. That little drop joins others, and eventually, it joins our creek. Eventually, that drop of water flows right by our property. Maybe you even splash it on your face one day.*

And then I know. This is my watershed moment. I can use it to turn Ash in, hold her accountable, try to make the past right or at least make it make sense.

Or I can look to the future and try to keep her safe. Focus on Silas instead of my own anger and grief.

Maybe there's time for both, eventually. But in this moment, I have to choose, one or the other.

The past or the future.

Justice or mercy.

Dad or Ash.

She sits on the rock, wind whipping her hair in her face. She doesn't bother to pull it back or turn her head. She's given up because I've taken away every bit of the control I promised her. I try to tell myself that calling the police is what's best for her. Best for both of us. That she'll understand someday. That I really don't have a choice here.

I choose him.

I set the gun down behind me, well away from Ash, and pull Officer Hunt's card from my pocket to make the call.

But when I touch the shattered screen, nothing happens.

"Please," I whisper, pressing harder and harder until I'm striking with so much force, I can barely hold on.

Still nothing.

Hold on, he says.

So I do, squeezing the phone until the shards dig into my skin.

The screen may not work, but the phone itself can still call one number if I press the sides long enough.

Three long, blaring notes, then a woman's voice.

"Nine one one, what's your emergency?"

Tears of relief sting my eyes.

"I'm near the Lone Tree cabins. I'm in danger. Please send somebody."

"Hello? Is someone there?"

The microphone doesn't work. I squeeze the phone harder, yell right into the receiver. "I'm up the mountain at Lone Tree—"

"Can you hear me? Is someone trying to hurt you?"

I almost laugh. "It's a little late for that," I say, knowing the words won't reach her.

The voice on the other end is muffled now, but I catch some of the words: ". . . ghost call . . . got the location . . . Lone Tree . . . send someone up there?"

But it's a question, not a guarantee. What am I supposed to do now?

"Please come," I say, just in case, by some miracle, she can hear this part. "Please hurry."

When I hang up and turn around, Ash is still on her rock, watching me warily. The distance between us cracks something inside me, but I won't break open yet.

"Do you know what a watershed is?" I ask.

She nods.

"Good," I say. "Because this is our watershed. You've been calling the shots, but that ends now. You either go down that way and see how you do in the wilderness, or you come with me and I run the show from now on. I'll keep doing what I think is right, but I can't guarantee that won't mean telling the police your whole story." I pick up the gun and take a step toward her. "So what will it be?"

Ash stands and surveys the divide. Takes a step in one direction, then the other. Looks up at me with pleading eyes, but I stare back, keeping my face like stone.

"I thought you were on my side," she says.

"I was," I say.

She nods toward the gun. "If you see him, will you be brave enough to use it?"

"Of course," I say. The lie slips out easy as breathing.

Because if Silas looks enough like my dad that Ash mistook one for the other, I might be afraid of making the same mistake. I might not dare pull the trigger.

You'd be surprised.

This time, his voice leaves me cold. It doesn't even sound like him anymore.

As we start down the hillside, I shake the thought from my mind and focus on the hope that help is coming. First responders in Harmony might be on their way, even now. Hopefully Hunt, but maybe Kasen Keller, or maybe someone else. Maybe even Bishop Carver.

But no. It wouldn't make any sense for Bishop Carver, as a wildland firefighter, to be the first responder to my call, even if it's outside city limits. Why would I even wonder?

Because, I realize, Bishop Carver was the first one on the scene after my dad died, even though the fire had burned itself out by the time anybody got there. It hasn't struck me as strange until now, but I'm not one hundred percent sure that makes sense, if there was never a threat of the fire spreading. Shouldn't law enforcement have answered that call?

A new possibility murmurs inside me. My instinct is to dismiss it, but something stronger whispers that it's time for me to truly trust myself. Didn't Maggie and Hunt both tell me almost exactly that? And Bishop Carver himself?

So as we wind toward the cabin, I allow the memories and questions to follow, one after another, like mountain spring water finding its way to the surface, then wherever the terrain takes it.

I see Bishop Carver's face, lined and weary, when he came to tell me what had happened to my dad. And I remember my first thought when I opened the door: *He looks so much like Dad when he's upset.*

That memory is replaced by a silent scene playing out in front of me: The last time I saw them together, their forced smiles nearly mirror images of each other, and a realization that things had been strange and strained between the two of them for a long time.

I think of Ash's terror after the barn yesterday, and it's followed by a hundred memories of Bishop Carver in that very same place. If there's anybody who'd go out to the barn without notice or permission, it would be him. If there's anybody who'd be easily mixed up with my dad—because of their shared looks, sure, but also because of their shared wisdom and charm and charisma and leadership—it's him.

And then I remember Ash's anguished words that first night, repeated again and again like a river rushing down the mountainside. My own thoughts join with them, only this time, the watershed has taken everything in an entirely different direction that makes me sick to even consider.

It's him. It's him. It's him.

I don't want to believe it, but the current is too strong to deny that Silas could be Bishop Carver—the closest thing to family I have left.

And there's a good chance he knows we're here.

run

When she woke after the explosion,
she was looking at the sky.
When she tried to move, everything hurt.

But she sat up anyway and saw
the burning skeleton of the barn,
the heap of Mama's sweater smoldering beside it.
She ran over, barely aware of the pain,
dropped to her knees beside Mama.

Run,
Mama said,
    eyes wide,
    barely breathing,
    her face a mask of burned flesh.
You have to run.

Then
    eyes blank,
    not breathing,
    mask unmoving.

No, the girl said.
You're not dead.
And I'm not a monster.

But it all tasted like lies on her tongue.

She had to see Silas too, though.
Had to know.
She shielded her face with her arms,
walked as close as she could
until she saw him lying there
and thought she saw him move.

Then, in the distance,
the goat bleated,
and the face before her changed.

He didn't look like a monster anymore.
Just the man who came to help with the goat.
But they were the same person,
weren't they?

It was so hard to recognize him,
she almost wondered
if she had made
a terrible
mistake.

Run, *she heard,*
more in her mind than in her ringing ears.
West.

It was almost in her daddy's voice.
Or was it her mama's?
Or maybe the voice
of her monster?

Follow the creek, *it said.*
Take the gun and disappear downstream.
If you have to go into town, stay on the edge.

So she did.
She was gone by the time
the first responders came.
Long gone when the two victims
were pronounced dead
and the authorities decided
it looked like an accident
and agreed
they were grateful
the trees hadn't caught fire and
nobody else lived here.

Nobody else had been hurt.

22

I'm on edge all the way to the cabin, watching for any sign of Silas, not wanting to believe that Bishop Carver is capable of such a betrayal—of himself, of his family, of God. But it feels like all my certainty of belief has been eroding over the past two weeks in ways that can never be restored.

When we get back to the cabin, Ash goes straight inside to be with the hares. Meanwhile, I sit on the front porch with the shotgun in my lap like somebody from an old Western, second-guessing myself.

I can hear Ash moving around inside: scooting a chair across the floor, cooing at the hares, clattering softly in the kitchen. After what feels like forever, she brings me a peanut butter sandwich like an apology.

I don't hate her; I can't. But I don't think I'll ever be able to forgive her. It will never be like it was between us, because even though it was a terrible mistake, and no matter how sorry she is, she's still the one who pulled the trigger. She's still the reason Dad won't get to see me off to college in the fall or finally build the deck of his dreams or just grow old.

Still, I eat the sandwich, partly because I hear Dad's voice telling me that even a Ferrari can't get anywhere without fuel in the tank. I'm finishing the last crust when I hear the sharp crackle of tires on gravel.

Someone is coming.

I'm too frozen with fear to bring the gun to my shoulder even if I wanted to. But when the car comes around a corner, I'm grateful I didn't.

Officer Hunt's gaze flicks to the gun for a moment, but then his eyes are back on mine. Steady. "Hey there, Calli. I was keeping an eye on the road up the canyon when I got word of a nine one one ghost call from right around here. Everything okay?" he asks.

"I have something to tell you."

"Go ahead," he says. "I'm listening."

I mean to tell him all of it: The story of Ash and the accident. My suspicions about Bishop Carver. But some kind of twisted loyalty inside me won't let me form the words.

Love means loyalty, I can hear Dad saying. *It means we stick together, come what may. It means your name is safe when I speak it, because I would never betray you. Remember that, Calli: We protect the people we love.*

I love Ash, I realize, and even though I'm sick at what she did and I may never forgive her, I don't think she deserves to suffer. And I love Bishop Carver too. So until I have some sort of proof that he's Silas, I'm not sure I can risk the ruin he might face if I were to raise suspicion and I'd somehow gotten it wrong.

Hunt is still staring at me, and I know I have to give him something.

"Ash isn't who you thought she was," I say at last. "But she isn't who I thought she was either."

His jaw tightens. "Okay."

"She's not my cousin. It was Kasen Keller who told you that, but I let you believe it. I didn't want to lie—I just couldn't stand to think of her being taken away. She was so, so scared of you guys, and I thought I knew why. I thought she was Charity Trager."

"Officer Keller thought the same thing," he says. "He already came clean when the Trager girl's body showed up. Told me he'd been by your house to clear things up, only it seemed you'd left town."

"I have something to ask you too," I say, biting my bottom lip. "Something hypothetical."

"Okay," he says, a little cautious now.

I hesitate. "What if a minor commits a crime?" The words surprise me even as I'm saying them, the watershed breaking in a way I hadn't anticipated.

"Calli, you shouldn't have lied, but I don't imagine we'll press charges. Not against you, anyway."

"That's not what I mean, and I'm not a minor anymore anyway. I'm asking: What if a kid killed somebody, but it was self-defense?"

"What's this about?" he asks, not unkindly. "Is somebody hurt? Are you okay? Did something happen to the girl?"

Did something happen to the girl?

Of course it did. Isn't that always the story? Something happened to Ash and to her mom and to Charity Trager and a hundred girls like her in Ash Creek and in every other town too, again and again and again, and nobody did anything about it until finally, *Ash* tried to do something about it.

But she got it wrong—horribly, irreversibly wrong. And now she'll probably be locked up, and I'm just one more person taking her choice and her control and her life from her, like everybody's done all along.

Tell him what she did, my father's voice urges.

Whether I don't trust Hunt or I no longer trust the voice, something stops me. "His name is Silas," I say finally. "The man you're looking for, from the barn."

"And you saw him up here?" he asks.

"No," I admit, "but I think he's been here before. We've got a pretty good view of the other cabins around the pond at night, and we didn't see any other lights or anything. Not even Fluffy and LuEllen's."

He nods. "Good. How's Ash?"

"Okay too, I guess." There's a small shuffling sound from inside,

233

and I wonder if she's near the window, trying to listen. "Do you want me to bring her out here?"

"Not yet," he says. "I'd like to talk to you first, if that's okay. But if you want somebody here with you at any point—Ash or Trish or anybody else—just say the word. I'm not on anybody's side here; I'm just trying to find out the truth. And at this point, you're not under investigation. I want to make that perfectly clear."

It hadn't even crossed my mind that I would be, but I guess it makes sense. I lied and left town, which must have looked suspicious as hell. Maybe harbored a fugitive too.

"Sit tight for a minute. I'm going to search the system for anybody named Silas," he says.

I nod, and he goes to his car and starts typing into the computer. When I follow, he shuts the car door. So I take the hint and wait a few feet away until I can't take his silence any longer.

I gesture to Hunt to roll down the window, and when he does, I ask, "Did you find him? Do you know who he is?"

Hunt scrolls down the screen, and I'm beginning to wonder whether he heard me when he swears under his breath and turns toward me. "No," he says. "There's nobody by that name with any sort of criminal record around here."

"Do you think it's an alias?" I ask, wishing I could see what's on his screen.

"Maybe," he says. "Makes it harder to track you down, and harder for victims to identify you too. It's pretty common to use another name when you have things to hide."

"Like Fluffy?" I ask, maybe because I'm still desperate to have Silas be anyone but Bishop Carver. The idea of Fluffy as a criminal is so ridiculous, I'd laugh under any other circumstance, but nothing's particularly funny to me right now.

Hunt doesn't laugh it off either, and I'm grateful. "I'd be surprised, but at this point, I'm not ruling anybody out. In terms of the alias itself, though, sometimes there's more to it," he says. "A psychological level. Sometimes it's easier to do things you wouldn't normally do if you can dissociate from your normal life. If you can trick yourself into believing it's somebody else doing them. And sometimes, the name itself is a message or a symbol. One of the guys on the force is always putting up theories like that, so I ran a quick search in that direction too, and I'm wondering whether he might actually be right on this one."

"Why?" I ask, letting my eyes dart once more to his computer. "What does the name Silas mean?"

Officer Hunt gives a little up nod toward the aspens and the spruces surrounding us. "Of the forest," he says.

I shiver, hating that this place that has always felt so safe has suddenly turned so sinister. Hating that Silas—whoever he is—has made me feel like anyone and everyone I used to trust could be capable of terrible things.

Hunt turns to face me. "Can you think of anybody who matches that description?"

"No," I say, secretly wondering, *What description?* Except that I already know who fits it. My stomach roils at the thought that Bishop Carver really is Silas. He has spent his career in the forest, and it's the subject of at least half his spiritual metaphors. Silas. Of the forest. How could I have missed it?

No evil speaking of the Lord's anointed. Dad's voice is almost mocking now, but I wonder if he could have suspected something wasn't quite right with his cousin. It would explain why things had been different between them the last few years.

Hunt's still studying me, like he knows I'm holding back. So I straighten up, deciding it's my turn to ask the questions. "What haven't you told me?"

He gets out of the car and walks to the cabin, cupping his hands to look through the window. Maybe he wondered the same thing

I did: Has Ash been listening? Whether she's in there or not, he's satisfied with what he sees. He locks eyes with me, though, and keeps his voice low as I step up on the porch beside him.

"We still haven't found evidence that anybody else was in the barn with her, back at your place. In fact, at this point, we're pretty sure she locked herself in."

Again, my suspicions want to burst from me, but I can't quite bring myself to give them voice. "How do you know?" I ask instead.

"Well, for starters, there were no footprints beyond the three of ours."

I picture the blackened shell of Ash's barn, then push the picture from my mind. This doesn't have to mean that Silas is Bishop Carver. Isn't it possible that being in a barn—even a different one—triggered a traumatic memory that made her believe she was still in danger?

Officer Hunt watches me. "I get the feeling you've got some of the same questions we do. I'm hoping we can finally work together to find the answers."

In spite of myself, I do too. Because I'm so tired of trying to do everything on my own, of carrying the weight of the secrets I'm supposed to keep: first the secret of Ash herself, and now the secret of what she did. Silas depended on secrets, which only makes me want to crack things open even more.

I know that there are terrible police officers out there, just like there are terrible doctors and coaches and priests. But there have to be good ones too. And you can trust the good ones, right?

"Is there anything else?" he asks. "Even if something doesn't seem related, it might give us a clue."

If I'm really going to tell him the connection between Ash and my dad and my suspicions about Bishop Carver, I wish I didn't have to do it alone. I wish I could be telling this hardest story I've ever told to the person I've shared everything with—hopes, fears, crushes, all of it—for the last five years.

So I imagine Ben beside me. Weaving his fingers through mine. Telling me it'll be okay, promising to stay with me until I kick him out. Again. Nudging me to start with the part I know for sure.

"About my dad," I say, watching for some sign as to whether Hunt is making the connection already. But he only nods, waiting for me to say more.

Tell him. I've been imagining Ben beside me, but it's Dad's voice I hear. Not gentle—almost like a challenge. I can't imagine he'd want revenge, but he'd want to make it right. Maybe that's all this is.

I gesture to the two rocking chairs on the porch, and we both sit before I start again. "You probably know that he died not far from here," I say. "Ash took me there today."

Officer Hunt waits, so I tell the story on my own terms.

"She lived up here," I say. "Before she came down to town. I don't know how long. Maybe all her life. I don't know if you've been up there, but it's awful. And I guess Silas knew about the place. I guess he'd come up there and . . . he'd hurt Ash's mom. She can tell you about that part. So even if he's not up here now, he knows the mountain. When I found that out, I wasn't sure if we should stay put or come down. I keep going back and forth on a lot of things."

I don't even realize I'm playing with the gun, snapping the safety on and off as I rock, until Officer Hunt puts a hand over mine. "Would it be okay if I asked you to put that down?" My eyes flash to his own gun on his belt, and something in me doesn't want to give him that advantage.

But I shake it off. Remind myself that everything he's done so far has shown me he's one of the good ones. And I'm playing with a loaded shotgun without even realizing it.

"Sure," I say. Once I've set it safely behind my rocking chair, he leans forward in his.

"I'll admit, I'm still trying to see how this all fits together. You said you've been going back and forth about a lot of things," he says. "Tell me another."

When I look into his eyes, I wonder if he's known some of these secrets all along, or at least suspected.

"Ash . . . ," I start, blinking back the tears. "She was so scared. She'd been hurt and neglected for so long. And I think . . . I think she might have made a mistake."

I listen, but there's no sound from inside. No indication that Ash has heard this betrayal.

Officer Hunt nods. Waits. Not unkindly, but he's not going to let me off the hook, and he's not going to speak the truth for me.

I try again, but I can't say it. Maybe I haven't forgiven her, but I can't forsake her either. Can't turn her over to a system she's so terrified of. In this last thing, I have to let her be in control, no matter what Dad's voice tells me.

"I'm sorry," I say, because I really am. "I can't tell you the rest. But I hope she will."

It takes a second, but Officer Hunt seems to accept this. "Let's go inside and talk to her, then."

There's really no way around it, so I lift myself from the rocker and pick up the shotgun. The screen door squeals in protest as I open it, and I'm surprised to find the wood door closed behind it. Ash must have shut it after she brought out my sandwich. I half hoped she'd been listening in so that it wouldn't be so much of a shock when we asked her what we need to ask her.

"Ash?" I call as I walk inside. "Can we talk to you?"

No answer.

No Ash.

Officer Hunt shuts the door behind us.

"Let me check the bathroom," I say. But there's already a sick feeling inside me that tells me she's not there.

"Maybe she's in the loft," I try next.

But when I spin from the empty bathroom to rush up the stairs, I'm stopped in my tracks by the sight of Officer Hunt with his gun drawn.

migration

She followed the creek for days,
feet aching, heart breaking,
relieved
the monster was no longer beside her,
until she realized
it was
inside her,
and dangerous things happen
when two things mix themselves up in your mind
that were never meant to be mixed together at all,
like Silas,
the man who hurt Mama
but also came to help.

But wasn't she the one
who had hurt Mama most?
Every time she closed her eyes,
she saw Mama's face,
heard her voice,
curled up like a cutworm
at the pain of remembering.

> I am a monster, she whispered,
> but instead of power, it filled her with shame.

When the sun was up,
she waded in the creek,
as if the flames were still coming for her
and only the water could keep her safe.

During the nights,
she huddled in tall grasses when she wanted to see the stars
and under trees when she couldn't bear the stars' beauty.

What did she deserve of beauty,
or kindness
or comfort?

But kindness and beauty and comfort
and even shame
don't last long in the mind and heart of a monster.
Soon, it was only about survival.

She ate berries and pine nuts
but also
the soft pink flesh
of a raw trout.

She stumbled through the brush, half blind,
until a searing pain caught her leg,
and another sliced her belly.

Barbed wire.
She'd walked straight into a fence.

Then she noticed the house in the distance.
She'd almost gone straight into town,

but it wasn't too late to stay on the edge.
She could bring the gun,
sneak into the house,
take what she needed,
whatever the cost.

The biggest gap was between the wires,
so that's where she went,
with a long gash across her back to show for it
and the gun dropped on the other side.

But then she noticed
the crowd in the yard,
and milling through it—
was that Silas?
It couldn't be.
She blinked,
and then she could see
it was only someone
who looked like him.
It was only her eyes
playing tricks on her again.

And then she could smell
the air
so thick with the scent
of ham and potatoes,
she could practically taste it.

Patience, she told herself.
Maybe tonight.
Right now there were

too many people
and she was so tired.

Even going for the gun
on the other side of the fence
seemed too far.
Too heavy.
Too risky, with the wires.

There was an old piece of burlap under the tree,
and she burrowed under it,
grateful for the shade.

Waited
in the cool quiet of the cottonwood
for the strength to sneak into the house
or for her own last breath,
unsure which would be more welcome.

23

"No," I whisper, wondering if it's been Officer Hunt all along.

Scenes and words flash through my mind: the red flag in his personnel file that he was quick to explain away, his insistence that there were no footprints but ours in our barn, his subtle revelation that sometimes, people can have more than one identity. The fact that he let Ash stay with me, which probably gave him easier access to her than if she'd been in the system.

And then: Ash's story of the man in uniform who forced her to disappear in the first place.

But then I follow his gaze to the kitchen floor, where the dark smudge of dirty boot prints leads into and out of the room. The treads are much too big to belong to Ash.

"No," I say again. "No no no."

"I'm calling for backup," he says, straight-arming his gun toward the floor. "Stay down."

I'm about to tell him it's no use, there's no signal, but he has a radio, not a phone, and it crackles to life right away. There's a rapid-fire exchange of information before he clicks it back into place on his belt. "Apparently somebody is already on the way," he says.

"I thought you guys were watching the road." My voice is tight and desperate.

"He must have been up here already."

"But that doesn't make sense," I say. "Whoever it is, why would he wait until the police are here to make a move? We've been up here by ourselves for almost twenty-four hours."

Officer Hunt considers this. "It may be a suicide-by-cop scenario. He may have been waiting for me all along."

"So what if I go out there and—"

"No," he says, cutting me off. "Nothing good could come from having both of you in the crossfire. I'm going to see if I can follow the tracks." He's still got his back against the wall, but he takes a quick look out the window. "You stay put and stay down, okay? When the other officers arrive, tell them what I've told you. I've got to mute my radio while I do my initial sweep to avoid drawing any attention, so they won't be able to communicate with me. I'm counting on you to fill them in. Can you do that?"

"Of course," I say. There's something powerful in the assignment, in feeling more like his partner than simply potential prey. Maybe that's why I call out to him before he leaves. "If I had to guess," I say, pointing toward Nowhere, "I'd guess they went that way. The Tuttle cabin is up there."

He nods. "Good to know, in case I lose the trail." Then, urgently, "Keep the shotgun close, but do everything you can not to use it. And remember what I said: Stay down and stay safe, okay?"

"Okay," I say. "You too."

Once he's gone, I lean against the wall and wait, braced for gunfire. *Suicide by cop.* When I try to picture how this will all play out, I can only see a future filled with heartbreak. So instead, I turn my mind to memories of the past.

Of coming here with Dad when I was little. How he hated the sound of the generator and would sometimes light old kerosene lamps instead. We'd cook our dinner in the fire, beef and carrots and potatoes wrapped in foil, and it made me feel like I was living in a storybook.

Of coming here with Mom and sitting out on the deck, listening to the aspens. Sometimes she'd bring sketchbooks and pastels and we would draw the forest, and I'd marvel at how she could capture the trembling of the leaves on a still piece of paper. That too feels like a scene from a fairy tale.

But storybooks and fairy tales have monsters. Dragons. Bad guys in disguises and dark secrets hiding in the woods. Maybe that's exactly the kind of forest this has been all along.

No one is alone.

Even in the quiet of the cabin, there are still sounds.

The leaves are drier than they should be, making the sort of papery rustle they usually don't make until they're about to turn. When the forest is like this, all it takes is one lightning strike to spell disaster.

I am a tinderbox too, waiting for the shot, the strike. I can feel it coming as I hold Notch to my chest, her fuzzy body and rapid heartbeat doing little to slow mine.

When all you can do is sit and think and wait, there is danger in that too.

Suicide by cop. It still doesn't quite make sense to me. Because why involve Ash and me at all?

And because of something else I can't quite identify. Some presence, even though I'm alone. Some absence, even though the whole place feels heavy with the weight of all that's happened.

Then, by the door, I see what's not quite right.

The presence: Ash's canvas shoes, the soles nearly falling off, are still here. If someone took her suddenly, that wouldn't be suspicious all by itself.

But the absence: Dad's hiking boots are gone.

A chill runs through me. Did Ash herself take the boots and leave these tracks? Was there ever anybody else here at all? And if she's out there alone, who and where is Silas?

I'm the one who told her we had other shoes for her, but I

meant my old boots, which I can still see inside the closet door. I stare at the dirty footprints on the floor, trying to tell if the pattern is familiar, wishing I'd paid more attention to the tread of Dad's boots.

I've been wishing things like this ever since he died. Wondering why I didn't ever ask him how to fix the signal booster, or when a baby hare is really ready for solid food. Regret pricks at me for never trying to have the harder conversations either. I never dared ask about his childhood, and I know there was pain there. If I'd at least tried to talk about it, could I have helped him past it? And could we have helped each other through the loss of my mother better if we'd been able to talk about it more—not only the happy memories, but the hard parts too?

One night, I overheard him talking to someone on the phone. "I'm past the point where I believe I'll ever heal from losing her," he said, his words heavy and slow. "I'm the same bulb, but I'll never burn as brightly. I'm the same song, but I always slip back into a minor key, no matter how hard I try to be strong for Calli's sake."

Another night, years later, I watched from the dark of the hallway as he snuck a bottle from the corner cupboard in the kitchen and took a swallow straight from it, then took another to wash down a pill he pulled from his pocket. At the time, I couldn't shake the feeling that it wasn't really him leaning against the fridge. It couldn't be him holding the bottle of whiskey. Because wasn't he the man who, back when he was bishop, had preached from the pulpit that alcohol was a tool of the devil? Who had cautioned me all my life (and especially after I'd imitated Trish sipping beer at a barbecue with my own root beer) to never drink a drop, even though there were plenty of people who seemed to drink responsibly? Who cautioned me against painkillers, even when I broke my collarbone?

I was almost nervous the next morning, wondering whether he was my dad at all or had turned into someone completely different. But he still seemed to be himself, humming while he made breakfast, strumming the chords of an old John Denver song on his guitar while he waited for me to gather my homework. I could almost convince myself I'd imagined the whole thing until I saw the bottle buried in the recycling.

On our drive to school that morning, we passed a man smoking on the street. Dad made a point of saying to me, "We have to remember not to judge those who choose to sin differently than we do." But the smile on his face was so peaceful that I wasn't sure whether there was another layer of meaning. Whether he knew I'd seen him.

Either it never happened again or he got better at hiding it—and I got better at looking the other way. In the months before he died, I heard him in the kitchen late at night more often, but I never went out to look. Why didn't I, just once, walk out there and see? Take the bottle from his hand and ask him if he was okay?

He would have been humiliated if anyone in Harmony had found out about the drinking. They would have understood, at least some of them. But he never would have forgiven himself for being anything less than their bishop, their example, their savior in small things.

Which is why he did stuff like drive up the mountain to help some sick goat for some lonely woman with no way to pay him, even on the night of his daughter's graduation. I can't help but wonder if asking him my questions that day could have made a difference, because he would have known that, even though I was graduating, I still needed him. Just the smallest butterfly effect, so he wouldn't have gone to see *that* goat on *that* day, when Ash was at her breaking point. If maybe I should bear some small piece of this burden of guilt with Ash and Silas after all.

I never saw him drink up here, though. Or heard him raise his voice. He was always different at the cabin. More himself up the mountain, among the trees. "I'm like the prophet Enos," he would say. "Coming to the forest to commune with God."

To the forest.

Of the forest.

Silas.

No. No no no.

As I scramble backward from the edge of that moral, mental cliff, the ground gives way beneath me, and I hold Notch closer in spite of her squirming to escape.

The boot prints. The bottles. The fact that Ash pulled the trigger when Dad stood in front of her, and that Silas is someone who knew this mountain well. There is one clear explanation for all of it, echoing from the very first words I ever heard her speak, like a reflection off a surface I didn't dare look at until now.

It's him.

It's him.

It's him.

It's a dangerous thought, burning through me and intent on destroying everything I've built my life upon. Horror pulses inside me as I try to unstrike the match that started it, deny my own thoughts and truths.

But maybe I've been doing that all my life. Maybe I've been living in denial, ignoring what's in front of me, for so long that I'm nothing but dry kindling, waiting to burn. Knowing my whole world could go up in flames.

Like Officer Hunt, I can't be on anybody's side but the truth, no matter how much it might hurt. Loyalty can be every bit as dangerous as deception.

So how do I find out the truth? I pace the cabin floor, trying to think what I'd do if I had a gun and a badge and access to criminal records.

Maybe I do have at least some of that. I look up at Hunt's car outside, laptop attached to the console—and window still open. I have no idea what information they have or what would happen if he caught me trying to hack in, but I can always say I was trying to call him because I thought I'd figured out where Silas went.

It won't even be a lie. If I'm right, I know exactly where Silas went. I visited him there just two days ago.

I never would have dreamed of any of this. Losing my last parent, then becoming a surrogate parent myself. And now, leaving the small comfort of Notch's warm, soft body behind in the cabin to climb into a police car with the intent to hack into the computer somehow.

As it turns out, there's no hacking necessary. The doors are locked, just like I suspected, but it's easy enough to slide through the window. And Hunt's computer fires up the second my finger swirls against the touchpad with a banner at the top that shows exactly what I'm looking for: National Criminal Database.

With trembling fingers, I type Dad's name into the search bar. Just as I'm about to hit Enter, the radio crackles to life.

"Officer Hunt, we have backup en route. What is your current location? Any need for additional support?"

There's no way I'm touching the radio or answering at all, but then I hear Hunt's voice, whispering and urgent and almost buried in static.

"Still pursuing suspect and hostage on foot. I lost the trail, but property owner recommended searching the Tuttle place. I've completed a sweep there with no signs of additional activity."

"What's your next step?"

"Will head back to the cabin to meet the arriving officers."

"Roger that. We'll be here if you need us."

I haven't dared breathe, and by the time the radio falls silent,

I'm lightheaded. But there's no time for weakness. Both Officer Hunt and his backup could show up any minute.

So there's no time to second-guess before I hit Enter, hoping I'm wrong about all of this and the screen will be blank beneath my father's name.

It's not.

suspicious activity

She should never have been found,
hidden so completely
under the tree
and under the burlap.
But then
there is light,
and she wonders if maybe this girl is an angel
come to bring her to the next life.

She lets herself believe it at first.
That maybe there is forgiveness
for what she's done.
That maybe she'll find rest now.
Maybe she'll be safe.

But then,
in the kitchen,
a picture
 of the monster
 or the man
 or maybe both
printed on every piece of paper,
and later, a butterscotch candy
hidden in the pocket of one of his shirts,
and the only words she can say are

it's him
it's him
it's him
and the only conclusion she can draw
is that she is still alive after all
and he is here to haunt her.

All along,
she thought she was escaping him
and what he'd done
and what she'd done.

But maybe it was him
all along,
bringing her straight
to his house,
to his daughter.

Maybe it wasn't her daddy's voice guiding her here,
but the monster's.

24

It takes me a minute to sort through the unfamiliar terms and abbreviations, but the fact that there's anything here at all tells me I wasn't wrong to wonder.

Two arrests, but no convictions.

Disorderly conduct three years ago.

Breaking and entering at a residential address six months after that.

And just last year, a scanned copy of a hastily scribbled warning when he was picked up for drunk driving. Again, no actual conviction. Whoever this scribbled signature represents, they got him hydrated and brought him home.

How did I miss this? I check the date, and the memory is immediate: closing night of the school musical. He'd said he couldn't come because he had to catch up on paperwork, that it broke his heart to miss it. But clearly, he wasn't doing paperwork. Clearly, none of what he said was true, except maybe the broken heart part, which doesn't feel like much of an excuse. Not when he was hiding secrets like this and using other people to help him.

I've been thinking every lie I've told and every truth I've withheld these last few days has made me less like my dad. But what if the opposite is true? What if every dishonest word or action makes me *more* like him? The fact that my own lies have all come so easily, so naturally, roils inside me.

I had hoped to see him more clearly now that he's gone.

And now I am getting exactly what I deserve.

I open the door and lean out of the car, gulping the mountain air as his own words come back to me, spoken before the show that night—and just hours before what should have been his DUI.

It's a strange and powerful feeling, to become another person for a while.

I stumble away from the car and am sick in the gravel.

Because everything that seemed sacred now seems sinister—or, at the very least, sanctimonious.

All the times we pulled over to help someone fix a tire.

All the lessons of love I heard him speak from the pulpit.

All the wounded animals he nursed back to health in our barn.

Was it all his way of making himself feel important? Of justifying the things he had done? A façade for who he was underneath?

He never hurt me, though. Never. He was a good dad. The best, really.

As long as someone was watching. As long as I made him feel important and didn't touch his things. Or ask him about his childhood—or ask too much of anything, really. As long as I turned around at the first sight of storm clouds.

Was he a good dad because I had learned to be the right kind of daughter? Or because he was afraid of what would happen if anybody found out he wasn't? With an exam room right at our house and the potential for anybody to show up at any moment, our lives at home became part of his public persona too. Maybe he doesn't fit the stereotype of taking it out on his own family because even that wasn't quite secret enough. He had to find another family that he could isolate and control even more.

Now that this wound is open and bleeding, I can't stop picking at it, digging further no matter how it hurts me. Because if this is true, then on some level, shouldn't I have known? But maybe I wanted to believe the illusion so badly that I missed what was right in front of me.

Like all the times he'd come home with injuries he attributed to animals.

Were any of them from Ash's mom?

Ash herself?

And are there others he hurt who I don't even know about?

Others who covered for him, even beyond the scribbled signature?

If Ash hadn't fired the gun, would he ever have paid any price? And what price did he deserve to pay?

The questions have gutted me, and I sit on the gravel with my back up against the police car, not caring if Hunt comes back and finds me here. Not caring what becomes of me. I have only ever felt this empty and alone once before: on the day we buried him. I think back to how relieved I felt then to have his voice and his memory inside me. Now it feels like a sickness. Something to be cured of.

And just like that, his voice returns, as if the thought has called him forth.

Have mercy upon me, O Lord, for I am in trouble: mine eye is consumed with grief, yea, my soul and my belly.

He always did have the perfect verse for the moment.

How oft shall my brother sin against me, and I forgive him? . . . Until seventy times seven.

It's not our job to judge those who choose to sin differently than we do.

Forgive me, Calli.

"You don't get to demand that of me," I say, my voice disappearing into the forest. The only voice I want to hear in this moment is Ash's.

She's going to tell you her whole story one of these days, Maggie said. *And when she does, you do two things for me: You listen. And you believe her.*

I tried, but I fell short. But maybe it's not too late. The fire within me grows; I have to find her and try again.

Gravel scatters as tires scramble up the drive. I stand and turn to face whoever this is, not caring if it's more police or some other predator or God himself.

And maybe it's all three. Kasen Keller seems to believe he's a god in this town. He climbs from his sheriff's truck, red-faced and spitting with every word.

"What the hell are the police doing here? We're well outside city limits."

"What are you doing here by yourself when they said they were sending officers—plural?"

My question takes him down a notch, but only for a second. "I thought I made it clear to Hunt I had this handled."

"Yeah, like you made it clear to him that Ash and I were cousins?"

Kasen stares me down. "Trust me, I regret that. Still doesn't explain what he's doing here now."

"I called nine one one, and Officer Hunt responded. He headed up behind the cabin," I say, anxious to get him on his way. "You can start with the boot prints in the kitchen, but when you lose the trail, keep going about half a mile in that direction. He was heading for the place where my dad died."

The mention of my dad works; Kasen's willing to temporarily let his territorial pissing match go for the poor kid who's mourning her dad. "Any more information on who we're looking for?" he asks.

"Just the two of them," I say. "Officer Hunt and the girl. Ash." I swallow a sob. "There's no one else."

Kasen swears and heads off into the trees. I stumble over to the garbage can outside the back door of the cabin, sure I'm about to be sick again. When I open it, the beer bottles glint up at me, reflecting back a truth I've refused to see but can no longer deny.

There was no squatter. These are his.

The thought makes me so angry, I throw the silver lid at the cabin wall, the crash reverberating through the forest. I don't even care who hears it anymore. I take the bottles, one by one, and shatter them against the side of the cabin, shouting new versions of the same question each time.

"How could you lie to me like this?"

"How could you leave me like this?"

"How could you hurt her?"

"How. Could. You?"

When I'm down to the last bottle, I grab the neck and turn, hurling it into the trees. Instead of a resounding crack and shatter, though, it only catches in the branches of a ponderosa.

I stare up at it, fuming that I've been denied even this small satisfaction.

"Are you mocking me?" I yell, to Dad or God or whoever might be listening.

But no.

This one has brought me something even better than a satisfying crash and shatter.

There's light glinting off glass, and it's not just from the bottle.

"Dylan," I whisper.

I scramble up the tree to where he's secured the trail cam facing the front door. I don't know when he put it back up here, and in this moment, I don't care. The needles scrape against my body as I climb, digging into my hands as I pull myself upward and yank the memory card loose. There's a flash of warning within me that only pain can come from following this, but I don't care. There is pain enough already, and at least this pain will carry truth along with it.

Back inside, I shuffle through the junk drawer until I see what

I'm looking for: an old digital camera that has just enough charge in it to power up. I hold it up, fiercely triumphant, as I slip the card inside the slot.

There are hundreds of images, so it takes some time for everything to load. First, I see the last twenty-four hours play out in reverse: my own face, discovering the camera, Kasen leaving, then arriving, Hunt heading off, Hunt and me looking for tracks.

Ash stumbling away from the cabin in Dad's old boots, nobody at all anywhere near her.

Hunt arriving.

Ash and me together, coming and going in the blur of the last twenty-four hours.

Then the time stamps jump backward, whole days at a time. There are deer and marmots, like last time. One night-vision picture doesn't seem to show any animal at all, and I wonder if something blowing by in the breeze tripped the sensor—until I see the sleek curve of a mountain lion's back at the edge of the frame. A shiver runs through me, and I swipe to the next photo.

And there it is. There he is. My dad, leaving the cabin not long after my graduation—the very day he died. I know him by his shirt and his old sneakers and the same truck that's parked outside the cabin now. By the slim wallet tucked into his back pocket and the swing of his arms when he walks. I know that walk so well, I see the full motion of it even in these few still photographs. And since I am still scrolling backward, he appears from the same barely there trail where Ash and I walked yesterday, as though time itself is being rewound.

In that moment, I would trade anything and everything for the power to be able to truly spin the hands of the clock in reverse, to go back to this moment. To draw him back into this room so that maybe he'd be able to explain all of this to me somehow, to make it make sense.

And even though that is what I want, it's also what I'm afraid of. I've spent my whole life listening to his stories, taking his word as gospel and his actions as inherently good. Letting him set the limits of my own world and my own truth. I think back to Dylan's revelation that he never felt Dad liked him until we broke up. Was he kind to people only as long as they didn't get too close? Or as long as he could serve them in some way that sustained his moral superiority?

I swipe backward again.

He wasn't even supposed to be here that day. After graduation, he was headed over to Cedar Falls to help a friend set up a new clinic. It would take an extra day, but his friend needed him, and there was no one else to help. He actually made me feel guilty for asking him not to go. And that wasn't the first time he'd left me alone to help some old friend who seemed to come out of nowhere. The borders between one trip and another, one lie and another, then and now and truth and terrible fiction, are porous, bleeding. None of it makes sense, because none of it is where it belongs anymore.

I force myself to focus on what I do know. What I can see with my own eyes.

He came here, carrying the carton of beer, when he would have sworn to anybody, including God, he'd never drink a drop.

And somehow this one lie laid bare, the one I knew all along but pretended not to, crystallizes so much of the rest of it.

Of course I could have missed or justified all the other bread crumbs he left. Of course he could have been hiding a whole secret life from me. Because I have already proven myself to be someone willing to look the other way.

If it'd been a snake, it would have bit you.

Ash saw him clearly when she took the shot—maybe more clearly than I've ever seen him in my life. I'm sure of it now, and as much as I wish this could have all gone down differently, I can't blame her anymore for taking it.

There are sounds in the distance, Hunt and Kasen no longer trying to keep their voices down. Which means they've got her or they've given up. When I brush my face with the back of my arm, it comes away wet with tears.

Then the figures step into the clearing.

notch

For a while, she gives in.
Lets Calli bathe her.
Feed her.
It feels good,
but she can't admit it.
Not even to herself.

Sometimes, she still feels her own monster
living inside her.

Snipping the notch out of the hare's ear
to punish her for trying to run away.

Tricking her into seeing Silas in the barn,
even though she knows he's dead,
knows exactly who killed him.

Picking at her burns until they bleed
to punish her for what she did to the hare
and Mama
and Silas.

She can't tell anymore
whether her own monster
was there to hurt Silas

or only there to hurt her
all along.

And she wonders
if she can ever be free from it
or if trying to get free
would ruin her first,
because if there's one thing she remembers,
it's this:
The monster always wins.

25

Officer Hunt's badge sparks in the sunlight before the clouds close in. "No sign of her," he says. "No sign of him either."

"We need to keep looking for her, as soon as we can. But there's no him. Not this time."

"What?" Hunt asks.

I pull out the camera, hurrying to scroll back to today's pictures. Maybe someday I'll show Hunt the others, but I can't even begin to sort that part out now. "I need to show you something from a trail cam I found in that tree. This shows pretty clearly who left the boot prints."

The officers lean in; when Kasen reaches for the camera, I jerk it back just enough to send the message that I'm not handing it over. I swipe for them, and they swear almost in unison when I get to the picture of Ash running away in the huge boots, alone. Kasen's is a curse; Hunt's a regret.

"Would she come back if she thinks we've left?" Hunt asks.

"Oh, I intend to leave, all right," Kasen says, rolling his eyes in disgust. "I'm done. I risked my whole career to protect this kid, and now she's playing hide-and-seek in the woods?" He steps in so close he nearly spits in my face. "I never should have trusted you, Calli."

There was a time it would have made me blush to hear him say my name; now, I just stare back at him.

"Maybe not," I say. "For what it's worth, I never really trusted you."

Hunt has ducked into his squad car. He's been typing something into his computer, barely paying attention to us, but he glances over at us as Kasen fires back at me.

"Your dad would be ashamed of the way you've handled this. You know that, right?"

In spite of everything I've uncovered, the words sting. "You might be right," I admit. "But it's hard to feel like that matters anymore. You know *she* still matters though, right? Even if she's not as high-profile as Charity Trager?"

It started as a smart-ass question, but somewhere between my mind and my mouth it turned genuine. Kasen eyes me for a minute, like maybe he's trying to figure out which way I mean it.

"If you think I care about what happened to Charity Trager because the case was high-profile," he says, his voice thick with emotion in a way that surprises me, "then I got nothing more to say to you." He stalks to his truck and opens the door. "I hope you find her," he says. "But you won't, if she doesn't want to be found. She'll run and hide. And I hope you take some responsibility for teaching her that."

I watch him drive away, turning my mind to Ash herself—and then to Officer Hunt, who is still sitting in his squad car, facing away from me.

"Will you help me?" I ask. "I don't know how long Ash will survive on her own, or if she trusts me enough to come back."

The words rush out, so urgently that I don't even notice until I'm done that he is only now turning away from his computer screen.

"Were you in my car?" he asks carefully. "Were you on my computer?"

I step back, stammer a reply. "I was trying to contact you," I say, realizing how ridiculous the lie I've prepared sounds as I scramble for another excuse. "I wanted to show you the new evidence and tell you it's just Ash we're looking for. . . ."

"You looked up your dad," he says, his face stony, his words simmering. "You searched his name and found his record. Why?"

My voice is desperate, pleading. "I don't know what you're—"

"Calli. Please," he says. "We could bring you in on obstruction of justice, and now that you've tampered with my equipment, we could be looking at other charges."

"Do I need a lawyer for this?" I ask, hoping the steel in my voice masks the fear. "Because I thought we were working together to help Ash."

Hunt climbs out of the car and steps toward me. "You won't need one if you tell me the truth. The whole truth, nothing but the truth, all that. Got it? Because the truth as I see it is this: You've hidden things. And lied. And run. To be honest, I'm not entirely sure we shouldn't be investigating *you*."

"Maybe you should," I say, and I mean it. "But whatever you're going to charge me with, can't it wait? I'm done running. All I want is to find Ash."

Hunt sighs, his head tipped back toward the sky.

"I don't want to bring you in, Calli. I want to find Ash and figure out what's best for her." He glances back at the computer. "Does your dad have something to do with all this?"

I almost tell him. It's a secret that feels so ugly to keep inside— but uglier still if I show it to anyone. Not only will that make it true, but it will tie all my father's sins to me in ways that can't be undone. And, selfish as it is, I don't think I have the courage to do that. Not yet, anyway.

"No," I say, finally. "He has nothing to do with finding her. He's dead. Looking him up was a mistake. It didn't change anything. I typed his name in the search bar and I read the results. That's it. I'm sorry. I wish I'd never touched your computer."

I have to swipe the tears away again, and I don't dare look at him. He may have known about Dad's record already, but if he didn't, he sure as hell knows now. Who will he tell? What will the rumors be—and worse, how many of them will be true?

When he rests a hand on my shoulder, my whole body tenses. I force myself to look at him when he speaks.

"You're right. Maybe for now, we focus on Ash, okay?"

I nod as a few light drops of rain strike the top of my head. We've been waiting months for this. For the rain to come and finally wash things clean.

"I did a quick sweep of the hillside and checked in at the other cabins, but there's no sign of a break-in anywhere. The only one that's not empty is Fluffy and LuEllen's, but they haven't seen anything. You don't think she'd go down by the creek, do you?"

I think of Ash after the accident. "She might," I admit. "If she didn't want to be seen on the road, the creek is the most logical path."

Hunt's face darkens at that. "She'd better not be down there if it really starts to rain. There's a flash flood in that canyon at least once a year. I'm going to take my car, try to see what I can from the road. Walking it isn't safe. You stay here in case she comes back, okay? And stay inside. These afternoon storms carry lightning too."

A low rumble sounds in the distance, as if to underscore his point.

"I should go," I say. "It's my fault she's in danger."

"You saved her," he insists as he opens the car door. "And you being here might be what saves her again. Just wait here and keep yourself out of harm's way. You promise?"

I hesitate, uncertain. But then a crack of thunder, closer this time, splits us apart, and Hunt is gone.

"Ash?" I call into the dark, empty cabin, just in case she snuck in while we were talking. I look in every corner and check under every bed, scanning for footprints as I go. Even though the hares have free run of the cabin, they're huddled in the corner of their bin. I want to pick them up, hold them. But when I approach, they burrow farther into the blanket.

I am alone. Afraid. Again. I climb to the loft and sit at the window, scanning the trees for any flash of color. Water begins to ping the leaves and pool in the gravel. A dark bird darts from the shelter of one tree to another.

There is no sign of Ash.

I've heard so much conflicting advice about what to do if you get caught in a storm. Stay under a tree for shelter. Stay away from trees because they're more likely to be hit by lightning. Minimize your surface area by curling up. Minimize your height by lying down. Look for shelter and retrace your steps, but always, always stay in one place. The impossible paradox of it all feels so much like what I've been asked to do with Ash: Respect her boundaries, but tell law enforcement everything. Keep her safe, but also let her be in control. Trust the authorities, but trust yourself. But how can I trust either? How can I trust anyone anymore?

The rain stops not long after it began; only a microburst, not a real storm. But the clouds still loom and thunder overhead. I watch until I can't take it anymore. Until I'm shaken free by one bolt of lightning too many.

I never actually promised Hunt I'd stay this time, which is good, because I can't. Not when Ash is somewhere out there. She would have died if I hadn't found her the first time, and I didn't save her once just to lose her now. She tried to tell me her story. But I didn't listen, and I didn't believe her. Or maybe I didn't want to listen because, somewhere deep inside me, I already did believe.

Ash has been letting me in, little by little, and I know her well enough now to understand this: Even though she ran, I think Ash wants to be found.

If I'm right, she'll be somewhere I know to look. So I pull on an old raincoat, leave a quick message in Ash's notebook in case she comes back, and prepare to head out. The clouds crackle with electricity as the last rivulets of water work their way down the slope—and it's then that I know where else Ash might have gone.

My shoes slip along the path as I make my way up the hillside. "Ash," I scream into the forest, again and again, but the only answer is the echo of thunder.

I think she was running away from everything: the house, the cabin, me, Hunt, her former home, the depth of her own pain and past. She just had to walk up the ridge to turn her back on all of it; I showed her the watershed myself. If I don't come for her, at this watershed moment, she'll walk the other direction.

And now, another paradox. The only way to call for help and my best chance of finding Ash both require me to do the thing I should absolutely not be doing: going to the top of a ridge in a lightning storm.

I scramble up the hillside, climbing over deadfall, the undergrowth scraping a web across my legs. Once again, the trees start to thin when I near the top, and that's when I see her, perched on the very same rock where she sat earlier.

"Ash! Get down from there," I call, but the wind is so strong that she doesn't hear me.

I inch forward, out of the trees. "Ash!" I yell again, and she lifts her head. "Come down. Please." She's searching the trees, but in the wrong direction. The wind has thrown my voice down the ridge. I jump and wave my arms, realizing as I do so that I'm turning myself into more of a target for the lightning.

Finally, she sees me. "Come down here!" I cry, gesturing wildly. "It's dangerous up there."

Ash nods, her face blank. She knows.

Thunder cracks again in the distance as I make my way toward her. "I know why you did it," I shout, a sob catching in my throat. "I know who Silas was. He can't hurt you anymore."

She seems to shrink at this. Shouts back, "You don't know the whole story."

"You're right. But you can tell me the rest." Even if Maggie's right and we never truly know anyone else, I want to try. I think it matters that we try.

I'm close enough now that I can lower my voice a little, but it's still more of a shout than I want it to be. "I can handle it. I promise. And I didn't tell anybody the parts you told me already."

"The worst part . . . ," she says, and then she's sobbing, shaking. I reach a hand toward her, even though I'm still too far away to actually touch her, and she recoils. She tries again, and her voice is hard now. Determined. "The worst part is I'm a monster too."

"No," I say, but she's lost in herself again, and I'm not sure she hears me.

"No," I say again, crossing the last of the distance between us as she curls up, hiding her face in her knees.

But also, she leans into me, so I slide one hand under her knees and the other around her shoulders, picking her up like the very first time I met her.

"You're not a monster," I say. "No matter what happened, you're not a monster." She buries her head in my shoulder and sobs harder as I struggle to stand. She can't be much bigger than the day I found her, but her clothes are soaked, and I'm exhausted already, and we're on steep, rocky terrain instead of the smooth landscape of the fields behind our house.

"Hold on," I tell her as I start to make my way back toward the trees.

Then a burst of light, an explosion of sound, and everything goes black.

watershed

As they drive to the cabin,
she is torn in two:
    the girl,
    the monster.

Or maybe not torn in two
but exactly the opposite.

Maybe two components mixed together again:
    the fuel,
    the catalyst,
waiting to explode.

But she can't let that happen again.

Not when Calli cared for her,
saved her,
somehow doesn't hate her,
even when she learns
what she did.

She wants the two of them to stay together,
but if they do,
Calli could get hurt
and Trish

and Sofia
and Ben
and Maggie
and Dylan.

It doesn't matter if she doesn't mean to hurt them.
She never meant to hurt Mama either.

So when the police officer comes—
the spark that could ignite everything—
the girl knows
she has to go
and take her monster with her.

They take the too-big boots
since their own shoes are falling apart,
leave as carefully and quietly as they can
in the opposite direction,
up instead of down,
no plan past that,
beyond Calli's word in their mind:
watershed.

Splitting apart sounds so much safer
than coming together:
    girl and monster
    fuel and catalyst.

That is the moment
when she hears the first crack of thunder,
loud as gunfire,
and knows this is right.

This is the only way
to choose another path
and leave her monster behind
for good.

26

When my eyes open to a roiling dome of thunderclouds, it takes me a moment to get my bearings. But only a moment. With my first breath, I know exactly what has happened, because even the smell is electric.

The rocks against my back prod me up off the ground as my eyes hurry to take in the scene before me. The lightning struck one of the tallest of the ponderosas scattered along the ridge. A hundred yards away, it burns like a torch against the gray sky. But the fire is spreading, and I am right in its path.

"Ash," I call, maneuvering my foot from under a rock as I spin to find her. Wasn't I holding her when the lightning struck? My voice sounds muffled and distant in my own ears, like I'm underwater and far away instead of inside my own head. The lightning has shocked her out of her sorrow, and she's crouched nearby, watching me with wide, scared eyes.

"Come on," I say, hoping she will move on her own now.

But can *I*? As I take my first faltering step forward, a sharp pain sears through my left foot. A circle of blood blooms at my ankle where it must have wedged under the rock when I fell.

I spin to see the flames spreading, licking their way from one tree to the next. We have to keep moving, no matter how it hurts. Ash pulls her shirt up over her nose and ducks under my left arm, trying to support me as much as she can with her tiny frame. Somehow, it helps, and together, we hobble down the ridge.

The aspen trunks rise like pillars of salt before me, reminding me to keep moving and not look back. I send a quiet *Thank you* to God or the universe for a crosswind rather than a tailwind. If it holds, we'll escape it, and the fire might not come anywhere near the cabin. But it's not a chance I'm willing to take.

"Hurry," I say, knowing how ridiculous it sounds since I'm the one slowing us down. And sure enough, Ash finds a way to help us go faster, joining in with a deer trail I've never noticed. I'm beyond grateful for her knowledge of the mountain I thought I knew myself.

After a few agonizing minutes, we come to the shack. Ash slows as we approach it. As much as my ankle screams for me to stop, we won't be safe here if the fire turns.

Ash ducks out from under my arm. "Keep going," she says. "I'll catch up."

So I do, for a little while. I hobble to the edge of the clearing, then turn to make sure she's coming. I wait long enough that I'm about to go after her when she bursts from the door, the violin case clutched in her hand. She reaches me in a few quick bounds just as I feel a definite shift in the wind and the sting of smoke in my nostrils.

Neither one of us needs to say a word as we scramble toward the cabin. Running from the fire is an instinct so primal that, as I look down the narrow path, I see squirrels and marmots crossing ahead of us, pursuing the same goal of safety, probably at the pond or the creek. I startle when an elk appears beside me, but it disappears down a slope before I can even be sure I saw it at all.

I'd planned to go straight for the truck, but the animals' presence reminds me of one important thing we need to do first.

"Ash," I say, releasing my arm from around her, "go ahead of me and load up the hares. We'll leave everything else."

She breaks away but watches me for a few strides, making sure I'll be able to make it on my own. Finally, satisfied, she sprints ahead.

When I focus on it, I can tell that the pain in my ankle is getting worse. So I don't focus on it. Instead, I force the growing roofline of the cabin ahead and the eerie glow of the sky above to spur me onward.

A few agonizing moments later, I reach the clearing of the cabin. When I risk a glance back toward the forest, the flames look like they may be reaching the spot where Ash's shack stood. I'm glad she got the violin out of there while she had the chance.

And this, I realize, is my chance. If there's anything inside the cabin I want to save—besides Ash and the hares, of course—it's now or never. The fact that the trees are cleared away ten feet from the walls in every direction might be enough to save it—or it might not.

The memory card is the main evidence of what happened, and it's right inside my pocket. I touch the edge of it with my fingertips, wondering: What should the rest of the world know? There is power in those pictures. Power to take him off his pedestal with nothing but the truth. How do I want him to be remembered? And is that even my decision to make?

My ankle buckles beneath me as I watch Ash run to the truck, the pain of my injury fully eclipsed by the pain of this place as I stumble forward, the heat of the fire pressing against my back. A mechanical rumble nearly as loud as the thunder makes me turn my eyes to the sky. Impossibly, there is already a single helicopter flying over, a bucket of water dangling below. Even so, this may be the last time I see this place. Or it may survive, unscathed.

It's in God's hands now.

This time, when I hear his voice in my head, I want to be sick. But then the door to the generator shed swings open, caught by the hot breath of the fire itself. Before I can stop myself, I've picked up the gas can with one hand and curled my fingers around the cap with the other. In that moment, I am ready for it all to burn.

Then I think of Ash. Of her destructive, split-second choice that changed my life forever, made in a moment of fear and pain.

Not in God's hands, I answer with absolute clarity and purpose. *It's in mine.*

And I make my choice.

⁀

Moments later, I hurry forward to throw the tailgate down for the hares—and only then do I notice Ash's hands are empty.

"Where are they?" I shout. The helicopter is flying back now, low and so close that it's hard to hear anything.

Ash's eyes swim with tears. "You left the door open."

"I'm so sorry, Ash," I say, my eyes and throat stinging. "But they know how to stay safe. And they have each other." I take her hand in mine, choking on the smoke and my words. "We have to go now."

So we get into the truck, and I drive. As we skid down the gravel road, I'm hoping the hares' instincts are as strong as those of the rest of the animals we saw running on our way. They've survived once already.

"STOP!" Ash yells, and I slam on the breaks just in time to avoid a head-on collision with Officer Hunt, who's turning off the main road. He rolls down his window and shouts something I can't quite hear—but when his face glows orange in the light of the oncoming flames, and he starts waving wildly for us to drive, I get the message anyway.

I hit the gas, my tires screaming onto asphalt. Seconds later, he's tailing us as we race down the canyon, nothing between us and the sheer cliffs but a thin metal guardrail, the tires burning below us and the orange sky burning above us. When I look over, Ash's eyes are closed, her face oddly calm. She may have shut down; it may all be too much.

Or maybe it's a relief to be on this side of the watershed. To have all of it in the rearview mirror, even if it's going up in flames. Maybe especially then.

"I'm so sorry about the hares." There are about a hundred other things to apologize for, but now isn't the time. So instead, I say, "I'm sorry about all of it. I believe you. And I'm ready to really listen now."

I can take my own eyes off the road for only a fraction of a second, but even so, I see that the person beside me isn't a monster or a victim. She's just Ash, reborn.

"Drive," she says.

So I do.

coming home, part 2

As the girl from Harmony drives,
she remembers
something she'd forgotten
so long ago.

She curls one hand around the steering wheel,
almost into a fist.
Rests the other over her heart.

You have power,
she reminds herself.
You have truth.

That's right,
she almost hears her mother whisper
from somewhere
beyond.

27

Officer Hunt follows us all the way to my house, and I half expect a lecture when I climb out of the truck. For speeding, for obstruction of justice, for about a dozen other things I've done these last few days. He might as well pull out the cuffs and cart me away. Somehow, the thing that makes me saddest about that prospect is having to leave Ash.

"Holy shit, kid," he says, crossing the driveway toward me with his hands out. But I stand my ground, even when he grabs me by the shoulders. "You okay?" he says, leaning down to look me in the eye. I nod, but I'm not, and the next thing I know, my ankle gives out, and he's catching me and keeping me from falling to the concrete.

"Hey, now," he says. "Let's get you inside." And then he's passing me to someone else, and the someone turns out to be Maggie, and I nearly fall to my knees all over again.

"Get yourself through that door," she commands as she props me up, "and then you can pass out entirely if you like."

It's such a Maggie thing to say that I almost laugh. I'm safe. I'm home. And by the time I hobble through the door, Ash is already there, waiting for me with Mom's quilt, stretched taut by her skinny arms.

Ash guides me, limping and choking, down the hall of the only home I've ever known. As we walk by his room, I reach out from under the quilt and close the door, half wondering if I will ever open it again.

Maybe it doesn't matter. Even with my eyes closed, I can still see every image from the memory card as though it's right before me. And even with the door closed, I can picture every detail of the room, from the worn handles on his side of the dresser (he never did put anything in her side) to the log cabin quilt on the bed, handmade by the women in our congregation as a gift to my mom when she first got sick.

Will the sharp edges of these feelings dull with time, fading like the scent on his shirts? Or is it more like my handprint in the concrete, still showing every detail of the day kindergarten Calli pressed it there? Maybe more like that, I decide. A perfect replica in relief of what was there but will never be restored again.

Now I am in the little corner bedroom I've slept in all my life, shaded by the tree we pick cherries off every June, looking out over the street where Dad taught me, patiently and painstakingly, to ride my bike, jumping and whooping and running behind me when I finally got the hang of it.

I'm willing to bet he learned to ride his bike on that very same stretch of road. "I tried to escape," he would say with a laugh. "But I never succeeded." The words send a chill through me now as I realize it wasn't only the physical house he could never leave behind, but the trauma and destruction he learned here too. If I could turn back the clock on all of it, what answers would I find? Would I find absolution there too?

Not entirely, I think. Because if Mom and Maggie both got themselves out of bad situations and changed the course of their lives, shouldn't he have been able to do it too?

Ash guides me from the window to the bed, her grip soft but firm on my shoulders. "You should sleep," she says, concern etched onto her forehead.

She's right. I try to answer but instead fall to the bed in a fit of coughing.

Ash sets a glass of water on the nightstand and tucks the quilt around my shoulders. "This will heal," she tells me. "God will help."

I want to believe her.

So I do.

As she closes the door softly behind her, I let my eyes fall closed and turn away from the whispers and voices of the past, even as they beckon me.

in the beginning: silas

He wasn't always a monster.
It's important to know that.
He was once so small,
he curled into the space
beneath his sleeping mother's chin.
So helpless, that was the only place
he felt safe enough to close his eyes.

As he grew,
the cottonwood reminded him
of safe haven
but also
great pain
and the kind of man
or monster
he swore he'd never be.

Years later,
he met a woman,
married her,
had a baby,
loved them more than life itself.

But one day,
when he found his fly rod broken,
he snapped too,

raising a hand to his daughter,
striking his wife instead
when she stepped in.
Nearly losing everything
in that one blow.

That will never happen again,
his wife said,
her palm cupped against
the handprint he'd left on her face.
Or I will leave you
and I will take her with me
and I will make sure
everyone
knows
why.

I promise,
he said,
and the cottonwood
bore witness.

He kept that promise
for a very long time.

But when his wife died,
it opened all his old wounds,
broke him along all the same cracks
in ways that just wouldn't mend.

And even though he'd never meant to,
he had learned things from
the monster of his own childhood.

Things that found their way to the surface
at a little house in the forest
once the time was right.

How to bury his fear,
      but also
      how to bring it out in others.

How to build a cage made of all the right questions,
      like Who would believe you?
      and Where would you go?
      and How would you ever survive without me?

How to stand over someone
      and make them believe
      it was their fault he'd hurt them—
      how he never would have
      if only they hadn't made him so angry.
      If only they'd listened.

But also
      how to apologize,
      shower them with gifts,
      swear he'd changed,
      so the cycle could begin again.

How to take the strings of yourself
      and wind them
      around someone
      and make them believe
      that he and they
      are tied together
      no

matter
what.

But also
  how to divide himself in two
  as the only way
  to keep himself whole.

He wasn't always a monster.
And that is always the case.

28

The rain comes back the next afternoon—and the next, and the next—an ominous absolute as time seems to bleed and blur around it. The whole valley smells like sage every afternoon, and Ash and I sit together on the front porch, breathing it in together.

But we're not alone. Once again, a parade of characters enters and exits the house, like actors in from the wings to deliver their lines.

Fluffy delivers a fresh batch of LuEllen's brownies. Ben comes by every day, almost as regular as the rain, but Trish, Sofia, and Maggie are the main players on this stage, cleaning and cooking and fussing over Ash. Now Trish props my ankle up on a kitchen chair, wrapping it so tight I feel only an echo of the original pain. As she tears one last piece of athletic tape with her teeth, she sees me watching out the window.

"I know he's late, but he's coming," she says, knowing somehow I'm thinking of Ben. "He has something to tell you, but he made me promise I wouldn't even give a hint."

"Trish," I plead, knowing how much she must be wanting to spill right now.

But she tears another piece of tape and slaps it across her mouth, shaking her head with mock seriousness. A laugh breaks free from deep inside me, the first one in a while, and when Ash peeks around the corner to see what's going on, she joins in, throwing her arms around Trish's neck.

Maggie comes over and shakes her head at the whole thing.

"Let's go check on the garden. Bishop's here and would like a minute with Calli. That okay with you, Calli?"

I nod, even though I'm sorry to see them go. Bishop Carver holds the door for Maggie, then comes to the kitchen with enchiladas and apologies. "I would have come sooner," he says, "but, well . . . the fire. It sounds like you had a close encounter with that yourself. I'm so glad you're safe, and that it didn't spread any farther."

He puts the enchiladas in the fridge, and we sit on opposite ends of the sofa, not quite facing each other. Back in my bedroom, Ash starts playing the violin.

"What's going to happen to her?" he asks, maybe as bishop or maybe just as someone who's curious. It makes me wonder how much he knows, about Ash and Dad and Silas and all of it. About what we were doing up the mountain in the first place.

I decide to stick to his question. "Maggie says the social worker is coming back today," I tell him. "We're still not sure what the recommendation is going to be, but Maggie says it's a miracle they've let Ash stay with me this long."

"Whatever it is, you're going to go along with it?" he asks, a hint of a smile at the corner of his mouth.

"Of course," I say. "I always cooperate."

He laughs. "Well, I think we both know that's not the case. Can I tell you my first memory of you?"

"Of course." I swallow back a sudden wave of emotion. With my parents gone and everything that has happened the last few days, it feels like a gift to hear a piece of my past from one of the few people left who have known me well all my life.

"You weren't more than two or three, I think. We'd gone sledding and come back here for hot cocoa. Your mom tried to help you out of your car seat and into the house, but you wanted to do it yourself. You made us all go inside while you buckled yourself back in—snow pants and all—and then got yourself out again, then climbed under the fence when you couldn't open the gate. By the time you showed up at the door, you'd given us all a solid five minutes of entertainment. But you never once looked up at us in the window. You just focused on the task at hand, and you got the job done your way, without any help at all."

I swear, somehow, I do remember that day. Mom zipping me into my new snow pants, the impossible sensation of feeling warm and snug, even when I jumped into a snowbank. The rush of going down the hill at a thrilling speed but still feeling safe with my back pressed against my daddy's chest.

It hurts so much now to recall even the happy memories. Is missing him, loving him, a betrayal of Ash? He was good to our family. He was terrible to hers. Both of those things can be true, but if I want to be part of Ash's life, I can't ask her to understand that. It feels like there's a choice to be made: hold on to his memory or to her. But is it even possible to let him go when he's woven into every part of who I am? When there are a million things that will always remind me of him, from the arc of a fly line to the strum of a guitar to the smell of sage after it rains . . . no matter how hard I try to forget?

Maybe the only way to let him go is to finally understand how I lost him.

"You were the first responder," I say, my voice small but steady. "When my dad died. Why? How?"

He tightens the papers he's holding into a tube. "During your graduation, I kept looking over at him. Thinking how hard it must be for him to watch you grow up and know you'd be leaving soon. Things hadn't been the same between us for a while, but still, I thought he might want to talk. I saw him head up the canyon, so after I'd gone back and forth on it for a couple of hours, I decided to grab my fishing gear and see if he wanted some company. I was almost to your cabin when I saw the explosion." He shudders and stops, bowing his head and breathing slowly like he's trying to keep his emotions in check.

"Did you tell me all this before?" I ask, trying to remember.

"No," he says. "I told you the truth, but only the very basics. The whole thing is seared into my memory, even though I wish I could forget. I didn't want you to have a picture any more vivid than was absolutely necessary."

"Thank you," I say, and I mean it.

Bishop Carver nods, unrolling the papers he's been holding coiled in his hand. "But I'm here to answer any questions, anytime. And in that spirit . . ." He holds them out to me, an official logo at the top. "I thought you might like to see this."

Because Bishop Carver is, of course, Chief Carver too. The papers he gives me are a printed summary of last week's fire: nearly a thousand acres burned, initially caused by a lightning strike, two homes destroyed but no lives lost. Nothing in the report begins to capture the terror of the flames, the singe of the air, the suffocating thickness of the smoke.

"A natural, low-intensity fire like this one can be the healthiest thing for a forest. Fewer trees means less risk of diseases and insect problems, better light on the forest floor, lower levels of surface fuel to prevent catastrophic fires in the future. Fire can be a good thing. I'm just sorry you were so close to it."

I'm stuck on the first part of what he's just said. "That was a low-intensity fire?"

"I'm sure it didn't feel like it," he says. "But as forest fires go, yes."

I shake my head, then read the last line of the report again: No lives lost. For the first time, I remember that Fluffy and LuEllen were up there too. Even though it was Fluffy who brought back the truck that got us out of there, I never spared one thought for the fact that they were up by the pond when it happened too. That they were in every bit as much danger as we were.

Bishop Carver clears his throat, and when I see the look on his face, I can tell there's something he's holding back.

"What else?" I ask, the hair on my neck prickling.

"Well," he says, stalling. I wait until the silence makes him uncomfortable enough to start again. "You see there were two structures lost, right?"

I brace myself for the impact—but turn to face it head-on too. "I'm guessing you're about to tell me that one was ours."

"Yes," he admits. "The stone chimney survived, but that's pretty much it."

I picture it, a blackened chimney standing guard over the charred remains of the safe haven of my childhood, the seared skeletons of the trees bearing witness to it all. I half expected this already, maybe even wanted it on some level when I was consumed by grief and betrayal. So how does it still hurt to lose the cabin? How can it all hurt so damn much?

"It's not your fault," I manage to say, because at least one of us deserves to hear something comforting. "It was insured, I think." There is all sorts of insurance on what I've lost in my life.

He nods, but he still looks like he's treading lightly.

"What else?" I ask again.

He taps a finger against the table nervously, and I do feel some sympathy for him. He wants nothing more than for all of us to get along and love each other and be the best versions of ourselves. But something tells me this conversation won't fit into any of those categories.

"There's one thing that's a little . . . unusual," he begins.

"Okay," I say, remembering the shotgun shell he almost wouldn't tell me about at the Dairy Freeze. "What now?"

"I think you saw the chopper," he says. I nod, unsure where this is going. "It was headed to another fire when it saw the lightning strike and went off course to see if it could stop yours before it spread. In situations like this, we always protect any cabins we can. The Tuttle shack was a tinderbox ready to go up. It didn't have the required clearance around the structure. We might not even have known it was there if the barn hadn't gotten their attention, but still, he figured it was abandoned. What I'm saying is, that shack was bound to burn."

Again, I wait, and eventually, he goes on. "But the pilot didn't drop the load near your cabin because there was no reason it should have caught fire. He flew right over because it had such a wide clearance. There wasn't much wind, so the fire shouldn't have hopped to it. It should have been safe."

"But it wasn't," I say carefully.

"No," he says. "Somehow, the flames made it all the way across."

"It's okay," I say, trying to reassure him. "Fires are unpredictable, right? I have a lot of good memories at the cabin, and I can still hang on to those, even without the cabin itself. And I guess I could rebuild with the insurance money, if I wanted to. But honestly, right now I'm just trying to make it through today."

"I understand," he says. "But in terms of rebuilding . . . the insurance won't cover an intentional fire."

"Intentional fire! What the hell?" I've just sworn in front of my bishop, but I'm too worked up to care. I point to his own report. "It says right here that the fire was caused by a lightning strike."

"That's true, and that's the report I hope to submit. But, Calli, there were remnants of a gas can recovered in the forest beyond your cabin. Almost like somebody had spilled a trail from the cabin to the trees." He clears his throat again. "I don't suppose Ash would know anything about that?"

My heart races. "Of course not," I say, my eyes right on his. "She was with me the whole time. We were both just trying to get out of there."

"That's what I thought," he says. "And there's no way anybody else could have done it? You didn't see anyone else at all up the mountain?"

"Nobody except Officer Hunt, and he came up the road as we were going down it. Even if he had a motive, which I can't imagine, there's no way he could have made it to the cabin and then back to the road. Not without us seeing him, and not during the time you're talking about."

Bishop Carver nods, satisfied. "That's all I needed to know. In that case, it's not going in the report, because there's nothing to it. Like the shotgun shell, I suppose."

"I suppose," I echo, trying not to let any of the emotions roiling inside me reach the surface. I have learned how to hold things inside from the very best.

"Is there anything else you want to tell me?" he asks, not unkindly. "I'm still your bishop, you know, and clergy can keep things confidential. If there's anything you want to talk about."

My mind flashes from Dad to Ash, from the shotgun shell to the suffocating smell of smoke, and for the briefest moment, as I look into Bishop Carver's wise, warm face, I almost give in. He's proven himself for years now as someone who loves our family. As someone who is loyal to us, for better or for worse, and the only person who has known both me and my dad all our lives.

The memory card is buried in the back of the junk drawer, not ten feet from where he's standing. I could show it to him and tell him everything I know. It would hurt like hell to open this wound further, but maybe having it out in the open is the only way for it to heal. Maybe it wouldn't hurt so bad if we could do it together, and he could even fill in some of the missing pieces for me. Maybe he would understand. And doesn't he deserve to know?

We watch each other. We might even be thinking the same thing: Either we come clean about everything, follow both the letter and the spirit of every law, or we don't.

"Not today," I say at last. "But thank you for coming."

"Of course," he says. "Let me know if there's anything else I can do. And can I ask you to do one thing for me?"

I nod, even as uncertainty jolts through me.

"Would you call me Travis again? It's never felt quite natural, you and your dad calling me Bishop."

Relief washes over me. "Absolutely. And me too." As he stands to go, one sentence escapes from me. "I was mad at God for a minute there."

Travis shrugs it off. "He can take it."

There's a crackle of connection that makes me think we can still communicate. He's been talking about integrity lately from the pulpit: about making sure our words and actions align with our truth. And suddenly, that's something I want so badly.

Maybe I can trust him. Tell him. I fill my lungs, ready for the littlest nudge to start me down this slope, unsure I'll be able to stop once I get any momentum at all.

But somebody knocks on the door, and the moment is broken.

"I'll get it," Travis says. Then, as he opens the door, "Dylan! Come on in." It's so much in his nature to welcome everyone, always, that it just comes out. But I see the moment when he realizes maybe it wasn't the right call.

"It's okay," I say, ignoring both of their outstretched hands and getting to my feet on my own.

I turn to Travis. "Let me know if you remember any other stories," I say. "Especially about my mom."

quarterback

The bishop and firefighter.
The young hunter and the old mechanic.
The deputy and the officer.

Here is one thing they have in common:
they all played football in high school,
but none of them played quarterback.

So after a big loss,
they could feel sorrow,
wonder whether they could have done more,
but also
take some assurance
in knowing it hadn't been them calling the plays.

On some level, they all knew about Silas,
even if they didn't know him by that name.

But it's easier to turn away
or to point fingers and place blame
than to admit that whole systems are failing
again and again.

Easier still to say
it's not our place to judge

when what we really mean is
we're not willing to change.

Until, finally, someone is.

integrity, part 2

The bishop opens the door to his truck,
the handle nearly too hot to touch
in the afternoon sun.

He's spent his career trying to understand fire
and a lifetime trying to understand people,
and he's still not sure he knows a damn thing
about either one.

He starts the engine and drives east
almost without thinking about it,
and soon he is in the mountains,
slamming an orange prescription bottle
into the rubble left by the fire
and working through his anger and betrayal
in the safety of the empty forest.

She's a good kid.
Better than you deserve.
And I hate that I'm keeping
anything from her.

I turned in your wallet
when I found it in the Tuttle place
after the . . . accident.

But I kept this
because it looked bad that
you'd left your own prescription bottle inside,
and I was sure
if you were there,
you'd have the perfect explanation
and make it all make sense.

But I guess without you to spin the story,
I found the truth instead.

Because I got curious. I went online.
The pills don't match the label,
and when I paid your credit card bill
for Calli,
I was almost sick
when I saw
that the bottle of whiskey
I'd found next to the pills
was bought with your card.

I would have sworn I knew you,
but instead of believing my own instincts
you made me question whether I even knew myself.

How did we all miss it until it was too late?
You've made a liar out of me
and out of Calli too.

But I can't be the one
who lays your ugly truth out there
when it's your daughter
who will really pay the price.

Back in his own driveway,
before he goes inside,
he pulls out his phone,
which glows with a picture of his wife and kids,
and reminds himself again
that integrity is aligning your words and actions
with the truth inside you
instead of the mental and moral gymnastics
of the other way around.

He pulls up the two versions
of the official report on the fire:
one declaring the loss of the cabin intentional,
the other declaring it
"a natural ignition, lightning-caused fire,"
which, back in the day,
even the official forms called an act of God.
He thinks of God then,
and of Calli.
Submits one.
Deletes the other.

Leaves behind the person he spent
his whole life looking up to
without looking back.
Looks ahead instead.

Sometimes integrity
is being willing to burn it all down.

29

After Travis leaves, Dylan and I walk the property side by side without saying a word. It's kind of nice. But I can't keep quiet forever.

"I'm sorry," I say.

Dylan looks at me with genuine surprise.

"For what?"

"For sending the cops after you." It seems so ridiculous now that I can barely get the words out. "I never really thought you'd done anything wrong, but—"

"I know," he says, and I'm grateful he didn't make me finish my sentence. "I swear, Calli, you know every time I've been on your property. Well, besides when I walk along the border to hunt."

"And when you put the trail cam back at the cabin?"

He blushes. "I meant to tell you, I swear."

"My dad wouldn't have been very happy about that." I don't tell him why, but the way he tenses, I wonder if he knows something. So I ease up to the difficult conversation, the way I've tried to do with Ash. "You said he never liked you when we were dating. But I guess I never asked you if you liked him."

Dylan swallows hard, then forces himself to look me in the eye. "I did, at first. I mean, everybody knows what a good guy your dad is, right? But, Cal, remember that first time we went to look at the memory card at the cabin, and there was nothing there? That's because he swapped out the card before we took a look. It was so quick I almost missed it, but I swear . . ." Dylan drops his head. "Ugh, now that I say that out loud, it sounds creepy as hell. I'm sorry, Cal. I should have trusted both of you better than that."

"It's okay," I tell him. "You should trust yourself, Dylan. Or at least try to. If there's anything this whole nightmare has taught me, it's that. I'm not sure how much they told you, but the guy from the barn turned out to be a ghost, or a memory, or something like that. There's nobody after Ash anymore."

I try to say it with enough finality that he won't ask any questions, and it works. He nods and leans back against the fence—just as Ash bursts out the back door. When she sees us in the distance, she breaks into a run. She's had a restless energy ever since we got back from the cabin, but whether it's from escaping the fire or finally feeling safe from her own secrets, I'm not sure. Even so, I'm surprised how anxious she is to get out to me, and I open my arms in case she needs it.

But she bounds straight past me and up to Dylan. "Horses," she says, fierce determination written across her face. When he just looks at her blankly, she rolls her eyes (an entirely new move for Ash) and says, "Calli says you have horses. I want to learn how to ride them."

"Umm . . ." He's so trapped and helpless that I want to laugh, but I just shrug; this is his to deal with. I can picture them out there riding horses together, though: him helping her learn the ropes, her leading him up the canyon.

"It's okay," I tell him. "If you want to."

"Well, sure," he says. "I can't get my little brother to do anything but play video games. I'd be happy to take you instead. You probably fart less too."

Ash laughs, loud and long and right from her belly. I'm not sure it's a sound I've ever heard before, but I can't wait to hear it again. "Tomorrow night," she says, then scampers off before he can protest.

"That kid is something else," he says, a note of admiration in his voice. "I don't mind riding with her. It might be good for her to have a guy around she can trust." He digs his toe into the dirt. "By the way, I'm kind of with somebody else now. From Cedar Falls. Wanted you to hear it from me. Any advice so I don't screw it up this time?"

He's so earnest about it all that I roll my eyes, just to get him out of his head a little. But the advice I give is the best I can think of. "Just be honest. Let her see your whole self."

Dylan, ever a Rigby boy, starts to turn it into a dirty joke, but I shoot him a look, and he catches himself. "Okay, okay," he says. Then, with a small up nod at something over my shoulder, he adds, "Speaking of moving on, anything new to report on your end?" I turn to see Ben's car in the distance, pulling into his personal parking spot beside the house.

"I don't think so," I say. I know I don't owe Dylan an explanation, but it's almost like I'm trying to explain it to myself. "Not right now, anyway. There's too much I have to figure out on my own first."

He nods. Fills in the hole he's been digging with his toe and taps it level with the sole of his shoe. Making the ground smooth again, like he did for my dad the day all this began.

"Should I come by around seven?" he asks, and for a minute, I wonder if I imagined our whole conversation about moving on. My face must look some version of panicked, because he laughs. "Relax, Calli. Not for you. For Ash, tomorrow night."

"That sounds perfect," I tell him, because it does.

As he ambles away and Ben bounds toward me, they give each other a little nod, and I think how lucky I am to have had them both around for most of high school. At the cabin, it felt like my whole life had been a lie. But this is also true: Ever since I got back, I've been reminded by people I love that there is more to me than him.

When Ben reaches me, I have to study him for a moment before I realize what's different.

"You got a haircut," I say. "It looks really good."

"Thanks," he says, a little shyly. "I figured it was time. It definitely wasn't getting any better." He turns to stand beside me and just looks with me, over the fields toward the house, a new perspective on the place I've always called home. It's so perfectly what I need in this moment that I put my arm around his waist, and I welcome the weight of his arm when he puts it around my shoulders.

We stand like that for a while, and I can feel the way our breath matches up sometimes, then goes back out of sync. Maybe it's a metaphor for what we've been doing all along.

Finally, Ben breaks the silence. "What are we looking at?" he whispers.

I laugh as the whole scene comes into focus: the little house with its peeling red-brown paint, the run-down barn in the distance, the fields of wheatgrass and sagebrush. Home.

"What if I sold it?" I ask.

He turns to look at me without taking his arm from around my shoulders. "Sold what?"

"The house. The truck. The land. All of it. Just sold it all and walked away."

"Why?" he asks, genuinely confused.

I feel my armor going up, and I don't fight it. Someday I'll tell Ben the terrible new truth I've learned about my dad. But not today.

So I choose my words carefully. "I think I need to start over," I say. "This place holds so many happy memories—including with you—but it's always going to be stained by so much sadness and loss. Things I don't want to remember."

"That's fair," he says. "It's your choice to make. You could sell it all."

"But should I? Will I?"

"Calli, we both know you're the only one who can answer that question." He's quiet for a minute. Then: "I thought you were going to commute to college. I kind of thought you'd be here when I got back."

"Got back?" I ask. "Where are you going?"

Then, like a lightning bolt, it hits me. I know the last few weeks have been hard, but I still shouldn't have forgotten: Ben sent in his mission papers not long before Dad died. And when I remember Trish's taped-up mouth so she wouldn't spill his secret, I do the math and know exactly what the secret must be. Quickly, I pull away so I can look him in the eye.

The smile on his face tells me I'm right. "Holy smokes, Ben, when did it get here? Why didn't you tell me?" We stand there in awkward silence for a second, but it doesn't last. We both burst out laughing: When in these last few days would have been the right moment? It doesn't matter anyway. All that matters is the next question.

"Where are you going?"

"Argentina," he says. "Good thing I had Spanish in high school."

"Sí," I say, and we both laugh, because our high school Spanish teacher mostly played his guitar and told stories about when he was in high school, so *sí* is one of the few words we actually learned. We had some good teachers and some terrible ones, but it's hard to see how even the best teachers could have prepared us for everything that's happened since.

Except maybe we prepared each other.

"You're going to do so much good," I say.

"That's the goal," he says. "But it's terrifying to think that people might be looking to me for answers or direction in their life. I can barely find my car keys most days."

"You'll figure it out," I say, and I mean it.

"So will you."

"It's half a world away," I say.

"Really only a quarter. Plus, they have baseball there, not just soccer. And pianos. It's practically the same there as here."

"Pretty much identical," I say, leaning back into him. "If you get to leave, shouldn't I get to, too?"

"Well, I guess that's fair." I can hear the smile in his voice. "I've been kind of wondering if you would, to be honest."

To be honest. I've never intentionally held anything back from Ben.

"Want some practice?" I ask. When he looks at me, a little confused, I say, "For when you get the tough questions on your mission?"

He searches my face. I try to play it light, smile, but he probably sees right through it. "Shoot," he tells me.

"Do you think we all deserve a second chance? Like, everybody? No matter what?"

He pauses. "I think it's a little bit conditional. You have to be truly sorry. You have to confess, then turn away and sin no more. That kind of thing. Right?"

"What if you die before you get your second chance?"

Ben squeezes my hand and holds it against his chest. "Well, I guess that's where it comes in handy that death isn't the end."

I think of Dad having another chance to make things right. To repair all the harm he did—or at least try. And I can't help it. I want that for him. I want to remember him as the good father he was, to love him again like I loved him before. But I can't unless he fixes it, which is no longer possible in this life. And even though I've heard it preached ever since I can remember, it's hard to imagine there really is something beyond.

"But you also have to make it right with the people you hurt. How can you do that if you're already gone?"

Ben studies me again. He has to know who we're talking about, even if he has no idea why. "I do not know the meaning of all things," he says, paraphrasing the scripture. "But I know God loves his children." Then, gently, "Maybe this person can't make things right anymore, but God can."

"So I'm supposed to just forgive him," I say, blinking back tears, torn between my own love and anger.

"Only if you want to," Ben says, wiping a thumb across each of my cheeks. "And not for his sake. For yours."

"And forget?" I ask, not sure what I want the answer to be.

"Some things," he says, tucking my hair behind my ear. "But you can't force it. Hang on to what you need, and when you're ready, let the rest fall away."

Hang on to what you need. I take his hands in mine, wrapping his arms around me as I turn back toward the house. The tears keep falling, but I hold tight to Ben's hands—to all of him—because his faith means he's also made a promise to mourn with those who mourn. To comfort those who stand in need of comfort. Him keeping that promise is how our friendship began, really.

Ben doesn't try to soothe or shush me, just lets my tears roll off his arms as I look back over this place where I spent all my childhood. I can picture us out there, riding our bikes down the slope every summer, jumping off and throwing them to the ground at the last minute so we didn't end up in the creek. Cross-country skiing across the fields in the winter and awarding ourselves aluminum-foil medals on Podium Rock. Ben splitting his pants out here freshman year—because he tried to climb the cottonwood to get me the last yellow heart-shaped leaf that fall, the only one to hang on after a freak October snowstorm.

Hang on to what you need.

The question I asked the day Dad died comes back to me: Who am I without him? Now I know the answer is that I will never be without him. This little farm at the mouth of the canyon will always be part of me, for better or for worse. And so will my dad, whose DNA is in every cell in my body, for better or for worse.

In this moment, it's a hard truth to accept.

"Do you think things will turn out right somehow?" I ask.

I don't even realize I'm almost quoting the song until he answers me, almost singing until his voice breaks a little at the end. "We can make it so." His dark eyes are so kind and earnest that I have to believe it. I rest my palm against his cheek, overwhelmed with gratitude that, now and always, Ben is on my side.

calling

The girl from Harmony
continues to discover her truth,
little by little,
line upon line,
each step
illuminating the next.

The boy's path has been easier,
but even so,
he has found his truth
in much the same way
and is ready to share it
wherever God sends him.

Once you find your truth,
you too might feel called
to share it.

If you do,
know this:

It takes courage
and audacity
to leave your home,
to raise your voice

knowing
you are still young
and have much to learn
and no one,
not even God,
can guarantee
that any of it will go well.
That anyone will listen.

But they might.
And it might make a difference.
And your might
and your truth
might save a life.

And it might
be your own.

30

Ben and Ash and I celebrate his mission call with shakes at the Freeze. From that moment on, it feels like the whole world is on a sped-up sugar rush.

Officer Hunt and Maggie stop by with Ash's social worker to give us an update—and maybe to make sure we're staying put. (He's told me in no uncertain terms that he's willing to turn me in if I so much as think about bending the rules again.)

The social worker isn't messing around either; her no-nonsense tone matches her haircut perfectly. "We've already filed the paperwork to get her into the foster system, and we're looking for her dad." Ash reaches for my hand when she hears that. I glance over, worried that he's just another person who hurt her, but her eyes are bright and hopeful.

"As we read the list," Officer Hunt says, "there was one family that seemed like they might be a good fit."

As far as I know, it would be a pretty short list, and I'm not sure I'd be excited about any of them. But when Maggie slides the paper across the table with a smile on her face, it's not hard to see why.

"Sofia and Trish?" I ask, blinking to make sure I'm really seeing it.

"They've been working on the trainings and paperwork for a while, but they were suddenly motivated to finish up quickly," says the social worker. "If you both support the idea, they're ready for Ash anytime."

"Now," says Ash eagerly, releasing my hand. "I'm ready now."

Her answer stings more than it should. Of course Ash belongs with two responsible adults, not some teenager who drives her to a cabin in the woods during fire season when there could be a predator on the loose. "Everything happens for a reason," Maggie always says. "And sometimes, the reason is you didn't use your brain."

But without that trip, I might never have gotten to see where Ash lived, and she wouldn't have had anybody to bear witness to what she went through. I would never have seen what was on the memory card. I might never have known the truth.

Painful as it is, I'm glad there's no going back. Glad you can't unstrike the match.

Because I deserve the truth—and so does she.

We already spoke it to each other, lying on opposite ends of my bed last night.

"Tell me the story," I said, and then I listened to all she's been through.

"Once there was a girl," she began, "who went on a great journey to find her true home . . ."

She started it like Mom's story—the one I told her the first day she came to me. But the rest was all her own, told with strength and courage. When I asked her whether the man in the uniform from her story was anyone she'd seen since she came to live with me, she shook her head. "No," she said, before changing her answer to a steely "not yet." Some of the hardest parts she wrote in the little notebook, and I cried too when I read them. But something about giving it a beginning, a middle, and an end seemed to help. Making sure it was all set in the past.

"Tell me yours," she said to me when she'd finished, and I did.

Now I look at all the people around my kitchen table, every one of them wanting what's best for Ash.

"Tomorrow?" the social worker is saying, and Ash nods.

"One last day together," I say, and Ash agrees.

The social worker leaves for another appointment. Ash stays inside to start packing while I walk Maggie and Officer Hunt out.

"I know I made a mess of everything," I say. "And I'm sorry for that."

Maggie rolls her eyes like she can't believe this foolishness. "Well, of course you did. But I don't know anybody who could have done better. You became an orphan at the same time you became an adult. You were suddenly responsible and suddenly alone at the same time." She wraps me in a tight, no-nonsense hug. "That's a lot, honey. It'd be a mess for anybody." Then she drops a kiss on the top of my head, promises to bring dinner by later, and starts toward her car.

Officer Hunt turns to go too, but there's something I want to ask him.

"Do you think anything is going to change in Ash Creek after Charity Trager?"

He stops. Half smiles. "That bishop of yours seems hell-bent on changing the way we handle things around here, both on the church's end and on ours. And that's a good thing." Then he shakes his head. "As for Ash Creek, I wish I could tell you yes, but I don't know."

"Trauma and tragedy for two girls in the same small patch of nowhere in the same summer. What are the odds?" I ask.

Hunt looks to the horizon, his shoulders heavy. "Way too high," he says. "Just ask Officer Keller."

I look at him, too surprised and confused to watch my language. "What does that asshole have to do with anything?"

Hunt chuckles under his breath. "He can be an asshole. I'll give you that." But then he turns serious. "Do you know why he cared so much about this case?"

"Because he's from Ash Creek. He moved here when we were in high school, and he cared because he thought Ash was Charity Trager."

"That was part of it. But did you notice that he was still pretty . . . intense about everything, even after Charity Trager's body was found?"

It hadn't occurred to me, but he's right. "Okay, why?"

"I'll turn the question back on you. Do you know *why* he moved here from Ash Creek? What made him and his mother flee from the only life they'd ever known?"

I shake my head, my stare blank.

"Because he had a little sister. And then he didn't. And the Brethren would never say exactly what happened to her. It's all public record. He had to try to start over with all of that on his shoulders when he was still just a kid."

I sigh. "I guess something like that might make me an asshole too."

Officer Hunt laughs again at that. "That's very generous of you, Calli. We're all shaped by our own experiences and biases—including police officers. It takes courage to break free from what you've been conditioned to see and believe. Which reminds me: You'd make a good cop. I've been meaning to tell you that. Or maybe a victims' advocate. We could use one of those around here."

The words take me by surprise. Not just because they're un-expected, but because even when I turn them over in my mind, I'm not sure they're true—especially considering everything I'm not telling him.

"I didn't even see what was right in front of me," I say, letting him think I mean these last few days, when really it's been my whole life.

"We've all got blind spots," he says. "I know I do. But the first step is recognizing that, so you're already ahead of the game. Plus, you're brave. Smart. Observant—even if you don't catch every-thing. You see everyone as human but still hold them accountable. I mean, you'd have to learn how to respect authority, but even then, it's not so bad to have a little streak of rebellion." He looks around like we might be being watched. "Don't tell anybody I said that."

"Your secret's safe with me," I tell him.

⁓

Back inside, I help Ash pack up anything from my closet she wants to keep, plus the soccer clothes from Sofia and Trish. In the bathroom, she tries to pack her toothbrush, but I take it back out and remind her she'll need it tonight. I'm not giving up our last night together—but I'm also not sleeping by Ash with enchilada breath.

After that, there are a few hours of daylight left, and as much as I try to avoid the thought, I know where we should go. When I ask Ash, she agrees, and we drive to the cemetery. Not to the center, where Mom is buried beside Dad and his family among polished marble headstones, but to the south edge, where the graves are closer together and marked only by small plaques in the ground.

When we find the temporary marker with her mom's name on it, Ash drops to her knees. I kneel beside her and wait, wait, wait for her to say something. When she finally does, it's a refrain of a question I've been asking myself. One I haven't dared give voice to.

But Ash has always been braver than me.

"What if I'm like her?" she asks.

"What if I'm like him?" I ask, knowing the possibility of being like my parent is so much worse.

Anyone else—Maggie, Ben, Trish, Sofia, Officer Hunt, Dylan, *anybody*—would tell her she's not. Would assure me I couldn't be. So I'm grateful it's just me and Ash here, because there's something right about at least sitting with the question. You have to ask it—really ask it, keep asking it—if you want to be sure of the answer.

"I heard you talking to him," she says, startling me out of my meditation.

"Who?" I ask, worried that she means Silas again. That maybe she's not as well as I hoped.

"Bishop Carver," she says, plucking blades of grass, one after another. "Don't worry; I won't tell him. We can keep each other's secrets."

The hairs on the back of my neck prickle. "What secret?"

"You didn't lie to him," she says. "There wasn't anybody else up the mountain. Just me and you and Hunt. And Hunt really was down at the road, and I really was inside the cabin. He couldn't have made a trail of gas from the cabin to the forest, and neither could I. But you . . ." She looks up then, straight at me. "You did."

In a flash, I'm back at the cabin, blinking away tears from the smoke and the pain, but somehow still mesmerized by the way the flames of the forest fire lick the trees—until the door to the generator shed swings open, caught by the hot breath of the fire itself, revealing the great humming machine and the gas can beside it.

I blink myself back to the present and don't look away. In that moment, I know Ash better than I have ever known anyone in my life. Because we are the same. We know sometimes it feels like the only way to move on from a hell you didn't make and don't deserve is to burn it all down.

But I didn't.

In the end, I tossed the can into the forest so there would be *less* fuel, *less* chance of the whole thing burning. I didn't do it, because in that moment, I thought of Ash. And this is another way she and her story have saved me.

But now it seems like the gas can exploding—and any trail of fuel I inadvertently left—could have been the thing that helped the fire cross the clearance to the cabin.

"I thought about it," I tell her, the truth of it bringing tears to my eyes. "I almost did. But I was afraid I'd end up hurting someone I didn't intend to. Hurting *you*. If I'm being honest, though, I'm not sorry it happened."

Ash bows her head. "Even if you had, my secret would still be worse. I was a monster once. Maybe I always will be."

I hold her, and she lets me. "No," I say. "Never."

"Even after I go with Sofia and Trish, will you come if I need you?"

"Yes," I say. "Always." She curls into me then. Shudders. I hold her closer and repeat the word, my breath ruffling her hair.

"Always. Always. Always."

epilogue

The girl from Nowhere walks beside the creek,
no longer half dead.

Her life is rich now,
not because of the money
Calli put into a new account for her
when she collected the insurance payout
and sold the property.

But rich because of
Trish,
Sofia,
a therapist who listens
and helps her understand
that it was the fiercest part of herself
who saved her.

Rich because of clean clothes each morning
that stretch
from one laundry day to the next,
friends from school,
school itself,
her own Dairy Freeze apron

and paycheck
and unlimited ice cream,
horse rides with Dylan,

and a clear conscience
after she and Calli
gave Officer Hunt the memory card
and told him everything.

And after that,
a new beginning
that means she never feels
hunted
or haunted.

Almost never, anyway.

And Calli,
who still comes back from law school to visit,
sometimes with Ben
or sometimes just her,
and the two of them
go to the place Calli bought
with the rest of the insurance money.

The tiny cabin with the wide front porch
overlooking the pond and the forest
where they can sit
under the Night Stars quilt,
where they can see
the ponderosa,
still towering over the rest of the trees,

but also
new seedlings sprouting
among the ashes.

One night
when the old cabin
was still new to them,
she and Calli sat on the front porch
eating green bean soup,
drinking Cokes,
and two hares
loped through the trees.

Ash,
Calli whispered,
does one of those hares
have a notch out of its ear?

They looked closer
and it did,
and that was when they knew
for sure
and forever:
They survived.

ACKNOWLEDGMENTS

I am grateful beyond measure for all the people who helped bring this book into the world.

To Tara Dairman, Ann Braden, Jennifer Bertman, Tasha Seegmiller, Rosalyn Eves, Erin Shakespear Bishop, and Helen Boswell-Taylor, you make every page better, every time, and I am so grateful to have you in my life.

To my incredible agent, Ammi-Joan Paquette, whose enthusiasm, expertise, and advocacy make all the difference.

To my phenomenal editor, Michelle Frey, who saw what this book could be and wouldn't settle for anything less. What a tremendous gift it is to work with you.

To all the folks at Knopf/Random House, and especially Dana Carey, Lois Evans, Andriannie Santiago, Arely Guzman, Renée Cafiero, Lisa Leventer, Artie Bennett, Ray Shappell, Jake Eldred, Ken Crossland, and Shameiza Ally.

My gratitude also goes to the expert readers who answered questions on everything from victims' advocacy to police procedure to religious fundamentalism: Rose Hunter, Wendy Jessen, Tracy Fails, Steve Barker, and Aleana Compton. Any detail I got right is because of you; anything I got wrong falls entirely on my shoulders.

To the friends who have supported and championed my books all along the way, including Martene Barker, Charmayne Orton, Jessica Remington, Evan Vickers, Chris Vickers, Amy Rigby, Kati Simon, Gia Miller, Julene Weaver, Maggie Lewis, Elizabeth Funk,

Colette Neish, Charlene Busch, Rachel Christensen, Natalie Christensen, Lynn Hicken, Donna Law, Jennifer LaGarde, John Schu, Colby Sharp, Brooke MacNaughtan, Jenny Call, Bridget Lee, Robyn Orme, Summer Hodson, Jane McCallister, Allisa White, Sara Penny, Jennifer Jowett, the whole team at Bulloch's, and all the educators and booksellers and readers and librarians who have embraced my work and read and shared my stories.

To the teachers who taught me to ask questions and to trust myself, including Kathryn Ipson, Linda Wilson, Ty Redd, Huck Shirley, Janet Weaver, Laura Cotts, Vicki Challis, Carol Ann Nyman, Steve Steffensen, Richard Anderson, and Alice Braithwaite.

To Ally, Nic, and Hope, because you're awesome, and I'm so lucky you're stuck with me.

To my dad, who taught me to do what's right, and my mom, who taught me to trust my own moral compass. Thank you both for your feedback and for your endless support. You are two of the best people I know.

And to Robbie, Lucy, Halle, and Jack, for everything, always.

ABOUT THE AUTHOR

E. B. Vickers is the acclaimed author of the young adult novel *Fadeaway*, which appears on multiple state award lists, including a Top Ten on the Texas Tayshas Reading List. She is also the author of several middle-grade novels as well as picture books. She grew up in a small town in the Utah desert, where she spent her time reading, exploring, and asking questions. Several years and one PhD later, she found her way back to her hometown, where she now spends her time writing, teaching college chemistry, exploring with her family, and still asking questions. Visit her online at elainevickers.com and on social media at @elainebvickers.

𝕏 ⓘ